HOW TO
SEAL
YOUR OWN
FATE

HOW TO
SEAL
YOUR OWN
FATE

A NOVEL

Kristen Perrin

DUTTON

DUTTON

An imprint of Penguin Random House LLC
1745 Broadway, New York, NY 10019
penguinrandomhouse.com

LIBRARY OF CONGRESS CATALOGING-IN-PUBLICATION DATA
Names: Perrin, Kristen, author.
Title: How to seal your own fate : a novel / Kristen Perrin.
Description: First edition. | New York : Dutton, 2025.
Identifiers: LCCN 2024044053 | ISBN 9780593474044 (hardcover) |
ISBN 9780593474068 (ebook) | 9798217046348 (export)
Subjects: LCGFT: Cozy mysteries. | Novels.
Classification: LCC PS3616.E785 H68 2025 | DDC 813/.6—dc23/eng/20240924
LC record available at https://lccn.loc.gov/2024044053

Printed in the United States of America
1st Printing

The authorized representative in the EU for product safety and compliance is
Penguin Random House Ireland, Morrison Chambers, 32 Nassau Street,
Dublin D02 YH68, Ireland, https://eu-contact.penguin.ie.

HOW TO
SEAL
YOUR OWN
FATE

PROLOGUE

Castle Knoll Outskirts, May 13, 1961

HER NAME HAD ALWAYS BEEN TOO PLAIN, SHE THOUGHT, as she looked at the prison register in front of her, which required her signature. Ellen Jones didn't reflect who she was and what she'd done. Nor did it do a good job of foretelling what was in store for her—the things she planned to do. The things she knew she had to get away with.

A stern woman took her right hand and forced her fingers into the black ink, taking each of her fingerprints in turn. Her pockets were emptied, and small objects went into a cardboard box—a Swiss Army knife, several coins, a crumpled piece of paper with the name and address of a lawyer on it, and a mostly melted boiled sweet.

She was being *held*, she'd been told. Arrested, held, questioned. That was the order of things. The admittance form had several boxes for personal information. She'd filled in all of them except the one that said "Name." Her form read:

Name: _____ Hair: brown _____

Age: 16 years _____ Eyes: green with brown flecks

Height: 5' 4" _____ Address: 42 Ripple Lane, _____

Weight: 9 stone _____ Castle Knoll _____

Her left hand shook as it hovered over the last blank box. She had no ID on her, and no one to confirm or deny who she was. There had been no parents to sigh disappointedly when the police contacted them about her arrest, and no one to bail her out. She'd never be able to hire a good lawyer if she were to go to trial. But there wouldn't be a trial; she'd been caught in the act. There was no need to proclaim innocence. When they asked if anyone else had helped her commit her crime, she simply lied and said, "No."

Ellen almost laughed to herself, because whoever thought of using prison as an excuse to reinvent yourself? They knew her real name in town, of course, even the police who'd arrested her. But perhaps now all that was over. She'd just disappear in prison and emerge as someone else.

It was worth a try.

She wondered where the others were. Laura "Birdy" Sparrow and Eric Foyle. Eric was the one person she thought might come and visit her if she ended up getting put away. The thought was strange—*getting put away* made her feel like an object going into storage. Something out of order that needed to be slotted back into an organized system. She imagined that people entered prison like puzzle pieces with sharp edges and emerged rounded so they could be pressed back into the machine. Functional. A part of society. The thought made her shudder.

Eric Foyle understood her; he had that same violent fire burning inside him that she did. She knew he wouldn't abandon her; there was more in store for the two of them. They had a future.

She bit her lip, trying not to cry.

Because Ellen felt she deserved to be here, after all. The whole thing had been her idea. It just wasn't very well planned. When they saw his car, so distinctive, they'd decided to take their chance anyway. Everyone knew who that car belonged to, because no one else would dare drive a car such a garish shade of dark purple. And a Bentley, at that. A dark purple Bentley was such a villain's car, and the moment Ellen found out what kind of crimes its owner was committing, she vowed to do everything in her power to take him down.

When she noticed the car, parked and empty at the service station on the leafy road two miles outside Castle Knoll, Ellen made a snap decision. She told Eric to pull into a hidden drive next to it. Its owner wasn't inside buying petrol; they knew that already. He would be in the dilapidated pub next door. Eric opened the boot of his own car, and Ellen grabbed the tire iron from inside.

Ellen's legs fought through the overgrown bushes as she and Eric hurried down the lane that connected the drive to the petrol station. It had rained, and pink peonies brushed against her shins, heavy with droplets. Her worn saddle shoes and knee socks made her feel like a schoolgirl still, even though she'd dropped out last year at fifteen. She knew her calling already, and school wasn't going to teach her anything.

The petrol pumps were empty, and the station attendant was having a smoke break somewhere. Luck was on their side, or so it had seemed. Eric looked at her, his eyes a clear light blue that matched forget-me-nots, and gave her a smile of reassurance. He broke hearts, Eric Foyle did, but she was still happy to stand in line.

A crowbar was propped up against some old hubcaps near the door to the petrol station, and Eric sprinted for that. But even if they had nothing but their bare hands, their anger was so strong that they'd both do plenty of damage just with those.

The first smash of glass was the windscreen. Ellen screamed out a battle cry of satisfaction as she swung the tire iron. The glass spiderwebbed but didn't shatter, so she hit the same spot over and over until finally the windscreen gave way.

Eric had gone for the tires with his crowbar, swinging the hooked end at the rubber, hoping to slash them to pieces. Like Ellen, he was undeterred when his first blow simply bounced off. He found a weak spot, a groove worn down a bit, and beat it over and over again until the crowbar stuck in the rubber with a satisfying *hiss*.

He delivered a powerful kick to the metal of one of the doors, denting it. He gave the body of the car several more kicks before swinging the crowbar into the sides of it, over and over. Paint flew off in big flakes, and the sound of metal ringing made Eric into some kind of medieval blacksmith forging weapons for war. Somewhere between the first blow and the seventh or eighth, he broke several fingers.

But Ellen knew her plan wouldn't work unless she went for the engine. It was crucial that this car couldn't deliver its owner to where she knew he was bound. Ellen dropped the tire iron and wrenched open the bonnet, balancing on her knees atop the front bumper. A Swiss Army knife emerged from her pocket, and she held it in her left hand as she searched for the one essential cable Eric had taught her to find. She tore at the hoses first, pulling at every rubber pipe and wire she could find. Battery cables snapped, coolant connections were severed, caps were unscrewed and thrown into the bushes.

Ellen knew then that she would never feel more alive, more purposeful and powerful, than when she was on her knees ripping the guts out of that man's car.

As triumphant as that moment was, she kept her head. She was out from under the bonnet as soon as she'd severed the cable she was looking for, and she clicked the bonnet back into place with surprising gentleness. Three purposeful strides and she was back by Eric's side, picking up the tire iron from the pavement where she'd dropped it and hammering at the windows.

Even when the wail of the police sirens cut through the afternoon air, she didn't stop. Eric disappeared, not looking to see if she was following him, but Ellen was riding the wave of adrenaline so gloriously that she hadn't noticed. It wasn't until she was pulled away, covered in motor oil and sweat, and cuffed by powerful hands, that she saw a pair of outraged eyes boring into her. The owner of the purple Bentley.

"I'd do it again," she said, her voice low.

And she still felt that way, as her pen hovered over the "Name" box on the form in front of her. Ellen hoped that maybe Eric would make sure the truth came out, if she was locked away for a long time, but she knew he was in a precarious position. He had his younger brother, Archie, to look out for, and his employer was so powerful. He'd keep his head down if he knew what was good for him. She knew his future.

She knew all their futures.

Finally, she let the pen find the paper in front of her and wrote a name in careful, clear letters. The name she'd carry with her for the rest of her life.

Peony Lane.

Castle Knoll Outskirts, Present Day

Peony Lane didn't normally walk this route into town; it was a long way for someone her age. But when the bus that took her from her house through the winding country roads into Castle Knoll unexpectedly broke down three stops too soon, her stomach sank with the weight of something inevitable.

She couldn't quite place it—which premonition of hers was clicking into place? Her funny way of grasping onto images and words, squeezing them gently in her mind like handling oranges at the supermarket and then doling them out to people as fortunes . . . it was an imprecise art.

She stood on the verge in the wet grass and eyed the trail that took you past the old pub, the petrol station, and rows and rows of new houses, until it finally delivered you into Castle Knoll. The ghosts of old memories tugged at her, but she pulled her tartan shawl tighter around her shoulders. She was in good shape, so she steeled herself and trudged onward.

In no time she was nearing the derelict pub, which for a number of years had been missing a wall, replaced with insufficient chipboard that was now weathered and warped, graffiti-covered.

Her unease grew as she heard the wood of the old pub start to groan. That was all the warning the old structure gave before slate tiles began suddenly sliding off, cascading to the ground like oversized broken teeth falling from a whitewashed stone jaw. She stopped ten feet back, then moved several more feet away as the crack of a beam sounded and the roof spilled its contents inward. The front of the pub crumbled as if it had only ever been dust held in place by old paint. No glass shattered—there was none remaining in the windows after all these years—but the front door splintered before it was buried by the rubble of the walls.

The ghosts of her memories grew legs when she saw what was inside. The color of the car was impossible to make out under layers of dust, tiles, and rubble, but the shape of it was unmistakable. That old Bentley was waiting for her, horribly wrecked from the crash that had ended the lives of three people so many years ago.

And she knew in that moment that she'd been wrong. Decades before, she'd told a fortune, and only now had it become clear that she'd made a mistake.

Several minutes passed, then she observed someone coming toward the wreck, drawn to the site by the noise of the pub's collapsing walls. She should have worried about being spotted there, gawking, but she had too many big thoughts swirling around in her mind to think about that now.

She drew in a pinched breath through her nose, set her jaw, and nodded at the wreckage. "Enough, now," she said.

Then she continued on her way, this time at a slightly faster pace, because her destination had changed.

CHAPTER

1

November 1

AUTUMN HAS ARRIVED IN CASTLE KNOLL SO SUD-
denly that it's as if the elements rearranged the landscape
like set pieces in a theater while I slept. I'm so used to London's slow drizzle as the seasons change that this sudden
burst of color has me dressing quickly and racing outside,
like a child who's opened their eyes to see snow on Christmas morning.

I slow down only to let my coffee brew, but it's sealed in a
thermos in no time. I'm kitted out in an oversized Fair Isle
jumper and a pair of wellies I've yet to fully break in, determined to get them well and truly muddy today. Nothing says
"I'm playing countryside dressing-up" quite like a pair of
Wellington boots that are completely free of flecks of mud,
and lately I'm having to try as hard as I can to convince the
locals (and myself) that I'm not just here playacting as a
country heiress.

It doesn't help that all my pockets are heavy with the
nonsense of outdoors—I can't help but pick up every dropped

acorn and shiny conker that I see—something that people who have spent their lives in Castle Knoll certainly do not do, unless they are under the age of ten. This morning, I breathe in the earthy aroma of decay that hangs in the air as I walk, hoping I might find some inspiration for my writing. Mist pools in the gardens, with the promise of a crisp, clear day ahead.

I'm constantly telling myself that country life suits me. That it feeds the writer in me and I've finally found the place where I belong. Most days I can keep that mantra going throughout my walk from the Gravesdown estate into the village. I tell myself that the atmosphere in the pub where I write is perfect for drumming up ideas for new murder mystery drafts. It's dimly lit, leaky, and full of odd comings and goings.

Each day I take my usual seat at the Dead Witch, right by the open fire, and peruse the menu with the absolute security of someone with a bank account that has recently expanded by about forty million pounds.

And most of the time, when I say to myself that the half scribbles I've made just need time to develop into something great, I believe me. Most days.

Today is not one of those days.

My walk through the mist quickly becomes a stomp, due to how awkward and stiff my new wellies are. It didn't take any time at all for my morning eagerness to become restlessness, but the countryside isn't the easy transition I thought it would be. Not after a lifetime in London, hopping around art galleries with my mum and living off cheese sandwiches. It's silly, but I miss those cheese sandwiches. Not the actual horrible cheap white bread and Day-Glo mustard. I think I just miss who I was when I ate them.

The biggest problem is the house. Gravesdown Hall in

summer was an altogether warmer place—and I don't just mean temperature-wise. The light of full summer was constantly streaming through the diamond lattices of the high windows, making a kaleidoscope of the floor. The gardens were a work of art, and while I still employ the professional gardeners Aunt Frances used, her old gardener Archie Foyle has given up his hobby of shaping the huge topiary hedges that line the long drive. The lack of his whistling and endless patter makes the outdoors seem rather empty.

In August, Gravesdown Hall was this enigmatic place that was full of mysteries, full of just enough danger to make me feel alive, and most important of all—full of people. Archie's granddaughter, Beth, who used to cook for my great aunt Frances, was always popping in to bake something while we were all trying to get to the bottom of Great Aunt Frances's murder. A murder, I might add, that was foretold by a fortune-teller named Peony Lane in 1965, which Frances lived her life trying to prevent. Rather unsuccessfully as it turns out. I've tried to convince Beth to keep to her old schedule, but she says that these days the house makes her sad.

It has to just be in my head, but since I inherited the Gravesdown estate, I'm starting to feel like the village of Castle Knoll is giving me the cold shoulder. And this is a small place. If you're out and about, as I have been recently, you run into everyone. So if there are people you aren't seeing . . . there's a good chance they're avoiding you.

I unscrew the cap on my thermos and take a small scalding sip of its contents, wondering if it's just the fact that I'm an outsider here still. But once I solved Great Aunt Frances's murder, word definitely got around town that she had an entire room of files dedicated to town secrets.

Recently I thought of all the times I've wandered around the village trying to strike up a conversation with the postman

11

or the bar staff at the Dead Witch, only to have them give me tight smiles in return. It's clear they've been wondering just how many of their secrets Aunt Frances collected, and how far I've gotten in my reading of them.

My thoughts drift back to the house, and again I wonder if staying here is the right choice. As autumn wraps its chilly arms around the estate, I'm finding the sun leaves fewer kaleidoscopes on the floor, and the garden has shifted from a place of welcoming roses to become a collection of thorns with long shadows. At night, knowing I'm the only person in this sprawling house of seventeen bedrooms, a library, three drawing rooms, a formal dining room, a solarium, and a kitchen the size of an entire London flat makes me feel like the only thing I want in the world is Mum playing her loud music, and a cheap cheese sandwich.

My wandering feet have reached the edge of the formal gardens, and as I go through the ornate metal gate out into the grassy fields that border the estate's woodland, I see a shape through the mist. I squint for a moment to try to make sense of it, wondering if one of the horses from Foyle Farms next door has gotten loose. The lumpy form is moving with a lumbering gait, but as it gets closer, I can see the shape of hunched shoulders and the tartan of a wool shawl.

"Hello?" I call out. Technically this is private land, but that doesn't stop the locals from walking through here. The shape doesn't answer, but as it finally emerges from the swirling clouds of moisture, I see a rather striking elderly woman standing in front of me. She's got long pure-white hair, which she's wearing in one thick plait that crowns her head. She's only hunched because of the chill, and she straightens her shoulders as she meets my eyes. She looks to be in her late seventies or early eighties but seems like someone who's been health conscious her whole life. The way she stands makes me think that she could probably out-yoga me in a heartbeat.

I open my mouth to tell her kindly that technically, she's trespassing, but then I realize that I'm so lonely that if she's a nice enough person, I'll happily invite her to walk with me. She gives me a curt nod that's strangely . . . knowing. There's no other way to describe it, really. Looking into this woman's eyes is like traveling through time. Her eyes are light green, and I notice she's got brown freckles in her irises. I've never seen anyone with irises like that before, and it gives the impression that one is looking at something rare, like an uncut emerald or a vein of gold running through an ordinary rock.

"I knew I'd find you here, Annie Adams," she says. Her voice has a honeyed texture to it, thick and deep, but spiked with something sharper. Like a hint of strong whisky to balance out the sweetness. I notice she wears chunky silver rings on each bony finger, some set with turquoise or amber, others with polished ammonites or tiny leaves preserved in resin. I catch the glint of many silver chains peeking out from where she's pulling the tartan shawl tight around her neck, and I suspect she's got a host of interesting things dangling from the end of each one.

"I . . ." I falter, then try again. "Have we met?" I ask. I invited the whole village to Great Aunt Frances's funeral in October, so it's possible that we have and I've simply forgotten. Possible, but unlikely.

"I have a fortune to tell you, but you aren't going to want it," she says.

I feel the air stream from my lungs as I realize who this is.

This is Peony Lane. The famous fortune-teller, the person who set off a complicated chain of events in Great Aunt Frances's life, and mine. Her prediction of Frances's murder back in 1965, when Frances was seventeen, is ultimately why I now own the Gravesdown estate.

"You're absolutely right," I say. "If I'm going to meet some horrible fate, I don't want to know about it." But I'm not uneasy, exactly. I'm intrigued. This woman probably brings that out in everyone; I imagine it's been key to how she's made her living for all these years.

She smiles at me broadly, and it's not a malicious smile; it's an understanding one. "So you *do* know who I am," she says. "Don't worry, I won't tell you unless you ask me to."

I don't say anything in reply, because even though she's instantly captured my interest, Peony Lane is such a large character in the lore of Gravesdown Hall that it's rather like meeting someone who's just stepped out of a fairy tale. Besides, what do you say to the woman who told such a grim fortune—and turned out to be *right*?

"When a fortune comes true in such a huge and horrible way as Frances's did, I can be an intimidating person to talk to. But don't worry, I consider it unethical to tell an unwilling person a fortune. Whether it's theirs or not. But you . . ." She pauses and her eyes flicker behind me, toward the house. "You'll realize you need this fortune, and you'll come asking me for it. I just hope you come in time."

"Well, that's . . . cryptic," I say slowly. "But I suppose cryptic is your brand, right?" I laugh nervously and realize from her blank expression that I'm not being particularly funny this morning.

She gives me a tight smile. "You need to investigate the life and death of Olivia Gravesdown," she says. "Frances will have a file on her."

"Who's Olivia Gravesdown?" I ask. "And why do I need to investigate her?"

"Olivia's husband, Edmund Gravesdown, was the heir to the Gravesdown fortune, before both of them were tragically killed in a car accident," Peony says. "Along with Lord Harry Gravesdown, Edmund's father. And you need to investigate her death because I think someone might have murdered her. I can't be sure, but . . . Frances might have information on it, on that crash. It was an obsession of hers years ago."

"Wait, how could someone have killed Olivia if it's widely known she died in a car accident?" Part of me knows that she could be telling some sort of tale just to get my attention. But after the summer I've just had, I'm keeping an open mind.

Peony Lane doesn't say anything; she just looks at me with an unnervingly blank expression.

"The Gravesdown car accident," I say, thinking. "I remember the story." My mind races through facts that I only brushed by in my investigation into Frances's past. "The senior Gravesdown was in a car being driven by his eldest son. His son's wife was also a passenger, and the car hit a tree at top speed, killing all three of them."

"Perhaps you should find my file as well," Peony says. One hand casually goes to her chin, like she's thinking, but only of something of mild importance, like whose birthday is coming up or where to go on holiday. Not contemplating such a tragedy.

"Aunt Frances has a file on you?" I don't hide my surprise, because I feel like if there was a file on Peony Lane, I would have found it while investigating Frances's murder. That fortune became her whole life, and any insight into the woman who'd told it might have helped me understand Frances's conviction in its truth.

"Of course she does!" Peony actually laughs, like I was silly to think otherwise. "A sleuth like Frances? It took her a while to track me down. But once she showed up at my door, it was bloody impossible to untangle her from my life. She wanted to know *everything* about me. How my talents work, whether or not I was a fraud—anything to wriggle her way out of that fate."

"That sounds like Aunt Frances," I say. "I mean, the Frances I've learned about through her writings," I add hastily. "Because I never actually got to meet her."

"Well, once she met me, she sensed a whole web of lies. And she wouldn't rest until she worked out the truth of all of them, hoping she might expose me in the process."

"And did she?" I raise an eyebrow. Previously, I'd always been somewhat skeptical of fortune-tellers. But my belief system has been a bit upended as of late, and I've not really taken the time to think through where I stand now. Throughout my investigations last summer, I never once tried to decide if I believed Aunt Frances's fortune. It was enough that she believed it, and I felt like my feelings on the subject either way might bias my investigation.

"She didn't expose me as a fraud, because I'm not one," Peony says curtly. "But interestingly, she didn't expose me for anything else she found out either. I never discovered why. But you"—she points at me meaningfully, and I find myself backing up a step—"you need to do some digging. Start with Olivia Gravesdown. Frances kept her files alphabetical by secret, so try *I* for *infidelity*. Or maybe *F* for *fraud*. I'm honestly curious about whether Frances knew that whole story."

"And what is the whole story, then?"

Her face crinkles as she gives me a small smile. "Even I don't know all of it, and I'd like your help piecing it together after all these years." She reaches out and clasps my hand, squeezing it briefly before letting it drop. "We have a lot to talk about. And there's something that Archie Foyle has that you'll need. You're halfway to Foyle Farms already—why don't you pay him a visit?"

I should really just brush off everything this strange woman says. But so much in my world feels like it doesn't quite fit. I'm in a village that doesn't really accept me, alone in a big house I might not deserve, and this woman is basically the reason why. I suddenly feel my pulse in my throat as I start to understand that this is just what I need. Another mystery, something new for my mind to work on. My own writing hasn't been driving me enough. I haven't found my rhythm as a writer yet, and I'm struggling for the proper motivation in that quest.

But this? I'm already memorizing every word Peony is saying, to write it down later in the start of a new investigation notebook.

"I see," I say, trying to keep my voice even. It feels rather gross of me to be visibly excited about looking into the deaths of three people. Peony looks restless suddenly and shifts her weight from one foot to the other, with one hand in her pocket, holding an object I can't see. Wordlessly, she turns and starts to head back up the hill, in the direction I just came from.

"Where are you going?" I ask.

"I have something to do," she says, pulling a piece of paper from her pocket. "Frances taught me a thing or two about cheating fate," she says, and grins.

"What does that mean?" I call out, getting frustrated. It's one thing to be cryptic because that's your professional vibe, but this is just obstinacy for the sake of it.

Her smile widens. "Let's see how good you are at rooting out people's secrets. You're Frances's successor, after all. Check those files to see if she was onto any murderers hiding in our midst, while you're at it."

"Wait!" I call out. "There's no file for murder. If there was, I know I would have found it!"

She gives me a dismissive wave and yells back, "Then you need to look harder!" And then she's gone, swallowed up by the mist, as if she'd never really been there in the first place.

CHAPTER

2

January 18, 1967

IF YOU'RE TRYING TO STOP BELIEVING THAT DEATH IS coming for you, January is not the month to hold your hand and convince you otherwise. January is sharp, icy edges and dead earth, and it will remind you over and over again that in certain conditions, nothing survives.

I sound like an awful drag. I'm eighteen. I should be traveling or studying, or partying in London. But last summer my world was turned on its head. My best friend disappeared, and I was rocked by betrayal after betrayal from people I thought I could trust. The world isn't what I once thought it was.

So lately I am focusing wholly on my fortune—the eventuality that I will one day die by murder. This focus has spawned a curious education. I'm devouring books on ancient Greek myths (the Oracle of Delphi being of particular interest), astrology, ogham. . . . I'm even learning about casting runes.

I figure that the more I learn about divining the future, the better chance I have at dodging mine.

Or maybe dodging *is the wrong word. I find that what I'm actually trying to do is outsmart it. There are lots of these stories in mythology—a young girl finds herself at the mercy of a capricious god, or sphinx, or fae creature, and she has to use her cunning to get away. However, there is a difference between these mythical girls and myself. They each had the chance to bargain with their adversary. I need to find mine. I'm prepared to cut a deal.*

I've decided this quest is in two parts. One adversary is my eventual murderer, who could be anyone I come across in life—a friend, a family member, or someone who is currently a stranger to me, passing by in the street. So I must get to know them, covertly. What might they be hiding that could intertwine with my life in such a violent and final way?

The second part is my other adversary—fate itself. And because it won't do to go chasing after an elusive shadow, I've turned my focus to the person at the heart of this, who claims to speak on fate's behalf.

And that person is Peony Lane.

All I have to do now is find her.

CHAPTER

3

I TAKE A SMALL SHORTCUT THAT GOES DIRECTLY TO Foyle Farms, and as I walk, I wonder about Aunt Frances's other diaries. I found a stack of them in her house back in August, but there are huge gaps in the dates. Noticeably, she skipped the rest of the 1960s, and the earliest diary (other than the green one from 1965 to 1966) is from 1972. Either she didn't have anything else to write about for the rest of the sixties (doubtful, because come on, it was the sixties), or some of her diaries were stored elsewhere. Or they're missing.

My brain is flooding with ideas, so I find the nearest log to perch on and dig out one of my spare notebooks. It's then that I notice the green diary from 1965 is sandwiched among my other things. That diary has become something of a good-luck charm for me, and seeing as Peony Lane mentioned the death of the Gravesdowns, I decide to flip through it again. There's something in there about that car crash, if I remember correctly.

My fingers flutter through the pages eagerly. I know it's near the beginning. Aunt Frances and her friends were having a conversation in the woods on the Gravesdown estate, the first night they all sneaked through the fence. Aunt Frances's friend Emily said that Ford Gravesdown killed his first wife with a knife that had a ruby in the handle and then threw it into the River Dimber. Then they talked about the rest of the family. . . . Finally, there it is:

Four years ago, Lord Gravesdown's eldest son was driving his car, with his father and wife as passengers. He took one of the hairpin turns near the estate far too quickly, rolling the car and killing them all instantly.

I haven't heard any stories about Olivia's death being suspicious, and stories like that would have crystallized into village lore by now if there was any speculation. I decide that if the accident report for that car crash isn't in Aunt Frances's files, I'll pay a visit to Detective Crane and try to obtain a copy. I note down the reference to the crash in my new notebook, and then another idea for a book occurs to me. I spend ages sitting there, just writing excitedly, breathing in the smell of wet leaves and lichen. I sit there for so long that my knees start cramping from my awkward position on the log. But I feel energized, and I have the threads of a real-life cold case to chase, as well as a new idea for a murder mystery to write.

When I finally approach Archie Foyle's house, there's friendly smoke curling out of the chimney, and it's half past ten. I walk over the little footbridge that leads to his front door, the water from the River Dimber babbling beneath. A large waterwheel is set into the front of the stone farmhouse, turning slowly. The river approaches the house from the woods and has been tamed so that it flows around the entire house like a small moat. The two prongs of water then rejoin on the other side of the building, snaking off toward the village. Several breeds of duck are splashing about as I knock on Archie's front door, and I notice the Virginia creeper covering the front of the house has turned a fiery autumn red.

The door creaks open, and Archie's weathered face and keen eyes peek out from behind it. He's not wearing his flat cap today, so his white curls are a bit wilder than usual.

He cracks a broad smile when he sees that it's me. "Annie, what brings you here?" he asks. The door swings fully open and he beckons me inside.

"I was already out walking for the usual reasons," I say. "I'm extremely restless, for one. Rather lonely, if I'm honest. But then I ran into Peony Lane."

"Oh dear. I'll put the kettle on," he says, leading me to the kitchen. I bite back a smile when I see two teacups already out, and wonder if he was expecting me.

Archie's kitchen has bright yellow walls and is nearly the size of the one at Gravesdown Hall. He has a large set of windows over his sink that face the garden, where he used to be able to keep an eye on his polytunnels. The polytunnels were a source of trouble for Great Aunt Frances, because Archie was growing plants that weren't strictly legal. I personally didn't care all that much, but I didn't want to see Archie get caught in anything criminal. Which, given his very open nature, he would have been eventually.

The plants are gone now, though, replaced by some new permanent structures that function as garages. Great Aunt Frances's old Rolls-Royce Phantom II lives in one of them—a gift I was happy to make, as I don't see myself ever having use for that car. But also, along with that gift, I became a partner in Archie's new classic car restoration business. It's only small-scale at present, but I can tell he's enjoying traveling around, finding good deals on cars in need of rebuilding, and bringing them back here.

I'm watching him busy himself making tea when my phone buzzes from my pocket. I see that it's Mum calling, and since she almost never calls these days, I signal to Archie that I'm going to go outside to take it. He waves me off and I step back through the front door.

Weeks of relentless rain have swelled the River Dimber almost to overflowing, making heavy work for the water-wheel. It's started to make a funny hollow clunking noise as it moves, and I worry something has come loose. I take a step away from it so I can hear better.

"Hi, Mum," I say.

"Annie, hi!" Mum says. Her voice sounds light and breathless, like she's distracted but happy. "I'm sorry I haven't phoned in ages; I've been really busy."

"Busy is good," I say. "Have you got any new exhibitions lined up?"

Mum lets out a small laugh, and I hear her voice go slightly muffled, like she's turning away from the phone. There's the rumble of a low voice, and I hear Mum say, "*Not now.*" Then she comes through clearer and says, "Just doing lots of painting, you know."

"Mum," I say, stretching the word out in a playful drawl. "Have you got a guy over? You can tell me if you're seeing someone, you know."

She sighs. "I know, Annie, it's just . . . this one's a bit complicated. I will tell you about him soon, I promise."

"All right," I say slowly. "Just . . . stay out of trouble, please?"

Mum laughs, and it's a more genuine one this time. "That's rich, coming from you! You aren't getting tangled up in any more of Frances's secrets, are you? No more detective work? Because I finally got sent the full paperwork on Frances's estate, and this 'Good Behavior Clause' she's got in her appendix has me worried."

When Great Aunt Frances's fortune came true last summer, and she was found murdered on the floor of her library, it set off a competition for her inheritance that nearly cost me my life. Her will stipulated that whoever solved her murder would get everything—her fortune, her house . . . even the farm the Foyles have been living on for generations. Luckily I was victorious, which meant the first thing I did was make sure that Foyle Farms and its surrounding lands were legally given to Archie and his granddaughter, Beth. But Aunt Frances was meticulous in her forward planning, so her will has twists and turns in it that are still unfolding.

"That's obviously not going to apply to me," I say. "That's just Frances making doubly sure not only that her inheritor is a good person to begin with, but that they *stay* that way."

Mum sighs. "I guess you have that police inspector friend of yours," she adds. "Hopefully he'll keep you out of trouble."

"Uh-huh," I say. I'm not sure that's the way my friendship with Detective Crane works, but I'm not going to go into that with Mum. Last summer it was something of a tug-of-war between the detective and me, where I tried to find out who'd killed Aunt Frances, and he tried to do his job—which, admittedly, I constantly got in the way of. I pause, not really sure how to continue the conversation. But Mum fills the silence.

"I was calling to ask a favor," she says. "You know how last time you pulled a file for me from Frances's collection?"

"The one on Dad?" I ask. "That's still locked in Aunt Frances's files." And that's where I'm happy for it to stay, I think to myself. The last thing I want to be worrying about as I find my feet in Castle Knoll is whether or not my estranged dad is going to show up, asking for money.

"No, I was after another one," Mum says. "The one on the fortune-teller? Peony Lane was her name, right?"

The *thunk* of Archie's waterwheel is suddenly loud. It's

like something's rattling around inside the wooden framework, trying to knock its way out.

"Annie? Are you there?"

"Sorry, yeah," I say. "Why are you so interested in Peony Lane all of a sudden?" I don't mention that I've just met her, and there's a pinch of guilt in that. But I brush it aside, given that secret keeping seems to be part of the architecture of our relationship now. It's petty of me to crave more openness from Mum while reflecting her behavior right back at her, but I'm telling myself this is an act of self-preservation.

"I just wanted to know more about her," Mum says. "After you gave me Frances's diary to read last summer, I was thinking about incorporating some of the themes from it into my art—you know, like obsession and fate. Peony Lane would be the main inspiration."

Something feels strange about this. It's as if my refusal to hear my fortune from Peony Lane earlier has caused her name to echo all around me. Apparently she is not a woman to be ignored.

"I'll look into it," is all I say. The waterwheel suddenly lurches to a stop, and I can see that whatever was rattling in it has fallen partway out. It looks like an algae-covered stick, and it's wedged between the side of the wheel and the front of the house, where the Virginia creeper is particularly thick.

"All right, thanks," Mum says. "Call me when you find it, will you? And can you send it to me?"

"Sure," I say, distracted. There's something about that stick that catches my eye. "I'll talk to you later, okay?" I say to Mum, and hang up.

Archie appears through the front door with a cup of tea, but when he sees me pocketing my phone and reaching up to the waterwheel, he sets the tea on the window ledge and joins me.

"Something stuck there?" he asks. "Things are always getting pulled through that wheel—mostly pondweed and dead branches. With all the rain we've had these past few weeks, the river's been churning up more junk than usual." Archie is slightly taller than me, and he reaches up and pulls the object from where it's stuck in the wheel.

"Oh, you've got to be kidding me," he breathes as he looks at the object in his hand. He pulls out a handkerchief and wipes it dry, and I see the glint of well-polished gold and a scattering of small rubies, like droplets of blood. "You've got to be bloody kidding me."

"What is it?" I say, coming closer.

It's then that I see that although the object is stick-shaped, it isn't a stick at all. It's a very ornate antique dagger.

"She was right," I say, my voice breathless. "Emily was right all along."

CHAPTER

4

January 20, 1967

THERE'S A REASON I GOT TANGLED UP IN MORE GRAVES-
down secrets, and curiously, that reason is not Ford Gravesdown.

That reason is Archie Foyle.

Last week, the frost on the village green was so thick it was
almost like a coating of snow. I enjoyed the steady crunch of my
boots as I walked through it toward the little cottage that serves
as Castle Knoll's library. The cold air pricked at my cheeks, and I
felt grateful to Ford for the Christmas gift he'd given me the pre-
vious year—a thick wool coat of forest green, trimmed with fur
around the hood. I'd normally feel odd about such an extrava-
gant gift, but he's a lord after all, and the inheritor of the Graves-
down estate and fortune. What's extravagant to me is likely
nothing much to him.

The bite of the winter air can't touch me inside this coat, and
as I walked, I thought about what a clever gift it was. Ford is like
that—he'll have known that whenever I feel snug while wearing
this coat, it will make me think fondly of him. I do have a lot of

*growing affection for him, but he likes to plan and he takes plea-
sure in maneuvering people. This is possibly part of his allure,
which is all the more reason I'm determined to tread carefully
when it comes to him.*

*The library in Castle Knoll is so small that you can see almost
every book from the entrance. There are five freestanding shelves
that are about as tall as I am, but otherwise all the books are in
rows along the walls. I wanted privacy, so I nestled in the farthest
corner from the door, blocked by one of the tall shelves. I wasn't
wholly relaxed as I sat on the floor, and I realized it was because if
someone pushed hard enough on the shelves nearest the door, they
could fall like dominoes and crush me. My murder would be complete, just because I wasn't cautious about where I chose to sit.*

*So I readjusted myself, putting my back against the wall be-
neath the window so that if the shelf toppled over, I'd be under it
rather than crushed by it. Satisfied, I got lost in my latest project—
tracking down the fortune-teller Peony Lane. I had a stack of
Conan Doyles and Agatha Christies, which I moved to one side
as I spread out the news clippings I'd found about Peony Lane.
They were mostly stories about how one of her fortunes had led
to someone winning a raffle or avoiding a falling tree. So far there
was nothing about one of her predictions being darker, and certainly nothing about her predicting murders. If she had that particular talent, surely the police would be interested in her.*

*I also had flyers advertising Peony Lane's talents at a list of
fairs—the dates of which had all passed. I was hoping she did the
same circuit every year, so that if I failed in my mission to find her
this winter, I could at least see her in the spring when she made
her next public appearance.*

*What I wanted most was to find out where she lived, so that I
could speak to her in private.*

"That's not her real name, you know," a voice said over my

shoulder. It was so startling that I shrieked, causing the librarian to hiss, "Quiet, please!" in my direction.

In my distracted state, I hadn't noticed Archie Foyle walking toward me.

"What are you doing in here?" I asked him.

"What? You think I can't read?" Archie gave me a lopsided grin and sat on the floor beside me. I'd never noticed quite how curly his brown hair is, probably because he normally has it under a cap. He stretched his legs out in front of him, took my carefully folded wool coat from the floor, and wadded it up behind his back like a pillow. I gave him a stern look but didn't make a move to snatch it back, simply because Archie had me intrigued with his comment about Peony Lane's real name. "I started coming in here a few winters ago," he continued. "Just to be somewhere warm in the evenings. The farmhouse used to be freezing when we ran out of wood. Anyway, Miss Stokes—she's the librarian—"

"I know who the librarian is," I drawled, rolling my eyes a bit.

"Just checking," he said. "Anyway," he continued, "Miss Stokes said if I wanted to loiter, then I had to read while I was here. So, I started reading. I've made it through all of those"—he pointed to the stack of Sherlock Holmes novels I'd gathered to check out— "and all the Agatha Christies, and Dickens, Austen, Kipling, all the James Bond novels . . ."

"Archie, I don't mean to be rude, and I'm happy that you've found a way into the world of literature—even if it started as a quest for central heating. But I'm rather busy here. Unless you have some useful information about Peony Lane, then can you kindly leave me be?"

"Well, you see, I do actually. Have information about Peony Lane, that is." He looked at me, and I could tell he had something up his sleeve. The thing about Archie, though, is that he thinks he can hide his emotions, but he really can't. Watching him try to conceal information is like watching a four-year-old with a toffee in his hand tell you that he doesn't have any sweets.

"About her real name, you mean?" I asked. "Because that's what you said just now."

"I did indeed," he said, and he leaned farther back against my coat and tucked his hands behind his head. He closed his eyes as if he were settling in for an afternoon nap, and his face would have looked almost angelic if it hadn't been for the sun glinting off the surprising amount of stubble on his jaw.

"Archie," I said, my voice holding the crackle of impatience. "What do you want? I can tell you're going to sit here being smug until I meet some demand of yours. So you might as well get it out now."

Archie's eyes snapped back open, and he smiled. "Well, now that you mention it, I have a proposition for you."

"I'm not letting you try to break up Rose's engagement," I said. "Or giving you any information about what she's been up to lately."

Rose's romance with Ford's driver was currently the talk of the town, but Rose had had a fling with Archie just over a year before. So far as I was aware, there wasn't any great attachment on either side, but that didn't mean Archie wouldn't try to get her back, just because.

He put his hands in the air in pretend outrage. "I wouldn't dream of it!" he said. "Rosie is welcome to her happiness. I'll find mine soon, I'm sure." He winked at me, and it was so theatrical that I rolled my eyes.

"And I'm not going to take up with you so you can get back at her," I said.

"Again, Frances, you shock me," he said. Though I could tell he wasn't shocked in the least. "I know you're off the market, getting tangled up with Ford Gravesdown—"

"Excuse me, there is no tangling happening!" I huffed.

"I'm not passing judgment," he said. "All right, I am, but only because I hate that family. Ford in particular. He didn't have to throw my whole family out just because my father was having an affair with his wife. Eric and I didn't have anything to do with our father's choices." Archie shrugged, which seemed a strange gesture to punctuate the breakup of his family. "So here I am renting a leaky room above the Dead Witch and watching my childhood home rot from afar . . ."

I didn't know what to say to that. Archie's whole situation was really tragic, actually. I wondered if I could speak to Ford about it . . . but then it occurred to me that this was just what Archie was after.

"You want me to try to put in a good word with Ford, then? Try to change his mind and get you your farm back?"

"Why, Frances, what an ingenious idea!" he said, his voice full of feigned surprise.

"Archie, I'm not his wife—I don't have that kind of influence over him," I said.

"You never know. For the record, I oppose this relationship you have with Ford, on the grounds that I hate that bastard."

"Noted," I said coolly.

Archie shifted a little, prodding at my folded-up coat behind his back as if it was suddenly full of thorns. "What I have to tell you about Peony Lane comes right back to the car crash that killed all the Gravesdown heirs, with the exception of your charming new beau, Ford Gravesdown. But before I tell you what I know, you need to let me be your Dr. Watson."

"Pardon?"

Archie gestured to my notes and newspaper clippings. "I want in on this."

I gave him a long stare. "I sense that your motives in wanting to help me go beyond getting your farmhouse back."

"I'm not plotting revenge, I promise," Archie said. His words sounded genuine. "And I'm the perfect person to help you when it comes to Peony Lane."

"Why? What makes you an expert on her?" I asked.

"Because in 1961, when she was sixteen, Peony Lane was arrested. She was caught vandalizing Edmund Gravesdown's Bentley. She didn't do any real damage; the Gravesdowns had it fixed up almost immediately once it was towed back to their estate. But that Bentley crashed a week later, and there was something about Peony Lane's crime that the police never found out."

I was barely breathing as I listened to him. Peony Lane, in prison? Vandalizing property? Perhaps she was a fraud after all, because who would do that if they really could see the future?

"What did the police miss?" I asked, my voice barely a whisper.

"When Peony Lane was wrecking Edmund Gravesdown's car, she cut the brake cable."

"How do you know?"

"Because my brother, Eric, saw her. He was there when she vandalized the car—he helped. And as for the brake cable, Eric was the one who showed Peony Lane how to cut it."

My jaw dropped as I digested this information. Was Archie telling me that Peony Lane was responsible for the death of Ford's family?

"But surely there would have been an investigation into what caused the crash, and someone would have discovered the severed brake cable," I said.

"Like I said, after Peony smashed up the car and cut the cable, it was towed back to the Gravesdown estate. I don't know the extent of the repairs, but I suppose it's possible they didn't check under the bonnet, thinking all the damage was done to the outside of the car. But two days later that car sped out of the drive for the first time since the vandalism. When Edmund Gravesdown couldn't slow down at the first curve in the road, the car spun out straight into a tree."

"And no one pushed for a more thorough investigation into the crash? Examining the engine, the tire marks, the angle of the accident?" I asked.

"This is why we're going to be a great team," Archie said, looking impressed at my questions. "And here's where the plot gets thicker. There was no investigation because the family wanted everything buttoned up quickly. No questions, no inquiries. The car was just impounded straightaway."

He watched me while my mind worked through the implications of that. "The family," I said slowly.

"That's right. There was only one family member left, after that. And he did everything he could to sweep that accident under the rug. Your charming new beau, Ford Gravesdown."

My expression shifted into one of shock, but I pinched it back quickly with one of suspicion. "Look me in the eye and tell me your whole reason for talking to me today isn't about revenge on Ford Gravesdown."

Archie didn't even flinch. "All right, it's all about revenge against Ford Gravesdown. But, Frances, I can tell you smell it too . . . something's not right with that family, Ford included. If you want to know more about Peony Lane, you're also going to uncover a lot of Gravesdown secrets. You shouldn't deal with those alone, because people who know too much about the skeletons in the Gravesdown closets? They tend to disappear."

CHAPTER

5

I LOOK AT ARCHIE, WHOSE HANDS ARE SHAKING slightly as he holds the knife.

"Emily's story about that knife, about Ford killing his first wife. . . . She wasn't right, was she?" I ask him. His eyes don't leave the knife as he shakes his head.

"Let's take our tea inside," he says. He hands me the knife, and it's heavy in my hands. It looks like something that might have once been on display behind glass in the library at Gravesdown Hall.

We settle at Archie's kitchen table, and I place the knife between us. The handle is about five inches long, and there's an empty gem setting about midway down—right where your palm would be if you gripped it. If there were a stone in it, it would be about the size of my thumbnail, and when I reach out to flip the knife over, I notice there's a setting for a matching one on the other side, also empty. The spattering of smaller rubies I noticed earlier is transfixing in the light—they're in a strange pattern, like a constellation. The blade is long and thin—probably double the length of the handle—and it's still sharp and polished. It doesn't look river worn; it looks immaculately cared for.

"Have you ever seen this before?" I ask Archie.

His expression is curious, like he's in two places at once. "Peony Lane, you say?" he asks, as if I haven't spoken. "When did you see her, exactly?"

"About an hour ago, maybe? Archie, do you know anything about this knife? Peony instructed me to come here specifically—she said there was an object you had for me. Something that might shed light on the life and death of Olivia Gravesdown. Can you tell me how Peony Lane might be connected to all of this?"

Archie scratches the back of his neck, thinking. "As far as Peony's connection to this knife and the rumors surrounding it go, the person to ask about that would be my brother, Eric."

"I didn't know you had a brother," I say.

"He keeps himself to himself," Archie replies, and takes a long drink of his tea. "He's lived in one of the rooms above the Dead Witch for decades, but years ago he used to work for the Gravesdowns, like our father before him." There's a bitterness to his tone, but I don't press him.

"How does that connect to Peony Lane?" I ask.

"Well, Eric was a bit of a playboy in his younger years, and around the time of the Gravesdown crash, he had two girls he was seeing at the same time. One was Laura Sparrow—everyone called her Birdy—she was Emily's older sister. Birdy was his main squeeze. But on the side, he had Ellen Jones. You know her now as Peony Lane."

"So do you think the story about the knife and the River Dimber got started by either of them?" I ask.

Archie's expression closes down then, and he concentrates on his tea. "It's all so long ago, it's probably nothing," he says. "My memory's going. That was just the fuzzy recollection of an old man."

I don't believe it for a second; Archie's as sharp as ever. I can tell he's sifting through his memories, and it's clear that knife means something to him. His eyes keep flitting over to where it sits in the center of the table, before they dart back to his tea.

"Archie, someone must have stuck this in your waterwheel recently. It couldn't have got there by accident. Besides, it's so clean it could have been polished this morning," I say.

Archie purses his lips as if he's thinking hard about what to say next, but then just shrugs, saying nothing.

"So you won't mind if I take this dagger to Detective Crane and have him examine it?" I ask. "Maybe send it away for forensic analysis?" I'm half bluffing—I will take it to Crane, but I doubt he can do much about it. Other than Emily's disappearance, which I've solved, there are no missing persons cases related to Castle Knoll and the Gravesdown family. At least, none that I know of.

It takes Archie a moment to answer, but in that second of hesitation I see him struggle to hold his expression of nonchalance. "Do what you like," he says.

His thoughts are turning inward, and I want to ask him more about Peony Lane, but I don't know how to go about it. We sip our tea in companionable silence for a moment, and I look around the bright kitchen. There's a china cabinet to our left, full of ornate plates and knickknacks, and on the other side, a large oak bookshelf is overflowing. "I didn't take you for much of a reader," I say, trying to get him talking again.

He snorts. "Because I work on cars? Or is that opinion because of my past illegal gardening habits? You know, Annie, being judgmental doesn't suit you."

I start a little at his tone, because his voice is sharp. I've never known Archie to get short with anyone. I give him a sideways glance, and his expression doesn't soften; he simply looks out the window. I wander over to the bookshelves to look at the titles, curious now. Something has upset Archie, and I want to push him further to see if I can get to the bottom of it.

"I deserve that. I was an art student—I've had my fair share of people assuming I don't read either," I say, trying to keep the conversation going. I pull an old copy of *Sense and Sensibility* from the shelves and notice that the inside cover is stamped *Property of Castle Knoll Library*.

"Oh, I, uh . . . I've been meaning to take that back," he says. "I mean, everyone has the odd overdue library book hanging around, right?"

"Overdue from when?" I ask, raising an eyebrow at him.

"That one?" He runs a hand along the back of his neck, looking slightly embarrassed. "I think I've had that one out since about 1968."

I laugh, and it breaks what was remaining of the tension. "Don't worry, I'm not going to turn you in," I say.

"Yeah, well. I had a disagreement with the librarian a long time ago, but she's been gone for ages, so it's probably safe to go back in there," he says.

"What, talking too loud? Not paying your fines?"

"No, nothing like that. Our disagreement ended in divorce," he says casually, and his familiar wry smile is back. When he sees my puzzled look, he continues. "When I was twenty-three, I married Lucy Stokes, who was the librarian. She was a couple of years older than me, but it seemed like a good idea at the time."

"'A good idea at the time' is an interesting way to describe getting married," I say.

"Well. We were only married a year; I was in love with

someone else, really." Archie waves a hand like a whole marriage was nothing. "And Lucy left and moved in with a bloke in Bristol. Lucy had a daughter with her second husband, but we stayed in contact. Her husband was a useless sort of guy—he left just after his daughter was born. Later, Lucy's daughter got pregnant at sixteen and had a baby girl—Beth. Around that same time, Lucy got ill. She contacted me, almost in desperation, I think. Her daughter couldn't look after Beth properly, and didn't want to keep her. Lucy needed to know Beth would be looked after when the worst came." The lines in Archie's face deepen for a moment, but then his expression clears.

"So you're not Beth's biological grandfather?" I ask. "You adopted her when her grandmother died? Just like that?" I feel a rush of respect for Archie, and additional warmth floods through me when it occurs to me that Beth never left home—when she got married to Miyuki, they both moved in with Archie. They could have had all kinds of reasons for that, but I suddenly want to believe it was because Archie is their family, and they didn't like the idea of him being alone.

Archie's expression tightens a fraction. "'Just like that' is a funny way of putting it. Having Frances nearby made suddenly having a child of my own to look after a bit easier." He looks uncomfortable again, so I decide not to press him any further on it.

Perhaps hearing him say "Frances" while I'm staring at the shelf makes me look at the books there a bit differently. Because suddenly, the spines of several small leather-bound books on the very top shelf strike me as remarkably familiar.

I reach toward one, but it's just that little bit too high. "These look like the same kind of notebook Aunt Frances kept her journals in," I say.

Archie's out of his chair in seconds. "Oh, those are just

old farm ledgers," he says, walking swiftly around the kitchen table and coming to stand right next to me. "There's so much old junk on these shelves, I should really do a clearout."

I turn and give him a long look. "Archie," I say. "Several years of Aunt Frances's journals are missing."

When Archie doesn't react, I continue. "Specifically, everything from 1967 to 1972. Six journals . . . and up there, I can see six spines. The same size and shape of the others I have back at Gravesdown Hall. Frances liked a certain brand of diary; the others are all that same type too—though different colors."

I know in my bones that these are the missing years of Frances's journals, but Archie doubles down. "Frances was helping me stay organized for a time, and she gave me those books to help. I suppose she did like a certain brand—she must have bought a bunch for herself as well."

"Can I look at them?" I ask.

He narrows his eyes at me, and I can tell he knows I'm onto him. What I can't figure out is why he'd have the journals in the first place, and why he'd lie about them to me now. Was this what Peony Lane sent me here to find? Was the knife just a coincidence? I want to trust that maybe Archie's just sentimental, but Aunt Frances had a talent for collecting information. Her files are proof of that, but last summer I learned that the files only take you so far without the benefit of her own voice to guide you through them. Her journal writings gave me essential context for the evidence she'd squirreled away in her filing cabinets back in August.

"Nope," he says plainly, then he moves slightly so that his shoulder is edging me away from the bookshelf.

I sigh. "Look, I'm not about to get into a fight with you over these journals. I just . . . My encounter with Peony Lane left me unsettled, and I want to know if Aunt Frances had any more dealings with her."

Archie's face shifts a little, and he looks conflicted. "Well," he says after a pause, "I suppose it's only a matter of time before Peony tells you a thing or two about the past."

"It was my future she was particularly interested in telling me about," I say.

He smiles, but it's fleeting. "Yes, she seems to have this sort of *need* to tell people things about their future. I think it unburdens her soul a bit each time."

"What do you mean?" I ask. "Do you believe she can see the future?"

"Lord, no!" he says. "But I will admit that she has a way of talking about it that gets under your skin." A muscle in Archie's jaw twitches, and I notice his hand grip his mug a little tighter. "But more to the point, if Peony Lane is wandering about Castle Knoll telling you all sorts of cryptic things, you might as well know that Frances and I had quite a time tracking her down after she had her fortune told."

I feel my shoulders sag, because if I'm honest, I'm growing tired of Aunt Frances's fortune. It ruled her entire life; must it rule mine too? "I guess I should have predicted that Aunt Frances was seeking out Peony Lane because of her fortune," I say.

"The funny thing is," Archie says, "the fortune that started to matter to her most once we tracked Peony down wasn't her own." He crosses to the other side of the kitchen again, opens a cupboard, and pulls out a round cake tin. I think for a minute that it might contain something of the green and illegal variety, but when he opens it, I see a mountain of homemade shortbread.

"Whose, then?" I ask, taking a biscuit.

Archie lifts a finger of shortbread in my direction, in a silent toast. "Mine," he says.

CHAPTER

6

SO YOU'RE TELLING ME THAT FORD SOMEHOW KNEW the brake cable to his brother's car had been cut, did nothing about it, and then hushed it all up after?" I asked Archie. We were at a shadowy table in the back room of the Dead Witch, because Miss Stokes had told us off for being too loud in the library.

I'd realized then just how much Miss Stokes had observed from my comings and goings over the past few months, and I felt uneasy. She'd been the one I'd asked for newspaper clippings about Peony Lane, and she'd found a pamphlet for me on the history of the Gravesdown family.

Lately the whole village has been looking at me oddly. They don't know if they should treat me as some sort of chosen one due to Ford's involvement with me, or shun me as a gold-digging harlot. When I was sixteen, comments on my looks started becoming more frequent, but with Emily and Rose turning just as many heads, we could band together and declare war on anyone too lecherous. Spending time with the boys helped keep the older men from trying their luck, but now that I'm eighteen and Rose is engaged and Emily gone—and John and Walt are off to university (not that they'd be much use, as ex-boyfriends)—I've noticed more long looks than usual.

"I'm not saying Ford knew about the severed brake cable," Archie said, sipping a pint. I'd opted for a lemonade, but watching him sit across from me casually drinking like he belonged here, I suddenly felt a bit uptight for my choice.

"Then what are you saying? Actually, let's do this properly." I pulled out a notebook and pen. "Let's go back to the car accident."

Archie reached into his pocket and pulled out the folded newspaper clipping that we'd taken when Miss Stokes wasn't looking. It wasn't really my style to steal from the library, but technically it was Archie who took it.

"Perfect," I said, unfolding the clipping. "We'll go through the facts, compare town gossip—because sometimes there's truth behind the wild stories people spread—and then, if I can gather the courage, I'll see if I can get Ford's version of events."

CASTLE KNOLL GAZETTE

Wednesday, May 17, 1961

Horror Crash Leaves Three Dead: The Illustrious Gravesdown Family Tragedy

By Maggie Owens, village correspondent

On Monday, May 15, tragedy struck Dorset's most elite family when the lives of three of the senior members of the Gravesdown family ended in a car crash. This horrific loss comes only five years after Lady Gravesdown lost her battle with cancer, further proving the Gravesdown family to be marked by tragedy.

Lord Harrison (Harry) Gravesdown (58 years of age) was riding in the passenger seat of the convertible Bentley driven by his son Edmund Gravesdown (29 years of age), with Edmund's wife, Olivia (28 years of age), in the back seat, when the speeding car took a curve too quickly and crashed into a tree.

All three were killed instantly. The victims are survived by the youngest Gravesdown son, Rutherford (Ford) Gravesdown (20 years of age), brother to Edmund. Olivia and Edmund also leave behind a young son, Saxon Gravesdown (7 years of age). The guardianship of Saxon, as well as all the Gravesdown assets and lands, now passes to Rutherford.

An unnamed source has told the *Gazette* that Olivia wasn't wearing her wedding ring, a fact that adds weight to recent rumors of infidelity that have been swirling around Olivia in particular. In an unexplained turn of events, a stone found in the road appears to be a rough-cut ruby, which police speculate might have come loose from some jewelry, though nothing matching has been found.

London society is already talking about the marriage prospects of Ford Gravesdown. Even though he would be considered rather young to marry, it is suspected that given his new title and responsibilities toward raising his 7-year-old nephew, Ford Gravesdown plans to propose to his girlfriend, London socialite Etta Elle.

"This is very gossipy," I murmured.

"The Gazette *always seems to print whatever they like," Archie said. "I think there was even a follow-up article, where they talked about how there was evidence that Olivia tried to get out*

of the moving car—one of the rear doors was open when they were all found. It would explain how she was so easily flung into the road."

We were quiet for a few moments, because three people had lost their lives, and even when you factored in infidelity and scandal, it seemed wildly unfair and horribly tragic.

But then there was the alleged severed brake cable.

"Since the investigation was quashed by Ford—according to you," I add hastily, "I assume that meant no autopsies?"

Archie shrugged and sipped his pint. "No need—it was obvious how they died. And I suppose Ford wanted to protect young Saxon and bury his family as soon as possible without investigations dragging out their grief."

"You seem to know a lot about them," I said.

Archie sat back in his chair then and gave me a contemplative look. He drew in a long breath and let it out slowly. His eyes darted to the bar, then back to me again. "I don't think you realize just how entwined my family has always been with the Gravesdowns. The Foyles have been tenants of the Gravesdowns for generations. They've had their claws into each and every one of us, in their own ways. It's practically their family motto," he sneered into his pint glass, and let out a harsh laugh. "If you're a Gravesdown and you don't have a Foyle under your thumb, you're doing something wrong."

I sipped my lemonade, thinking. "You mentioned your brother, Eric, earlier, along with Peony Lane. Are you saying that Eric was close to the Gravesdowns, but then helped vandalize the car? He'd be an accessory to murder, if what you've told me about the brake cable is true. Do you know why he got involved?"

Archie ran a hand through his coffee-colored curls and shook his head, his expression tight. "All I know is this: Eric and Peony Lane vandalized Edmund Gravesdown's car while it was parked at a petrol station just outside the village. The police were called, and Peony Lane was arrested. Eric ran and hid in the pub next door when he heard the police coming. The damaged car was towed back to the Gravesdown estate for repairs.

"But Peony Lane went for the engine. When she'd finished with the brake cable, though, she slithered out from under the bonnet and closed it like no one had been under there. But Eric had seen her; he knew what she'd done."

"What happened to the car after it was taken away? Was it destroyed?" I asked. "This is the kind of detail that could be important. We should try to find where it went—which scrapyard, or was it sold?"

"I can look into that," he said. His expression looked less troubled and more purposeful, like he was pleased he had a job to do.

I paused, thinking. "Archie, three people died. What if Saxon had been in that car? How could they do something like cut the brake cable, not knowing who would be driving or riding in it? If they had a problem with Edmund, this was a horribly slapdash way to get revenge."

"Eric wouldn't tell me why they did it. But he let Peony take the blame for the whole thing."

"I'm making a note to look up her prison sentence," I said, scribbling in my notebook. "We should look at how long she was in for, and what that investigation entailed. Because . . . why didn't they find out about the severed brake cable then? I understand Ford wanting to move on with his life after the crash, so he didn't let anyone examine the car afterward, but that vandalism would have to have been investigated, if someone was caught in the act and arrested."

"I might know someone who works in the police station," Archie said. When I raised an eyebrow in a "tell me more" sort of way, he simply looked out the window and sipped his pint.

"Okay then," I said eventually. "You see what you can find out from your . . . informant. But the person I'd still most like to find is Peony Lane. This car crash investigation could be important, or it could be a distraction. I won't lose sight of my initial goal—to find her."

"I don't know where she lives," Archie said. "Or anything else about her, really. Other than the fact that she used to follow Eric around like a lost puppy. But then, so did a lot of girls, including Emily's older sister. Birdy, they all called her, before she ran away."

I felt a chill at the mention of Emily. I never knew her sister, just that she escaped out of her bedroom window in the dead of night, like the place was on fire. She left Emily a note, and it just said, "Come and find me when you're ready, love Birdy." There was no address, of course, so how could Emily find her?

Sometimes I wonder if Emily actually managed to track her down, and that's where she herself disappeared to. It's the most comforting theory I have, that she's just in the mystery place that Birdy ran to, living a new life with her sister.

"Is Eric still around?" I asked. "I'd really like to talk to him about all this."

Archie's expression clouded over. "Oh, he's around, but we don't speak anymore."

"Why not?"

"Long story. It's not just that we don't speak; it's more that we pretend the other doesn't exist," he said, draining his pint.

"Well, he might speak to me. Will you tell me where I can find him?" I asked.

Archie shrugged, and I could tell he was trying too hard to appear casual. "He might speak to you, who knows? He seems very interested in you at the moment. He's over there." Archie jutted his chin toward the bar. "Pulling pints."

When I looked over, Eric Foyle met my gaze and smoothed back a curtain of rich brown hair that had flopped into his eyes. He grinned at me, and I felt gravity shift slightly as I stood from my chair.

CHAPTER

7

BETH COMES IN THROUGH THE BACK DOOR AND CUTS off the question I'm about to ask Archie. "Oh, Annie, hi."

"Hi, Beth," I say warmly. "How is Miyuki enjoying Japan?"

"She's loving the chance to visit her family," Beth says. "Though I'm counting the days until she comes back. Not just because I miss her, but because she always fills her suitcase with amazing Japanese snacks."

"Smart woman—snacks are the way to anyone's heart," I say.

"Especially mine," Beth says, laughing. She's in one of her signature vintage tea dresses with a tan mac over the top of it. She's tall and broad-shouldered, with dark hair and distinctive facial features. Looking at her now, I see that her wide-set eyes and full mouth don't reflect Archie at all, though I instantly feel bad for trying to trace her parentage from her face. Her expression is friendly, but it darkens a touch as she looks between Archie and me, toward the knife.

"Am I interrupting something?" she asks.

"Your grandad was just about to tell me his fortune," I say.

Beth smirks and takes off her mac, hanging it on the coatrack near the door she just came through. She settles herself in one of the free chairs and rests her chin on one fist. "This ought to be good," she says. "Go ahead."

"Have you heard this before?" I ask. I'm curious about how much of Archie's past he's shared with Beth. I only have Mum as my blueprint for parental openness, and she's a crack you can barely get a fingernail into.

"Of course I have, but it was mostly Frances who brought it up over the years," Beth says. "I never get to hear Grandad's version."

Archie picks at a splinter in the wooden table, looking resigned. "All right then. The short version, though, because Eric's out with the tow truck and I need to call to check up on him to see if he needs a hand with anything. The gist of my fortune is, *You are the bringer of death.*"

"You . . . you're what?" I blink, not expecting something that grim to be connected to a person as jovial and harmless as Archie. "I know Aunt Frances had a long friendship with you, and I can't see her continuing that if Peony Lane linked you to death in any way."

He chuckles a little and nods. "You're right on that one. But Peony Lane was very clear on whose death I would bring, and it wasn't Frances's."

I look over at Beth, who has a knowing smile on her face. They both seem bemused by this story, so I gather that Beth isn't a great believer in Peony Lane's abilities either.

"I appreciate the dramatic pause," I say to Archie. "This is the part where I'm supposed to ask whose death you're going to bring, right?"

"Yes, Annie, you've got to play along," Archie says, grinning.

"All right—whose, then?"

"Peony Lane's," he says, and drains the last of his tea.

"Wait, Peony Lane predicted that you'd murder her?" I ask.

"She actually gave it to me written down on a piece of paper. And as for murder—you have to think very carefully about Peony's wording in these things. Even if you don't believe in them," he adds hastily.

"And you didn't listen to the wording properly, Annie," Beth cuts in. "She said Grandad would *bring her death*. That's different, isn't it? Maybe Peony Lane will be eating at a café next to Grandad, and she'll choke on a fishbone or something, and he won't do the Heimlich properly."

"I know how to do the Heimlich, thank you very much," Archie says indignantly.

"It was just an example," Beth says.

"Well, anyway, my fortune went like this," Archie continues. "*The bird returns, but it's you who are the bringer of death. You cannot cast the shadow of a shape that's not your own. One death with three to blame, or three deaths with one to blame— the circle must complete. The list you seek is the right one—the foil, the arrow, the rat, the sparrow. It begins with a secret revealed, and ends with the secret destroyed.*"

"Yes, and the way Frances told it, when you finally tracked down Peony Lane, there was *drama*," Beth says, and one corner of her mouth tugs upward, her expression amused.

Archie gives Beth an interested look. "I'd actually like to hear Frances's version, if you don't mind. How did she tell it?" His eyes dart to the notebooks on the shelf, but it's so quick it hardly even seems voluntary, just a tic he's developed. I wonder if, in one of those notebooks, the Frances from decades ago has written down this exact set of events.

There's something in that version that Archie knows and isn't sharing.

Beth clears her throat, and I focus my attention on her. "Frances liked to talk about how close she and Grandad always were," Beth says. We both look over at Archie, who looks away. "And she said that she was lonely when things started to change between her friends; everyone was drifting apart, but the one person who seemed to always be there was Grandad."

Beth reaches into the tin of shortbread and pulls a piece out. "One thing Frances did tell me was that it took her and Grandad several months to finally track Peony Lane down. And by that point, they'd dug up a lot of secrets about other people in the village—this was before she had started keeping official files—but they still didn't know much about Peony Lane herself. Frances also mentioned that by that point, she and Grandad had been through a lot together."

"'Been through a lot'—I suppose that's one way to sum up the winter of '67," Archie mumbles.

"Frances never told me what it was you'd been through," Beth adds, looking at Archie curiously. "Just so you know."

"Well," he says, "I suppose Frances did like to keep her secrets, after all." He looks rather relieved at this, like he's got away with speeding past the police.

"Anyway, Frances lashed out at Peony. She thought Peony was threatening Grandad."

"It's a bit extreme to threaten your grandad over a fortune *she* told," I say.

"That's what Frances said," Beth agreed. "Frances told me she got so angry, she said some things she could never take back. She just never told me what those things were."

I blink back my shock. The Frances I'd gotten to know in the pages of her diary didn't seem the dramatic type. But I suppose everyone has their limits. "Is that your version too?" I ask Archie.

He's looking at his hands, and then his eyes dart to the knife on the table again. He pauses a bit too long before he says, "Yes, it is."

CHAPTER

8

THE ONLY WAY I CAN THINK TO TEST ARCHIE FURther is to really follow through with what I said, and take the knife to Detective Crane.

Surprisingly, Archie simply wraps it in a tea towel and hands it over, then lends me a black 1960s BMW to drive straight to the police station. "You hang on to that car," he says, handing me the keys. "It's past time that you had one anyway."

"Thanks," I say. "Just tell me what I owe you for it—I'll buy it from you."

Archie waves my comment away, so I shrug but mentally plan to look up the value of the car later and send him the money.

If Archie is bluffing about not having seen that knife before, then lending me a car to take it to the police is officially doubling down. And besides, it gives me an excuse to visit the police station; I haven't seen Detective Crane in a while. I haven't had a reason, to be honest, though I've bumped into him a few times in Beth's deli. Our stilted conversations always skirt some key incidents. Namely, the part of our history that includes me sitting in his lap while vomiting in the car park after almost being drugged to death in the service of catching a killer.

Actually, I've had several experiences while in his orbit that I wouldn't exactly call first-rate. The discovery of at least one dead body and being nearly poisoned by hemlock both come to mind. Not that I'm looking to spend quality time with Detective Crane, but still. I'd much rather he knew me from a slightly more normal perspective.

As I drive back toward the village, it occurs to me that bringing him an antique dagger found stuck in a waterwheel doesn't exactly buck the trend of our previous interactions. But I suppose I'm already getting something of a reputation around Castle Knoll. Maybe I should lean in and become as ludicrous as my great aunt before me. I smile to myself, because I find I don't really mind being the person who drops potential murder weapons at Crane's feet like a sinister Labrador. Not when I'm the one ultimately solving the crimes.

The Castle Knoll Police Station is one of the first buildings you encounter as you approach the village from the Gravesdown estate. The drive takes you past an array of open fields before turning sharply onto a lane that's only wide enough for one car at a time and is completely enclosed by trees. I love this stretch of road—gnarled branches overhead reach across to one another like they wish they could knit themselves together. Today the leaves are a mixture of yellow and brown, thinning more each day. Soon it will just be the fingers of trees rattling with the winter. My adjustment to the countryside hasn't been seamless, but the thought of seeing these branches covered in frost makes me happy.

The tree cover disappears when the village draws close. You pass a falling-down building that I think was once a pub, with an abandoned petrol station next to it. I slow down because there's someone directing traffic here, along with cones closing off the road leading to the old pub. People in hard hats are talking while surveying what looks like the sudden collapse of the building.

"All right there?" the man in the yellow hi-vis suit says to me as I roll down the window. The 1960s BMW has a little handle that I have to rotate to get the window down, and it seems to take ages. The man smirks at my efforts—he looks the right age to remember when this was the only way to roll down a car window.

"Has something happened?" I ask. My mind is thinking up all kinds of interesting things—this old building would be the perfect place for clandestine meetings, or a hiding spot for stolen goods.

"The old pub finally collapsed this morning," the man says. "No one was hurt, thankfully." He looks over his shoulder at the pile of rubble where the pub once stood, a couple of walls still jutting upward, defiant. "Can't say I'm sad to see it go," he adds. "That place had a bad feel to it, a bad history. Anyway . . ." He pats the side of my car door like it's the horse I'm riding and he's sending me on my way. "You take care."

I continue, and before long, the lovely sandy stone of the cottages and townhouses of Castle Knoll starts appearing. The police station is nestled on a side road near the center of town, away from the bustle of the touristy high street but close enough to the heart of things to be convenient for people to access.

I recognize Crane's car as I pull into the police station: It's a silver VW that's new but not flashy. I still have my thermos of coffee from my walk this morning, and even though it's closer to noon now, I'm happy to find it's still hot. I get out of the car and try to gather my thoughts before heading inside.

I think what I'm really after is background information on Peony Lane, from an official standpoint. Has she been in any trouble before? What connections, if any, did she have with the three Gravesdowns who died in the car accident?

I'm standing there looking at Crane's car while all this is running though my head, so of course it's his voice that comes suddenly from behind me.

"Annie?"

I jump and nearly drop my thermos. "Nothing," I say, trying to think of a good excuse to be standing there staring at his car. I turn and notice he's wearing a fitted deep green jumper and dark jeans, which is one of his better outfits. He usually dresses like a university lecturer who dabbles in construction work—an incongruous mix of ill-fitting blazers with elbow patches paired up with Timberland boots. He's good-looking in a dependable way, with hair a sort of mahogany color and a fashionable beard.

"I'm sorry?" he says, and his eyebrows go up. I can tell he's hiding a laugh.

I let my shoulders fall and unscrew the top of my thermos. I take a slightly too large gulp of coffee that causes me to splutter a bit. "Ignore me," I say. "My morning has been extremely strange, so I'm not on peak form. It involves Peony Lane and finding a knife at Foyle Farms."

"Peony Lane . . . the fortune-teller?" he asks. He eyes my thermos slightly greedily.

"No, Peony Lane the landscape architect," I say dryly. "How many people have that kind of name?"

"Hey, there's nothing wrong with unusual names. My name is Rowan Crane; I have a nephew named Stix."

"Wow," I say, taking another sip of coffee. "Stix Crane, that's . . . He should start a band. Anyway, I'm sorry, I shouldn't make fun. My favorite book has a character in it

55

named Slartibartfast, and I really would name my firstborn child that. Boy or girl."

Crane just nods and says, "Forty-two," like he's answering a question I didn't ask.

I blink in surprise for a moment, caught off guard by the fact that he got my reference to *The Hitchhiker's Guide to the Galaxy*. This might be one of the only conversations I've ever had with Detective Crane that doesn't have to do with murder. I hand him my thermos without a word, and he takes it gratefully.

"Thanks," he says, taking a sip. "There's a new police chief, and he's an absolute coffee monster. He's been through the whole jar of instant on his own and it's not even lunchtime yet." He hands the thermos back to me, and as I take another sip from it, I try not to think about how the casual sharing of a drink is strangely intimate. The fact that I'm not thinking about viruses is surprising, but then again, I'm also the girl who got together with a random long-haired bass player on a dance floor in Clapham only a few months ago, before my Castle Knoll days. It was an effort to break loose and have a bit of fun, but it was obvious even to me that I was trying too hard.

Strange how quickly I went from reckless dance-floor snogging to solving murders in the countryside, and I discover that this is one thing about my London life that I don't miss. Good riddance to waking up at noon with a pounding headache and then having to text some guy named Alfonso about why I can't come and see his band that night.

My head starts to clear as the coffee warms me. "I came to ask you about something, actually. I mean, aside from also bringing you a weird knife." His eyes dart to the tea towel I have in my other hand, and he closes his eyes like he's already exhausted. "Is there any way you can check on an old file for me? It would just be an accident report, not an investigation."

Crane opens his eyes, looking relieved. "If it's an accident report, sure," he says. "Come inside. But if you see the new chief, don't let him know you have coffee."

SAMANTHA, THE RECEPTIONIST, gives me a hawkish glare as I pass her, but she doesn't say anything. She's in her late seventies, overdue for retirement but one of those people whose job is her whole life. I wouldn't even be surprised to find out she retired ten years ago and has been working here in a voluntary capacity ever since. She seems to be returning from an early lunch and is unzipping a fleece and settling back into her chair.

An elderly man holding car keys hovers near the desk, and I wonder if he's her husband. He absently twirls the keys around his finger, catching them in his palm as they swing around the key ring, then letting them go again. There are so many keys on it that the motion looks rather satisfying.

The man gives me a curious look, and I can tell he knows who I am. Most of the village does, so I'm used to it. But I can't say I've seen him before. He's got white hair slicked back 1950s-style and is wearing a mechanic's coveralls. "All right then, Sammy," he says. "I'll see you after work."

"Thanks for the ride, Eric," Samantha says.

I decide to invite Samantha's wrath and pry a little. I wonder if this is the elusive Eric Foyle. It's likely, given the mechanic's uniform. I think Eric must keep himself to himself; he's never come to say hi when I've been to visit Archie and Beth, and Archie has never even mentioned that Eric's been working for him. "Friend of yours?" I ask.

Samantha's expression goes steely, which I expected.

"Obviously. What a star detective you are, Annie Adams. Some of us like to give each other lifts—is that a crime now?"

I hold my hands up in surrender and back away. Today is clearly not a day to try to make idle chat with Samantha— not that I've found any other day to be better. Crane is already at his desk, so I hurry over. I know from experience that Samantha listens in on every conversation she can, so I drop my voice as he pulls out the chair opposite his desk for me.

"I'd like to know more about the crash that killed the Gravesdowns—Saxon's parents, Olivia and Edmund, and his grandfather Lord Harry Gravesdown," I say.

Crane enters something into his computer, clicks the mouse a few times, and then nods. "There should be a scanned file in the archives, but . . ." He clicks again, and his brow furrows. "It looks like this is one of the older ones that hasn't been scanned in yet." He sighs. "It's an ongoing project, getting all the old files digitized. Samantha's been at it for years, but things keep getting missed. The original is boxed up somewhere—I can put in a request to get it out of the archives."

"Do you know how long it might be until I can look at it?"

"You have to fill out this form, provide an email address and some other details, and I'll send you a copy after it's been scanned. Accident reports are available to the public; you just need to explain why you want them. Technically, you're family to the victims, however distant, so you could put that. Or maybe say you're a member of the public concerned with the safety measures of that stretch of road."

"Oh," I say, my head spinning slightly with how oddly connected to all this I am. "Thanks. I'm surprised Aunt Frances never asked to see it," I say. "I didn't check if she had a copy of it in her files, but that's only because I haven't been back to the house since Peony Lane told me to look into the crash."

"Peony Lane told you that?" Crane looks interested. "Why?"

"Why does Peony Lane do anything?" I ask. "I only met her this morning. She found me in the woods near the house, and I can already tell you that the woman is an enigma. But interestingly, Archie Foyle told me there's a rumor that Peony Lane caused that crash by cutting the brake cable of the car."

Crane's brow creases again as he types something else into his computer, and I watch him closely as he navigates through several pages of data.

"Peony Lane is an alias for Ellen Jones," he says slowly. "It confirms here that she was arrested in 1961 for vandalizing Edmund Gravesdown's car—the same one involved in the crash. But there's nothing that says she was held responsible for that. All the damage she did to the car was repaired before Edmund Gravesdown took it out on the road again."

I blink, disbelieving. Who *was* this woman? The woman who told fortunes about murder and was in and out of prison? "I've got to do a deep dive into Aunt Frances's files," I say. "I'll check the name Ellen Jones as well, and all those Gravesdowns. Frances has files on absolutely everyone. Does it say anything else in there?" I lean toward the computer.

We're interrupted by loud laughter coming from the front desk, and as I turn my head I see a smartly dressed man in his early fifties, with sandy blond hair and broad shoulders. He turns toward us, and his eyes narrow a fraction when he sees Crane and me looking at him. The man drains the coffee cup he's holding and hands it to Samantha without even looking her way.

"Incoming," Crane mutters. "The new chief inspector."

I look sideways at Crane. "Not a fan?" I ask.

Crane simply looks at the tea towel I've put on his desk and tries to change the subject. "What's the story of this knife, then?" He unwraps the cloth gingerly to reveal the blade inside.

"It was stuck in Archie's waterwheel," I say, then I start recounting the Castle Knoll legend about how the knife was used and then discarded.

"What an interesting object," the new chief says as he approaches Crane's desk. He doesn't pull up a chair; he simply looms over Crane. "I'm Chief Inspector Toby Marks," he says to me.

"Annie Adams," I say, extending a hand in his direction. He gives me a warm smile, and when he shakes my hand, I can tell he's one of those men who practice their handshakes to ensure they have the right balance of squeezy intimidation and firm confidence.

"Did I hear you say you think this was involved in a cold case? A murder, perhaps?" The corner of his mouth twitches, and I realize I'm something of a joke to him. He must have heard about my exploits last summer, and even though all my actions were genuinely in the service of solving a murder, annoyance has me grinding my teeth.

"I just thought it was worth showing to the detective," I say slowly.

Crane gives me a reassuring look. "I'm glad you did," he says. "Local stories can have surprising truths sometimes, so they're worth looking into. I can take this and have it examined by an expert," he adds. "Find out where it really came from, and who owned it last."

Chief Inspector Marks cuts in. "That's hardly necessary,"

he says, "and would be using resources we don't have. Miss . . . Adams, was it? If the knife was found on her estate, it's hers." He turns to me. "Take this back with you—you can arrange to have it appraised if you like. You never know, something like that, could be worth a lot." He guffaws then and gives me a shrewd glance. "Not that you need the money, though, eh?"

CHAPTER
9

I THOUGHT THE WINNING SMILE OF ERIC FOYLE WOULD mean he was easy to talk to, but I was wrong. As soon as I approached him, I could see small signs that he was covering up some deeper emotion with his casual hair tossing and warm expression. He gave me a wink as I crossed the room to the bar, but up close it looked more nervous than confident. His knuckles were white as he gripped the pump handle a bit too hard, and as I said his name, he wet his lips nervously; they looked chapped, and I wondered if this was a compulsive habit.

"Eric, isn't it?" I said. I kept my face neutral, but I felt my curiosity could be read pretty easily. This was the man who'd vandalized the car of the wealthiest family in town and who'd supposedly told Peony Lane how to cut the brake cable that had caused that fatal crash. What had Edmund Gravesdown done to earn Eric's double-crossing?

Eric's eyes darted to where Archie still sat with his pint at the table before he looked back at me. "That's me," Eric said. "And who might you be? Aside from possibly the next Lady Graves-

down?" The corners of his eyes crinkled a little, but the warmth was gone from them.

I felt my mouth form a tight smile. "So, the village gossip wheels are turning about that, are they? Then my guess is you already know my name."

His eyes left mine as he reached for a rag that was behind the bar and started polishing the taps with it, even though they were already shining. "Frances," he said finally. "And it isn't my fault the village is shocked at Ford Gravesdown taking interest in a local girl. Though I warn you, Ford is just as full of snobbery as the rest of the Gravesdowns were—he believes that society people are just plain better than the rest of us." Eric's mouth twisted as if he were biting back more words and they didn't taste very nice.

"From what I hear, you didn't object to that lifestyle either, until recently," I said carefully.

Eric pulled at the cloth in his hands and it slithered off the brass of the tap he was polishing until it snapped in the empty air. He slung it over one shoulder and leaned on the bar toward me. With his other hand he pulled a mother-of-pearl comb from his back pocket and ran it through his hair a couple of times, even though it was already smooth. Then he crooked a finger at me, beckoning me to close the gap between us if I wanted to hear what he had to say.

I looked at Archie over my shoulder, and his expression was cold. But he didn't make a move to come and join me, and there were things I wanted to know. I stepped up to the bar and leaned toward Eric. The smell of mint and light cologne wafted toward me.

He wet his lips again, pursing them in a way that was almost childlike. "I know things about that family that would have you running out of town. Same as Birdy did. You'd leave and never come back."

"Birdy . . . you mean Emily's sister?" I blinked in surprise. "Do you know something about what happened to Emily?" My heart started a drumbeat at the thought of it—of Eric being here at the Dead Witch all the time, seeing and hearing things the rest of us overlooked.

"I don't know what happened to the younger Sparrow, but I do know that Birdy saw something one night. Witnessed what she said was a stabbing, in the dark near our old farmhouse. Birdy went there looking for me, but I was up at Gravesdown Hall. I was working as Edmund's valet at the time, and he wanted me to help him get ready for a party he was driving to. His car had just been fixed after being vandalized."

My mind was moving at lightning speed. Peony Lane had vandalized that car, with Eric's help. But only she had been arrested for it, so of course he wouldn't admit to being a part of that. But my thoughts flipped through facts like they were notecards. The story Emily told—about the stabbing at the Foyle farmhouse and the knife thrown into the River Dimber—had come from her sister, Birdy.

"Who was stabbed?" I whispered, leaning even farther toward Eric.

"Birdy couldn't see," he said. "Not who got stabbed, or who did the stabbing. But it was no coincidence that the day after she witnessed that, everything went to hell. The next night, most of the family were dead, and Birdy had gone."

"Have you heard from her? Archie said you and Birdy were a couple for a while," I said. "Did she tell you why she fled?"

He hesitated. "I'll tell you three important things," he said eventually. His posture changed, and his classically handsome features looked different—he looked tired, but not the kind of tired that comes from lack of sleep. "And these three things are all I'll offer you; I can't get involved with this. I know what you're after," he said, and looked pointedly over my shoulder at Archie.

"Archie wants to destroy Ford Gravesdown, but I learned my lesson with them. I keep my head down now. I don't want his attention on me."

I bit my lip, thinking. I didn't want Eric to refuse to talk to me again—what if I needed to ask him more questions? Ford hadn't invited me out in a while, and as I got deeper into the Gravesdown family secrets, I found my feelings toward Ford were even more conflicted. That family was a hornet's nest, and I didn't feel like I could let my guard down around him. Curiously, after only one day spent investigating with Archie, I was calmer and more centered than I'd been in months.

I didn't know what that meant in terms of my shifting feelings about Ford—every time we went to dinner together or went for a drive somewhere, he always managed to convince me he was the most interesting man on the planet. But when he wasn't around, it was oddly easy for me to live a different kind of life— the village life I probably belonged in. Frances Adams, daughter of the local baker, who has hobbies like making her own clothes and reading. That version of Frances belongs in the library or having a pint with Archie Foyle, not at Gravesdown Hall, sipping expensive wine and listening to a lord talk about changes to his garden design.

I simply looked at Eric and said, "I'll make sure your name isn't spoken to Ford at all."

Eric seemed satisfied with this. "All right. Well. The first thing is that Peony Lane bashed up Edmund Gravesdown's car for a reason. And it was a noble one."

"How do you mean? Was she making a statement on wealth and privilege or something? A kind of protest?"

Eric's knuckles were white again from how tightly he was gripping the bar cloth. "I wish that were the whole of it. And I suppose that kind of 'statement' does underlie the whole mess. But it's not the only reason she wrecked that car." He drew in a long breath, then finally put the bar rag down, meeting my eyes again. "Ed Gravesdown used to drive that car of his over to the Old Nag's Head. You know it?"

I nodded. "The pub on the road out of the village. The one by the service station. It's in worse shape than this place," I said. If Eric was offended at my insult to his workplace, he didn't show it. "Why would Edmund Gravesdown go to the Old Nag's Head?"

Eric breathed in sharply through his nose, and I could tell his thoughts were angry ones. "Ed wasn't a nice bloke. I'll spare you the details, but he liked meeting up with women there. It was an out-of-sight sort of place."

My thoughts started to cloud over because I sensed I was about to hear something unpalatable that I wouldn't be able to unlearn. "Lots of men have affairs," I said cautiously.

"True," Eric said. "But Ed's affairs weren't exactly consensual. He paid the barman there to look the other way, but Ed was one of those men who slip things into drinks. Then he'd drive off with whoever he was with, to some unknown place."

My stomach lurched, and at the same time anger coursed through me—it was white-hot and made me ready to burn the whole village down. Then my thoughts went to Peony Lane.

"Peony—she found this out?" I asked.

Eric nodded. "And she became Ed's own personal ghost. She followed that car wherever it went. Ed had a whole host of car troubles—things that he didn't have enough car knowledge to realize weren't normal. His mechanic didn't bother to tell him someone was putting sugar in his petrol tank or stealing spark plugs. The mechanic just thought someone had it in for the Gravesdowns because of their money—which plenty of people did."

"So Peony Lane sabotaged his car so that he couldn't drive off with his victims," I said. A range of feelings surged through me— rage at the world in general, at men who would do such things. A strange kinship with Peony Lane, for her bravery in fighting this man in the only way she knew how. And horror at this twisted family—did Ford know what his brother was? Did their father? Christ, this was Saxon's dad. And what of Saxon's mother, Olivia? Wife to a monster like that, how many of his crimes did she know about?

And then I had a thought that I still don't regret. I was glad Edmund Gravesdown was dead.

"Exactly," Eric said. "Until one day, she got caught. I was there; we let all our rage out on that car, which wasn't Peony's usual style, but she had a plan: She wanted to disable it for good. I didn't know who he had in that pub. All I knew was that getting his car off the road right then meant someone could be saved."

"Archie told me Peony cut the brake cable in the car," I said.

"It was meant to be the fuel line, but yes. She did. She told me later that she cut the brake cable by mistake, and she's never forgiven herself for that." We both let a silence hang in the air between us for a moment, allowing the implications of Peony's anger to hover like three Gravesdown ghosts. "So that's one of the three important things you need to know." Eric was quiet for a short while and then eventually continued. "You already knew that Peony Lane was arrested for vandalizing the car. Now you know why she did it."

I gave him a solemn nod, not knowing what to say.

"The second important thing is that after a day in custody, someone paid her bail. Charges were suddenly dropped. The name on the bank transfer, according to my informant, was Edmund Gravesdown. But given how angry he was about his car, I doubt he was the one who showed up to bail her out and make the charges go away."

"Who, then?" I asked.

"That I don't know," Eric said. "But it was someone from that family. Now, I'm telling you this because you seem like a good sort. And Archie"—Eric looked back at his brother—"he and I don't spend a whole lot of time together these days, but I do care about him. He can act without thinking sometimes, but if he's hanging around someone with a cool head, that can only be a good thing for him. You try and be that for him, if you can."

"I will," I said. Eric paused to fill a pint for someone at the other end of the bar who'd signaled to him.

Finally, he came back and looked me straight in the eye, his face hard. "There's one more thing you need to know," he said. "The person who we rescued that day? The girl who was too drugged to know her own name? That was Birdy Sparrow."

CHAPTER

10

JENNY IS SITTING ON THE STEPS OF GRAVESDOWN
Hall next to three Louis Vuitton suitcases and an overlarge
bag from Ladurée. My shoulders unclench at just the sight of
her, and I realize that the lack of Jenny has been one of the
hardest parts of my move to the countryside.

"Please tell me you brought macarons," I say, eyeing the
bag as I rush toward her. She gives me a fierce hug, then
reaches straight for the bag when she lets go of me. Jenny
works for Harrods, leading the team that designs their famous window displays. She has a degree in set design from
Central Saint Martins, and though it might not seem like it
to the average person, the department store window displays
in central London are a seriously competitive space. Sometimes her job is like curating her own art gallery—they get
guest artists and designers in to make a real impact, or Jenny
and her team design their own masterpieces.

"I brought all kinds of goodies," she says, taking my arm.
"If you'll just let me into your mansion, we can get started on

unpacking this impressive haul." She gestures toward the array of bags waiting on the step.

I unlock the front door and we each take two bags. I'm extra careful not to crush the Ladurée bag because I don't want pulverized macarons. We step into the flagstone hallway, and I shut the large mahogany door behind us, locking it with the old skeleton key that's part of its original design. I then twist the modern dead bolt that Aunt Frances had installed while she was living here—just one of the many safety precautions she took due to her fear of being murdered. I admit, the front-door security does make me feel a bit better about being here on my own. I one-upped her, though, having a front-door camera installed, just to be extra safe.

In the foyer, Jenny takes a moment to look down the dim hallway and then toward the wide staircase that marches up to our right. "Wow, this place is a tomb," she says.

"Don't say that!" I slap her lightly on the shoulder. "Someone actually died here," I remind her.

"I'm aware," she says. "But even when I was here in October for Frances's funeral, it didn't feel this . . ." She shudders. "I don't know, it's got different vibes now."

"Yeah, now you see why I really need you here," I say. "So thank you for sacrificing your holiday to keep me from befriending the ghosts that I absolutely don't believe live here." I give her a look that says, *I'm starting to believe that ghosts live here.*

Jenny hugs me, though slightly awkwardly, as she's still holding several bags. "Christmas displays all go up at the end of October these days," she says. "Which annoys a lot of people but makes my life a little easier."

"Well, I think it's lovely. Bring on the Christmas tat."

"I think there are *many* Harrods shoppers who would resent your use of the word *tat* in that sentence. Anyway, I . . ."

She sniffs the air for a second, then sniffs in my direction. "Wait, why do you smell like wet dog?"

"What? I showered this morning! Oh, wait." I still have my backpack on, and I realize the dirty tea towel Archie wrapped the knife in is in the side pocket, and it's soaked with river water from when Archie dried the knife. The smell of the River Dimber is pungent and earthy, particularly around that waterwheel, which is slick with algae. I shrug my arms out of the straps, put the backpack on the floor, and pull out the knife. "Here's your wet dog," I say, holding out the tea towel. "Look what I just got out of the waterwheel at Foyle Farms. Or rather, what Archie pulled out. Which reminds me, I have so much to tell you—thankfully things have livened up around here as of this morning."

"Thankfully?" Jenny raises an eyebrow at me. "Let's not tempt fate." She snort-laughs, but when she does this it's almost delicate. "See what I did there?" I give her a deadpan look in response. "Anyway, I vote we light a big fire, have coffee and macarons for lunch . . ."

"Two of the most important food groups," I add. "But I need a sandwich or something; otherwise, all I'll have consumed today is caffeine and sugar. Ooh, and look . . ." I point to the basket on the hallway table. "Beth made her deli delivery while I was out, so we've got all the essentials." I lift the vintage scarf that Beth has tucked over the fresh bread, cheeses, chutneys, and scones and sigh contentedly.

We head down the long hallway and eventually wind our way to the kitchen, which is at the back of the house. I put the knife in the kitchen sink as I shuffle around the huge space, pulling together the makings of some sandwiches from the delicious things Beth has supplied. When I've cut several doorstop slices of bread, I place a jar of cider chutney next to them on a board, along with the wedge of smoked cheddar and some fresh salad leaves, and pick the whole thing up.

Jenny fills two mugs with coffee and lifts a mint-and-gold fancy box out of the bag she brought. "This entire box is pistachio," she says, "because I know you won't bother with any other flavor, heathen that you are."

"There is absolutely no point in eating any other flavor, because I'd just wish it was pistachio," I say. "Come on, let's eat in my new favorite spot." I gesture toward the solarium that's attached to the kitchen. It's a step down into a Victorian-style hothouse that even has cast-iron vents in the floor to let the heat from the hot-water pipes permeate the air to sustain tropical plants. Bright green banana fronds fill the center of it, where the domed glass ceiling is at its highest, and the rest of the space has meandering tiled pathways that take you past tree ferns, climbing passion flower, and exotic fruit trees I can't name. There's even a tree with bright orange pods that Beth told me is cacao, and somewhere else in here is a vanilla bean plant.

There's a very secret corner where a circular pond reflects the white metal crisscross of the ceiling, so deep that the water is nearly black. Lily pads are dotted around in it, and small fish make appearances when they sense people might be near with food. There's a pair of rattan chairs and a small Parisian-style café table nearby, and we take our seats.

"Okay, how did I not find this last time I was here?" Jenny asks, sounding impressed.

"Last time you were here, there was a funeral going on and you were too busy being the rock star that you are and helping me with all the details," I remind her.

We set our spread on the table and spend several delicious minutes eating before I dive into telling the story of my day.

Finally, I lick the remainder of the chutney off my fingers and say, "So now I'm just waiting on that accident report."

"And you're going to get your fortune told, right?" Jenny says. "I mean, I would. Mostly because it's spooky and sounds like a real once-in-a-lifetime experience."

I give Jenny a look that hopefully conveys just how ridiculous I find her. "You say this to me every time you drag me into some kind of bad idea. That zip line we did in Wales that made me sick? *Once-in-a-lifetime experience.* That time you made me take the Jack the Ripper tour with you and I nearly passed out just from the *descriptions* of those crimes? You sold that to me as *spooky.* Either of these selling points is bad on its own, but put them both together and it screams *absolutely not* to me."

"In my defense, who passes out when someone's just *describing* blood? I get that if you see the blood it sends you out cold, but that tour guide was just sharing some historical details," Jenny says.

"Your sympathy to my plight is overwhelming," I say, my voice deadpan. "But honestly, I *am* curious about what Peony Lane will say if I let her tell my fortune."

"Are you worried she's going to tell you how you'll die?" Jenny asks. "I mean, I'm sort of with Frances on this one—I'd want to know. And then I'd want to stop it."

I sigh. "Aunt Frances's whole life was essentially ruled by fear," I say.

Jenny shakes her head lightly. "I've got a different take on her, actually. After everything you've told me, and the bits and pieces I've seen the few times I've visited this place . . ." Jenny trails off for a moment, looking around the solarium.

"Something wrong?" I ask.

"Nothing," she says. "I thought I saw— Shit, there it is! It's a mouse!" She points to the ferns, where a frond still bounces lightly after something disturbed it.

I relax. "Oh, no, don't worry, it's a bird," I say. "There are these little guys that get in somehow; they hop along the ground under the ferns sometimes. They're cute, and they don't go into the house."

"Huh," she says, still watching the fern. There's a flutter of wings off to one side, and we both turn to see a mottled brown shape dart back under the plant cover. "I think it's a sparrow."

"Anyway, you were saying you had some different angle on Aunt Frances."

"Right, yes. I think that her fear of being murdered changed her life, but it didn't rule her. I think that once she got her feet wet in people's secrets, her life's work was exactly what yours is shaping up to be. Solving mysteries."

There is movement in the corner of my eye again, as the fern twitches. "I think that bird found the chutney some-how," I say, looking at the tiles near our feet: Tiny tracks of red that weren't there a moment ago now zigzag across the cream-colored surface.

"The chutney's been next to my hand this whole time, with the lid on," Jenny says slowly.

She stands up and cautiously takes a step toward the ferns. Two more quick steps and she's leaning over the fo-liage, lifting a row of fronds back with one arm. I hear her take a sharp breath.

"Jen?" I say feebly.

"Don't come over here," she says. "And call that police guy, like, *right* now. Or actually, just dial 999 because we need someone here *immediately*."

"What is it? Just tell me!" I say, my voice rising. I stand

and walk over to where she's still holding back a wall of plants.

Then I see it. The tartan shawl, torn and muddy, and the white crown of plaits belonging to Peony Lane. She's face down, her hands up near her ears. One hand has a scrap of paper in it, folded neatly.

My heart thuds, and I feel the familiar ringing in my ears that means I'm about to faint. I gulp air, but the sticky closeness of the tropical plants makes me feel like I'm underwater.

"Annie?" Jenny's saying, and I can feel her hand on my shoulder. "You need to hold it together for a few minutes because we need to get out of here. We're not safe—this must have happened *minutes ago*. Because, you see?" She points.

My vision swims, but I blink and try to focus. When I see the ruby-handled knife sticking out of her back, covered in blood . . . that's when I understand what Jenny means. It seems impossible, but it's the knife I was holding maybe . . . half an hour ago? I put it in the kitchen sink; I know I did.

How the hell did someone stab Peony Lane while we were sitting right here? Jenny is pulling me toward the glass double doors at the back of the solarium that lead out to the gardens. She rattles the handle but can't get the door to budge. "Is it locked?" she hisses, her voice a harsh whisper. "We have to get out of here, Annie, come on!"

"It just sticks. . . . Here, you have to—" I throw a shoulder against the heavy white-painted iron of the door and lift as I turn the handle. The door comes up from its frame slightly and swings outward. I hesitate. "What if she's still alive?" I whisper. "This has clearly *just* happened, and people survive being stabbed all the time!"

"Annie, she's very clearly dead," Jenny hisses.

"You're right," I say, and I step through the door and shove my shoulder back into it from the outside, as if simply closing it will erase the dead body lying inside.

Jenny drags me out onto the sloping lawn. Rosebushes pepper the smooth expanse of it, neatly pruned and ready for winter. "I felt for her pulse; she wasn't alive," Jenny says. Her hand is shaking as she dials 999.

I breathe in cold air like it's the only secret to staying alive. I hear Jenny explaining our situation to someone over the phone, and finally my brain catches up.

"Police are on their way, but they need me to stay on the line," Jenny says, the phone up to her ear.

Adrenaline shoots through me as she and I share a look of understanding. The police need us on the line because our situation is ongoing.

Peony Lane's murderer is still here.

CHAPTER

11

MY HANDS WERE SHAKING WHEN I RETURNED TO THE table where Archie was waiting. I felt my heart squeeze in on itself, wondering about Birdy Sparrow and Peony Lane. Had they worked together to get revenge on the Gravesdown family? Were Olivia Gravesdown and Edmund's father, Harry Gravesdown, covering up his crimes and enabling him to keep preying on unsuspecting women?

"I knew he'd talk to you," Archie said. His tone didn't give much away, but I could tell he wanted to know what had been said. The way Eric kept looking back at Archie, it was clear he expected me to relay all the information, so I did. When I finished talking, my hands were steady, but clenched in a quiet rage.

Archie was stone-faced, looking into his pint glass like the bottom of it had all the answers.

"Archie?" I said his name quietly, trying to shake him out of whatever spiral his mind was heading down. "What are you thinking?"

"I'm thinking that if we dig deep enough, we can find evidence that will ruin Ford Gravesdown."

I drew in a startled breath, but Archie reached over and gripped my hand.

"Think about it, Frances: This is important. If he had any role in covering up his brother's crimes, he needs to be exposed for it. That family is no good; you have to see that now."

I felt the last of my foundations crumbling. "Ford was only twenty years old when that car accident happened. You yourself were, what, fourteen? You're twenty now, right? You lived in that farmhouse at that point, with Eric and your father."

Archie's face holds something strange when I mention the farmhouse. A shadow I can't quite interpret passes over him, which is such an unusual thing to see on Archie that it stands out all the more. "We need to talk to Birdy, if we can find her," he says, changing the subject slightly. "And I want to know why that accident was hushed up so fast, with no investigation."

I felt uneasy, and I wanted to make excuses for Ford, but I couldn't. "If Peony Lane was arrested for vandalizing Edmund's car, why did someone from the Gravesdown family immediately bail her out?"

"Think about it, Frances," Archie said, his eyes blazing in the dim light of the pub. He removed his hand from mine and looked over at the bar. Eric was no longer there, so Archie raised his eyebrows at the woman who had taken his place, tilting his empty glass in her direction. She nodded once and starting filling another pint for him. "If the Gravesdown family knew Peony Lane was aware of Edmund's crimes, they wouldn't want her in prison; they'd want her in their pocket. People in prison have nothing to lose and are more likely to talk. But if she owed them? Or if they had a chance to get her out and threaten her further?"

I tugged at the end of a strand of hair that had come free from the long plait I wore. "I suppose," I said. "But I don't know what to do now. I wanted to find Peony Lane to learn more about my fortune and to see if there's anything I can do to stop it. This feels like a detour on that quest, like chasing down a mystery that might not matter."

"But finding out what really happened gives you facts about your new boyfriend that you need to know," Archie said.

An exasperated stream of air came from my lungs as I tried to pick through the shattered pieces of my thoughts about Ford and his family. It was like I'd been walking a normal road, only to have reality lurch sideways to reveal it was just a set of distorted funhouse mirrors all along.

I swallowed hard. I didn't want to admit it, but Archie was right. I needed to know. I could drop Ford from my life completely, without prodding further, but so many questions remaining unanswered felt like a betrayal. If the Gravesdowns hurt people, and Ford was part of covering that up, it should be exposed. I didn't care how many coats he bought me.

And underneath my need for the truth, there was the growing drumbeat of my future. Where there were secrets, there could be desperation, plots, and lies. And all those things could lead to violence. Violence leads to murder. It was like watching dominoes fall one by one, and I wanted to reach out and stick my finger in the line of them, propping one up before it knocked the rest down. Stopping the pattern.

"What do we do?" I asked. My voice cracked a little, which made me sound helpless, and I hated it.

"I think we should dig around in police records, see if we can find the accident report for the crash and the details of Peony Lane's arrest and release," Archie said.

"You mentioned an informant—care to let me in on who that was?" I asked.

Archie made a hushing motion at me because the woman at the bar was bringing him his fresh pint. "Thanks," he said, winking at her. After seeing Eric wink at me earlier, so self-assured, Archie's wink looked like playacting. "Put it on my tab." The woman rolled her eyes, then turned to me.

"That'll be two shillings, since you can afford it, love," she said to me. Her tone was acidic, and the way she looked at me told me I'd misread the village's feelings on the Gravesdowns. I'd thought the narrowed eyes and whispers at me were jealousy, because the heir to a wealthy estate was extending his favor my way. And judging by the barmaid's words, I could keep on thinking that if I wanted.

But what Eric had said changed everything. This whole village must have whispers running through it. What else did people know about that family? I reached into my purse, pulled out the money, and set it on the table without a word. I shot Archie an annoyed look as he simply sipped his pint.

"You could at least say thank you, or correct someone when they make a snide comment about me coming into Gravesdown money," I said.

"I figured you'd stand up for yourself, if you wanted to," he said. "But trust me, nothing you say will change their opinion. Especially because you're here with me."

"What does that mean?"

"Just that the village loves to talk about how a Gravesdown always has a Foyle on the side."

"I'm not a Gravesdown," I said.

Archie looked at me for a long time. "Then prove it," he said. "You're in the best possible position to find out what Ford knew about his brother. If Birdy said someone was stabbed, I'm betting it was true. Edmund's crimes and that car crash aren't the half of it. What if one of Edmund's victims was going to come forward, and what Birdy witnessed was the victim being silenced? There are more secrets about that family to uncover, mark my words. If you want to outsmart this fortune of yours, start by outsmarting Ford Gravesdown."

I prodded my feelings on Ford yet again and realized how complicated they were. I wasn't in love with him, and my trust in him had always been shaky. But then again, who were the Foyles? Archie and Eric weren't squeaky-clean either, and the family secrets boiling under the surface between them told me neither of them was telling me everything.

"All right," I said. "But I don't like being manipulated. And before you tell me how genuine you are in your interest in exposing the truth, I'm letting you know that I can see how you're using me. As long as both our goals align, I'll go along with it. But, Archie . . ." I leaned in and pointed a finger at him. "The second I find out that you're hiding something huge from me, or that your own hands aren't clean in this, I'll have no hesitation in selling you down the river with the other guilty parties."

"Understood," he said.

CHAPTER

12

COULD SOMEONE HAVE KILLED HER WHILE WE WERE sitting there?" Jenny asks, keeping her voice low.

We're huddled together in the gardens, watching our surroundings nervously while we whisper to each other. Jenny's still got the emergency operator on the line, but we're on mute so we can speak freely. The police are about ten minutes away, apparently.

"No," I reply. "You were sat facing those ferns where her body was hidden; you noticed the bird hopping around in the undergrowth. I'm positive that if a murder happened, or someone was dumping her body, it would have been a major scene. Which means . . ."

"She died in the house before we got there," Jenny says. "But the dagger in her back? Someone *had* to have put that there while we were in the house. Why do that?"

I shudder, thinking about the fact that someone was moving around in the house while Jenny and I were chatting over our bread and cheese. "I don't know. When I saw Peony Lane this morning, she was heading toward this house, while I was on my way into town. She specifically sent me in the direction of Foyle Farms and then continued toward Gravesdown Hall. I didn't think twice about it at the time; a lot of people walk the footpaths that circle the estate, and they often trespass just in search of a nice walk. But what if she wanted to make sure I wasn't going straight back home?"

"Okay, pause for a second," Jenny says, "because that's the first time you've referred to Gravesdown Hall as *home*. That seems momentous."

"Leave it to you to psychoanalyze me when we've just discovered a body," I say.

Jenny shrugs but looks pleased with herself. "What can I say? I treat multitasking like it's an Olympic sport."

"What I want to know is, how did Peony get in?" I ask, my voice rising. "And how did the killer get in? Beth's deli delivery is the only possible way—other than my cleaning service, who don't come today. The gardeners only have keys to the outbuildings."

"Well, it looks like someone made a copy. I'm not pointing fingers at Beth, but if she had the only spare set *and* we know she was definitely here today . . ."

"I saw Beth this morning, though, while I was talking with Archie. I mean, I guess technically she could have killed Peony while I was at the police station, but it would be pretty tight. But honestly, if I'm Beth and I've just killed someone, the last thing I'd do would be to leave that deli delivery right in the hallway, to spotlight the fact that I'd just been here." But then I think of Archie, and how cagey he was about those notebooks. "That knife showing up on Archie's property just today, though . . . what are the odds?"

Our thoughts are interrupted as three police cars come screaming up the gravel drive to Gravesdown Hall. The slope of the rear lawns means we can see the gates to the estate from here, as well as the white snake of the drive as it cuts through the rows of manicured cypresses that border it.

"They're coming around the side of the house," Jenny says, her ear back to the phone. She's unmuted us and quickly confirms something with the operator on the other end of the line. "We're to wait for the officers to find us, and then you can give them the keys to the front door, if you have them on you."

"Of course I don't have the keys on me!" I say, patting down my oversized jumper as if I might be surprised and find them buried in the chunky knit. "There aren't any pockets in this outfit, so all I carry with me from room to room is my phone."

Jenny reaches out and pats me on the head, clearly trying to lighten the mood. "And I'm proud of you for that, because otherwise you'd look like a psychopath. People who have the ability to forget their phones in different rooms need to be studied."

"It's more that I'm taking after Aunt Frances, and there's no way I'm hanging around by myself in this house without a direct line to the police. A strategy whose necessity has been reinforced today. Anyway, the police can get in through the solarium door—we left it open on the way out."

I point, and two uniformed officers appear from around the side of the house, approaching the back door.

"Wait, did you shut it behind us?" Jenny asks. The double doors are firmly closed, their glass panes reflecting the shapes of the bare rosebushes in the afternoon light.

"I . . ." I try to remember. "No? Maybe? I can't recall."

We watch the police try the handle, rattling it several times, and then they turn around to look our way.

"You wouldn't happen to be able to let us in, would you?"

The voice that comes from behind us isn't Detective Crane's, but that of Chief Inspector Marks.

"That door shouldn't be locked," I say. "We only came through it about twenty minutes ago, and you have to slide a bolt from the inside to lock it."

"Interesting," Marks says. "So you're telling me there's a body inside, and we've now got no way back into the house?"

I narrow my eyes at him. Something about this guy really grates on me. It could be that he's wearing an overpriced suit for his new job in the middle of the countryside (which, thanks to Jenny's tutelage in high fashion, I can tell is either a Savile Row custom job or something pricey enough to pass for it), but he's combined it with some very cheap aftershave. It's practically Lynx body spray and reminds me of the boys at secondary school. I clench my jaw and try to be polite.

"Try twisting the door handle the other way," I say, "while lifting the handle to pull up on the whole thing. It's just stiff, that's all."

"Well, *thank you*," Marks says, overemphasizing the words in a way that makes me feel like I've actually insulted him instead of being helpful. He motions to the officers at the door, and one of them nods, then slams a police baton into the pane just above the doorknob. "Look at that, we've found a way in."

I wince at the sound of shattered glass. "You're still going to have to lift it, like I said." I'm at least awarded the satisfaction of watching a police officer try the door several more times, only to then have to follow my exact instructions to get it open.

When it swings inward, I rush forward with all the officers, but one of them keeps me from entering while everyone else goes through.

"You need to stay outside," the officer says.

I was expecting this, but I'm still angry. Just before I go and join Jenny on a nearby bench, I poke my head in through the missing pane of glass in the door and peer up at where the bolt usually sits in the metal frame at the top of the double doors.

It's still in the unlocked position; the door would have opened just fine if they'd only listened to me. The Castle Knoll police force just wanted to willfully ignore me, which doesn't set a great tone for the future of my relationship with them, under Marks's new leadership.

CHAPTER

13

I SHOULD HAVE GRABBED THAT FOLDED PIECE OF PA-
per from her hand," I say.

"I mean, that's technically evidence, though, right?" Jenny
asks.

"I know, but . . . this started out as personal," I say. "Peony
Lane said she'd been looking for *me.* There were more things
she wanted me to know, but she wanted me to discover them.
She said even *she* didn't know the full story—whatever that
means."

Marks emerges from the solarium and notices us at that
moment, as if my defiance has summoned him. We're out of
earshot, but the intensity of his gaze makes me nervous.

"You two, stay outside," he says.

We quickly exchange a look that says, *Can't he see us sitting calmly on this bench?* He heads back inside, and I feel even
more convinced of the need to start my own investigation.

There's already a forensic team waiting nearby, dressed
in white coveralls, masks, and shoe coverings. It looks like
they'll wait their turn while the police do their thing.

I feel a light touch at my elbow. "Hey," Crane says, keeping his voice low. "You okay?" His eyes dart to Jenny, who is trying to covertly take photos of the crime scene on her phone. When she notices him, she quickly tucks her phone away.

"I *just* saw her alive. I brought that knife inside only, like, an hour ago," I explain.

"Annie, you really need to learn when to stop talking," he says, exasperated. "You've just admitted to me that you might have been the last person to see her alive, and that you've recently handled a weapon that is likely to be the murder weapon."

"You obviously know this! I brought it to you earlier, so you're going to find my fingerprints all over it!" I say. Then I notice that Crane's other hand holds a takeaway tray of coffees. "Wait, are you late because your new boss wanted coffee?"

His mouth forms a thin line, and he looks away for a second. "I was already picking one up for myself when your call for help came in. It was only polite to get them for anyone else who wanted one."

"I don't buy that for a second," Jenny says.

"I think you should put that tray down and wander into a crime scene with us," I say.

"I can't let you contaminate a crime scene," he says. But he shifts the takeaway tray into the other hand and sets it on the bench next to Jenny.

"We wouldn't be contaminating anything—we were in there half an hour ago eating lunch; our DNA will be everywhere already," I say. "Jenny even felt for Peony Lane's pulse, in case she was still alive and needed help."

"I can't," he says. "Technically you're both suspects, so letting you back into the crime scene gives you a chance to tamper with evidence."

"Oh, come on," Jenny says.

"Why do you want to go back in there so badly?" he says, narrowing his eyes at us. I can see that he's not going to let us in, so I move farther along the bench, making room for him.

"Let's drink your boss's coffee and I'll tell you," I say. He looks conflicted, which is kind of endearing. But when he doesn't move, I roll my eyes at him. "Oh my God, we get that you follow rules, okay? But when your boss makes you get coffee and then doesn't touch it, it's fair game!" I lift the tray of cups and hold it out to him.

"I suppose it is going cold," he says, and takes one out of the tray. "Here, you take that one, Annie—it's black."

"He remembers how you take your coffee?" Jenny whispers.

"Not the time," I mutter back at her.

Crane fishes a notebook out of his coat pocket and sits on my other side. "I suppose I can take your statements," he says.

We're just finishing up our description of events when Marks comes out of the solarium with a large clear ziplock bag dangling between two fingers.

"Annabelle Adams," he says.

The way he says my name makes me feel twelve years old, and I want to snark back, *Present*, like this is the school roll call, but I don't. When I simply blink at him, he continues. "Do you know anything about this?"

I squint at the thing in the bag and notice it's a piece of paper, creased from being folded up several times. "Is that what she had in her hand?" I ask.

"It is," he says. He starts reading, and my stomach flips with the first line. Even two words in, I know what it is.

It's a fortune, but it isn't mine. It's Archie Foyle's—the words match exactly what he recited when I visited him.

"The word *MINE* is scrawled across it in red pen," Marks says. "Does that mean anything to you?"

89

"Something tells me it will," I mumble.

"What was that?" Marks asks, eyeing me suspiciously.

"No, it doesn't mean anything to me," I say, not bothering to hide the annoyance in my voice. I look over at Crane and notice he wrote down every word the chief inspector read out just now, and I'm grateful for that. I'm even more grateful to Jenny for snapping a picture of the page of his notebook from around the back of my shoulders—she leans in like she's putting her arm around me just as Marks turns to point at something near the solarium door. If Crane noticed what she was up to, he gives nothing away and lets it happen.

"I see there is a surveillance camera on the front door," Marks says. "Is it up and running?"

"It is," I say. "I installed a state-of-the-art security system when I moved in, given that I'm living alone in a house where a murder previously happened. There's also a camera on the side door that leads to the boot room. But not one on the solarium door, unfortunately—the wiring was too complicated without a complete renovation." I'd forgotten about the security cameras—there's an app on my phone, but I turned the alerts off because I was constantly getting pinged when a badger or a fox set the motion detectors off. I make a mental note to go through it all, once I have a moment alone.

"Well, if you could be so helpful as to provide our tech team with access to that, we'd appreciate it." He rattles through a list of other things Jenny and I need to provide, like fingerprints and DNA samples.

"When can we go back into the house?" I ask. "I mean, even if the solarium is off-limits, I have things to do." I'm thinking of Aunt Frances's file on Peony Lane, which is something I want to grab as soon as humanly possible. I don't think Chief Inspector Marks will be aware that there's probably a ton of important details in that file, and I'd like to keep him in the dark on that.

But just as I'm forming some solid investigation plans in my head, everything starts to unravel. A uniformed police officer approaches us from the house with something very recognizable in his hand. He takes two steps past Marks, ignoring him, and hands a thick stack of paper enclosed in a file folder to Detective Crane. I don't have to see the name on the folder to guess that it belongs to Peony Lane. I see a muscle twitch in Marks's jaw, and color starts to creep up his neck when the officer says, "Here you are, sir—it was right where you said it would be."

"What's this?" Marks asks, reaching toward Crane for the file.

Crane keeps hold of the file, which makes me internally cheer for him. But then I feel immediately conflicted, because the detective has just thwarted my next move.

"Just a hunch I wanted to follow," Crane says casually.

"Don't you need a warrant for this kind of thing? You can't just take things from private property, right?" I ask.

"When a crime has been committed, and we think it's relevant, then yes," he says. "We can."

Marks looks at me, then back at Crane, his expression impatient. "Fine, we'll talk about whatever this is"—he waves his hand toward the file like it's a mess someone's made—"back at the station. A PC will be here while the crime scene continues to be processed, but for now the two of you can enter the house again from the front. We've had officers exiting that way, so the door is open now."

"We'll be in touch," Crane says, standing.

The chief inspector notices the coffee tray then, and looks to all our hands, where the takeaway cups are still steaming. He then looks back at Crane. In one smooth movement,

Marks reaches toward Crane and swipes the file from his hand.

The two of them walk off briskly, and Jenny tuts under her breath. "Now, there's a weird dynamic," she says.

"Honestly, I don't think it's weird. Something about that chief inspector seems . . . sort of how I've seen every in-charge cop on TV. It's like he's trying to act a part."

We start to walk around the side of the house to the main entrance, which takes several minutes because of how expansive it is. The gardens wrap around the estate, and we pass through a small apple orchard and a hedge maze and into the Japanese garden. Autumn colors are riotous here, with the bright yellow leaves of a ginkgo tree dripping down with every small breeze.

Jenny stops and bends over the koi pond, and several fish rise to greet her, thinking she has food. "Okay, before we end up back in earshot of the many police that are working inside your house, I have to say something. It's not Peony Lane–related—at least, I don't think it is. It's Laura Adams–related."

"Mum actually called me this morning," I say, and that phone call feels like days rather than hours ago, given all that's happened today. "And now that you mention her, she was acting a bit strange. Is she okay? Did you see her before you left London?"

"She's okay, but I went by the house in Chelsea to pick up some more of those books you left. And your mum's friend Reggie Crane—he's the detective's dad, right?" she adds. I nod. "Well, he was there with his taxi and, in a stroke of luck, on his way to Castle Knoll after a weekend with his boyfriend, so I was able to ride all the way here with him."

"When I spoke to her, I heard a man's voice in the background," I say. "She wouldn't tell me who it was, but if Reggie was over, I bet it was him. Did she say what he was doing?"

Jenny shrugs. "It probably was. Anyway, Reggie and I had a *long* chat on the way down—that man is full of juicy gossip. Apparently your mum's newest obsession is with Peony Lane."

"Yeah, she seemed very interested in that file . . . the one Crane just took." I feel my forehead crease in frustration, because I'm now left with nothing from Aunt Frances regarding her knowledge of Peony Lane. I'm going to have to either talk Crane into letting me see that file or find a way to get at those notebooks Archie has. Preferably both.

"Well," Jenny continues, "there was someone else there too, an elderly woman. Does the name Birdy mean anything to you?"

The sparrow fluttering around in the solarium plays in my mind like a film. "*The bird returns*," I say.

CHAPTER
14

February 10, 1967

I TASKED ARCHIE WITH THREE THINGS—SEEKING OUT *the wreckage of the car that the Gravesdowns were driving in that night; seeing what he could learn from his informant within the police, whoever that was; and finding Birdy Sparrow.*

As I sifted through the jumble of my thoughts after leaving the Dead Witch, I realized I didn't have much of a role in this investigation. I was relegated to being the spy—the girl who caught the eye of the wealthy but potentially nefarious man, who flutters her eyelashes to get him to give up his secrets.

This would not do.

Last summer, I learned that I have a horrible tendency to get pulled along by someone with a stronger mind than my own. With Ford, this means that he makes me feel like I'm losing a race that really, I probably shouldn't even be running.

But Archie? He's something else entirely. It's one thing to want your home back, but revenge . . . it's so tempting. Thinking about all the girls Edmund Gravesdown hurt, I could feel my blood boiling again. It made my feelings about Peony Lane shift, trans-

forming her from someone who gave me a grim fortune to a crusader for vigilante justice. Someone I wanted to know.

I used to regard her as someone almost unsavory, because who sees a future like mine and decides to actually share it with the victim? But after Eric's story, it's like a light has fought its way through trees and illuminated a side of her that was previously in shadow.

Perhaps she shared my fortune because she's trying to do some good. Maybe she feels like I'm someone who can be saved.

And that's the crux of it, really. The difference between Ford and the rest of this ramshackle cast of characters. Archie, Peony Lane, Eric, and I—we're on the lookout for secrets, on a quest to find out who can be saved. Ford has a bad tendency to look at people and wonder how they can be used. Knowing what I know about his family now . . . that does not sit well with me at all.

Three days have gone by, so I am restlessly making lists and writing theories. Here is where I've got to, in case I court so much trouble looking into this that my fortune comes true sooner rather than later. At least there will be some mark of my progress, some proof that I was onto something.

Important Facts and Questions

1. *Edmund Gravesdown was a criminal who sexually abused women and Peony Lane knew it. She did everything she could to stop him from preying on innocent women, including ultimately (allegedly) causing the crash that killed him, his wife, Olivia, and Edmund's father, Harry, by cutting the brake cable in his car.*

2. *Before the crash, Birdy Sparrow said she witnessed someone arguing near the Foyle house. Birdy claimed that someone was stabbed by a knife with a ruby in the handle, and the knife was thrown into the River Dimber. But how could she*

have seen what the knife looked like, and not the two people involved? Something about this story doesn't add up.

3. *After the crash, Birdy ran away. She told Emily about the knife, and Emily embroidered the story as the years went on.*

4. *Who was stabbed? Everyone involved in this is accounted for.*

Just as I finished writing this, a tapping sounded from my bedroom window and I had to bite my tongue to keep from screaming.

I relaxed only slightly when I saw Archie's face blinking at me from the other side of the glass, but adrenaline was still making my heart pound as I paused to tuck my notes away. There's a tree that grows very near to the front of the house, and if you're nimble enough, you can clamber along one of the sturdier branches to my window. It looked like Archie was nimble enough.

I raised the sash and pulled him inside but slapped him on the shoulder for giving me a fright. "We have a front door, you know! You could ring the bell!"

"At midnight?" he said, grinning. His curls were damp from the rain, and he was wearing a canvas jacket that was absolutely not right for the February chill. His shoulders were practically hunched up to his ears, and I felt a bit sorry for him.

"I didn't realize it had gotten so late," I said. "Here . . ." I pulled a folded quilt out from the chest at the foot of my bed and handed it to him. He took off his jacket and wrapped himself up, then sat cross-legged on the end of my bed like he'd been up here a million times.

"Thanks," he said. "I have something you need to see." And he reached inside his shirt and pulled out something rectangular. "I had to put it in there to keep it dry," he said. "If it gets ruined, my informant will have my head."

"I'm curious about why this inside informant is being so help-ful," I said. "Presumably they're risking their job."

"It's someone who hates the Gravesdowns as much as I do," Archie replied. "But that's all I'll say. Anyway, look at the photo." He handed me the paper he was holding.

"This . . . this is the wrecked car," I said.

Archie's face looked solemn. "Yes, and there are several things wrong with that photo. My informant said the bodies were found here, here, and here." Archie pointed to different locations in and around the car.

"Okay, so Edmund driving, Harry in the front passenger seat, and Olivia . . . in the road? That doesn't make sense." I stared at the photo, and the question of the stabbing and its mystery vic-tim swirled around with the problem of why Olivia had been found in the road. "Could she have been ejected from the car when it hit the tree?" I asked.

Archie was quiet; he could tell I was thinking. Finally, he cut into my thoughts. "Something important you should note—here." His finger traced the arcs of two dark lines on the road.

"Tire marks," I said, my mind reeling. "But . . . Peony Lane supposedly cut the brake cable. If there are tire marks, this means the cable had been fixed."

"Exactly," Archie said.

"So Peony Lane didn't cause the crash."

"She couldn't have," he added. "But then look, the curve of the road goes to the left, and the car hit the tree on the right side of it. Logically, it would look like the curve was taken too fast, which would cause the car to angle too wide and hit the tree. But the tire tracks—"

"They go to the right. Archie, oh my God, this is . . . this is a really significant piece of evidence. You genius!" I looked up at him; his cheeks had grown rosy from the sudden warmth of indoors after being out in the cold.

He ran a hand through his curls, flattening them a bit, then letting them spring back into place. He smelled like stale cigarettes and strong soap and had a small cut on his chin where I guessed he'd shaved hastily before coming over. I supposed I should feel honored that he'd decided not to show up looking disheveled, but I found the effort he'd gone to a little curious.

"I don't know about genius," he said. "I just like details."

"Well, those tire tracks are giving me all kinds of wild theories—and this photo tells all kinds of strange stories," I said.

Archie grinned. "I'd love to hear your wild theories—I think that's where we're going to shine as a team. I've got a mind for details, but you're the creative one."

"What do you mean? I'm not creative," I said.

Archie looked around my bedroom, which I suddenly noticed was a rather embarrassing mess. I jumped up hastily to stuff the strap of one of my brassieres back into a drawer, suddenly conscious that no man had been in my room before. I'd sneaked around a bit in the woods with my last boyfriend, John, and had kissed Ford a few times, but my romantic life had stalled quite a bit since my murder had begun to occupy my thoughts.

I didn't think of Archie that way, but it was still strange to have him up here in my inner sanctum unannounced.

He gave me a slightly patronizing smile. "That's nothing I haven't seen before," he said, putting a bit of false swagger into his voice. "But I wasn't looking at the mess; I was looking at all these things you make." He pointed at the dressmaker's dummy in the corner, which was half-covered in fabric panels and pins from where I was midway through a new dress design. Then his eyes darted to the magazine clippings all over my walls, where a mess of the latest fashions, travel advertisements, and interviews with Hollywood actors reigned.

"This is . . . it's all left over from another life," I said, rather sadly. "I don't belong in my teenage bedroom, but I don't belong in a big manor either."

Archie nodded. "I can relate to that. I stand out in the library, but Eric's crowd at the pub feels like a dead end to me. Anyway, cheer us both up with your wild theories," he said, his eyes finding mine with a new intensity.

I sat up straighter, feeling energized again. "Right. So, my wild theories. Can I see that photo again?" I asked, and Archie handed it to me. "So here, look at the boot—there are scratches around the keyhole there." I pointed, and Archie squinted to look closer. "Edmund had just had his car completely buffed and re-painted after Peony Lane vandalized it, right? And all the damage from the crash was to the front of the car."

"You're right," Archie said, not tearing his eyes from the photo. "Edmund was famously picky about that car—he couldn't stand a scratch on it. So those scratches on the boot had to have happened that night."

"Here's my theory, and it explains the tire marks as well. Because in order for the marks to be headed in this curve toward the tree, it means the wheel would have to be turned in that direction, right?" I asked.

Archie nodded. "But in that case, the tire tracks are a contradiction," he said. "It means the person driving both turned toward the tree—in defiance of the curve of the road going completely the other way—but also braked hard to stop. I'd say that maybe Edmund was trying to end it all in a rage, but then why brake?"

"I think someone else in the car grabbed the wheel, and Edmund slammed on the brakes to avoid crashing," I said.

"But who? And why?" Archie asked.

"My best guess is Olivia, though I can't think why. But she's the most likely person to have survived the crash. You say your informant said her body was here?" I pointed to the spot in the road that Archie had indicated earlier, a few meters into the center of the tarmac, and behind the car.

"If the car hit the tree and Olivia was projected out into the road, she'd have been thrown forward rather than back. Couple that with the open rear passenger door, and it looks to me like Olivia emerged from the wreck, probably quite injured and dazed, but alive."

"That makes sense," Archie said. "I mean, looking at it now, and hearing you talk through it like that, it's actually obvious that something's not right here. The fact that this wasn't strange enough for the police to flag it as suspicious is quite the oversight." He paused, and I knew what he wanted to add.

I sighed. "Quite the oversight, or quite the cover-up?"

"I didn't want to say it," Archie admitted, and he had the grace to look apologetic.

"I know. But honestly, I'm finding that I'm not the kind of person who wants the wool pulled over their eyes. If there's truth out there, I want to know what it is. Even if it's ugly. And even if it changes the way I see people I care about."

We were both quiet for a moment, looking at the photo. It was Archie who finally broke the silence.

"So after the crash, Olivia stumbles out into the road, and she uses her dying moments to grab the keys out of the ignition so she can try to open the boot?"

"It would explain the scratches," I said. "If she was injured and disoriented, it would make sense that she'd miss a few times while trying to get the key into that lock. But then that begs the question of what was in the boot that was so important that she was desperate to get it out, rather than run for help."

"I think she eventually did try to run for help," Archie said. "After she failed to open the boot. She just didn't get very far, and collapsed a few meters after she started to run."

I nodded, because the pieces were all starting to fit together.

"You asked why she'd jerk the wheel, aiming for that tree . . . I think I might know why."

"She wanted to run the car into a ditch so she could escape, and miscalculated?" Archie offered.

"Perhaps," I said. "But given what we know of Edmund Gravesdown's crimes, I think it's more likely she was actively trying to murder her husband. Which means she must have known about what he did. . . . Either that or their marriage was in such a bad state she was ready to end it all, for herself as well as everyone else in that car."

"That's an excellent theory, Frances," Archie said.

"Thanks." I beamed back at him.

"But I think we need to consider that your boyfriend, Ford, wasn't innocent in all of this." Archie's expression turned dark, the way it always did when he said Ford's name. "Because while I think your theory's a good one, we can't rule out the possibility that he and Olivia might have been in on this murder plot together."

I winced, both at the accusation and at Archie's statement of our relationship. "Stop calling him my boyfriend—I've decided to stop seeing him. At least while we're investigating all this. I'm not going to try to seduce information out of him; I'm not that kind of person."

Archie surprised me by reaching over and squeezing my hand. "I know you're not, Frances. I'm sorry, I've put you into a strange spot with him. But I really do think he's no good, and I'm glad you've decided not to see him anymore. Would you do me a favor and let me drive you there when you tell him? I just don't want you going there alone when you're going to drop that kind of news."

"He's not a killer, Archie," I said. "He wouldn't hurt me." I feel my eyes sting, because I do find I have some very complicated feelings about Ford. He wouldn't conspire to kill someone, would

he? True, he benefited from the deaths of his loved ones, in that he inherited the family fortune and the estate, but he always seemed sincere in his grief about it. But the facts were right in front of me, and they were screaming loud and clear.

"You said it yourself." Archie spoke quietly. "Once you start to look, the photo of the crash scene has some glaringly obvious inconsistencies. And yet somehow, the file was simply closed."

"And the person who is most likely to have pushed for that to happen is the remaining family member," I said, and I handed the photo back to Archie. I had to uncurl my fingers from its edges. I hadn't noticed that my grip on it was so tight that the paper was tearing.

CHAPTER

15

WE NEED THOSE NOTEBOOKS FROM ARCHIE'S," I SAY to Jenny. Evening has fallen, and we've ordered delivery from the family-owned Italian restaurant in Castle Knoll because neither of us wants to go near the kitchen. There's still police tape and plastic sheeting up in between the kitchen and the solarium, even though the forensic team took the body and all significant evidence away. Apparently, they need the room sealed off while they process all the fibers and things, in case they need to come back and collect more.

"The file is going to be out of our reach for the whole of the police investigation, I'll bet," Jenny says, folding a slice of artichoke and goat cheese pizza in half before biting into it. "That Marks guy doesn't seem like the type to share evidence. And I know Detective Crane sort of bent the rules for you last time, but it really doesn't look like that's going to continue. Not with Marks looking over his shoulder. Any luck finding Olivia's file? Because Crane only took the one on Peony Lane, right?"

"All the Gravesdown files are gone," I say. I let out a long sigh and reach over to refill my empty glass with red wine. We're in the library, picnicking on the floor in front of the fireplace. It isn't my favorite room in the house, given that this is where we found Aunt Frances's body last summer, but I'm trying to make new memories in here to override that one. Not that talking through another murder is the stuff fond memories are made of, but eating pizza and drinking wine with Jenny is.

"The thing is, I don't know who cleared the Gravesdown files out, or when. I found them when I was rummaging around during Frances's murder investigation, but I haven't checked on them since. I haven't had a reason to—and people have been in and out of this house since I moved in. Half the village was here for Frances's memorial, and I didn't think to hide the keys to the filing cabinets in a new location until really recently. But I think those diaries have things in them that the files won't have." I sip my wine thoughtfully. "Otherwise, why would Archie be so cagey about them?"

"Do you think Beth could help us get them? I know she's a prime suspect for Peony's murder, but if we can eliminate her, maybe she'll be an ally. Plus, if we go over there while Archie's out, and just ask nicely, she might simply hand them over not knowing what they are."

"Something tells me that's unlikely, but I guess we could try," I say. "The bigger challenge will be getting information out of my mum. The fact that she's suddenly spending time with Birdy and is asking about Peony Lane . . . it's more than odd. I mean, Birdy is technically her aunt, and when they met at Frances's funeral a few weeks ago, Mum did seem to like the idea of connecting with one of our only living blood relatives. But she hasn't mentioned her again until now."

"You think it could just be as simple as she said? That she's looking into it for artistic reasons? An investigation of past dramas for inspiration, against the backdrop of the area she grew up in? I could see her mining for creative material in that way, her signature style of crumbling pieces of the past but this time with a fortune-telling twist."

"That does sound like the kind of idea salad Mum would use to fuel a new series of paintings," I say.

Jenny holds Aunt Frances's green diary in one hand and gives it a thoughtful look. "Do you ever wonder why Frances married him?" she asks. "Ford, I mean. The sole remaining Gravesdown heir probably had the draw of money, but after reading the diary, I don't get the impression Frances was a fortune hunter. It's a rather curious match, don't you think?"

I take another slice of pizza and chew thoughtfully for a moment. "I do wonder about it, yes. I'd hate for it to have been for the money. I want to think she wasn't like that."

"It's a common reason, but I know what you mean. She seems like the type of person who cleverly tries to avoid love, only to fall really hard," Jenny says. Then she gives me a pointed look.

"Oh, don't start," I warn her.

"I'm just saying, you work awfully hard to avoid relationships these days, and I really feel like someone's going to come by and wreck all your careful choices."

In cinematically bad timing, the doorbell rings, low and resonant, almost like a gong.

"If that's him now, I'm taking appointments as the new resident fortune-teller," Jenny says, then bounces up to go and open the door.

"Don't open it," I say, standing up and following her. "Not until I've checked the security camera . . . which—damn it—I was going to look through all the recent footage from that whole system. So much has happened today. Don't let me forget."

I open the app on my phone and click between the cameras to the one labeled "front door." Detective Crane paces in the live stream, his hands in his coat pockets and his breath coming out in impatient clouds.

Jenny gives me an irritatingly knowing look, which I ignore.

"Annie, hi," he says when I finally open the door. "Jenny, good to see you again." He nods to her. "I'm sorry to bother you so late, I just . . . had some more questions."

I open the door wider and gesture for him to come inside. We all head back to the library, and Crane shakes his head lightly at the offer of pizza or wine. He looks tired but also rather on edge.

"You said you had questions?" I ask, settling myself in an armchair by the fire. Jenny goes back to sit on the floor near the open pizza box. Crane remains standing and moves his hands to his sides. It's almost like he's schooling his posture to be neutral, which worries me.

"Was this morning the first time you met Peony Lane? Please, answer me honestly." He looks almost angry, and I'm taken aback by the seriousness of his tone.

"Yes, it absolutely was. Why do you ask?"

The tension in the library is rising, and I feel strange about that. Jenny is looking from Crane to me and back again, like she's the umpire at a tennis match.

"What about seeing her from a distance, maybe on the estate?"

"No," I say cautiously. "Between her stature and her clothing, she was pretty conspicuous. I'd have spotted her if she was lurking around."

I'm treated to one of Crane's lengthy looks. I can tell he's taking the measure of me. "Well, the list of logged calls to the police station tells another story. We keep a record of every call and complaint that comes into the station—not 999 calls; those go through a separate system to a central dispatch. But when someone calls the station, the date and time and reason for the call get logged. And your name comes up as having called the station to complain about harassment from one Peony Lane. You're in our system as having called about her *eleven times*."

"Well, that's nonsense, then," I say, springing to my feet. "If I was complaining about being harassed, why wasn't it investigated? And I want to hear these alleged 'calls.'"

"I said they were logged, not recorded," he says evenly.

"Whatever happened to *your call is being recorded for training purposes*?" I fire back. "Anyway, you can't tell me you believe that I called all those times, and no one opened a file on it or came to check it out."

"Apparently they did," Crane said. His expression is more neutral now, which is somewhat heartening, but I can tell his confidence in me is still shaken.

I cross my arms and give him a hard look. "Who? Who came and dealt with my 'complaints,' because surely you can see how fake this looks."

"A PC named Asha is in the system as having followed up these complaints. Apparently you never answered the door any of the times she visited."

"I'm willing to bet no one answered the door because I wasn't home! Someone is setting me up, and they'd have watched me coming and going over the past few weeks, waiting to call and 'complain' when they knew I wouldn't be here to answer the door."

"Which number did the calls come from?" Jenny interjects. "Could someone have faked Annie's voice?"

"The calls came from Gravesdown Hall," Crane says. He rattles off a number I don't recognize. "It's been confirmed as the landline registered here."

"Well, there you go!" I say. "I'm twenty-five years old, why the hell would I use a landline? I didn't even know there *was* one here!" I take my mobile out of my pocket and wave it at him, as if to underline my point.

Crane looks relieved for a moment, then worried. "So you're telling me that someone set up a pattern of calls in order to fake some complaints from you, in the lead-up to murdering Peony Lane?"

"It's bizarre, but yeah," I say.

Crane puffs out his cheeks and lets the air empty from his lungs.

"You believe me, right?" I ask, my voice a bit softer.

His hesitation is so quick it's like a momentary breath, but it's there. "Of course," he says, and there's a softness in his eyes that's almost shy, and that more than makes up for it. "I don't think this is going to end here, though," he says eventually. "So I suggest you be on your guard."

After Jenny and I walk him to the door and say good night, I make sure to check all the locks and loop my house keys through a spare hairband I've got around my wrist. "I'm only wearing things with pockets from now on," I say. Jenny gives me a long look. "What is it?" I ask.

"I'm just mentally multitasking again. I'm thinking through the outfits I brought that have pockets, as well as deciding that we definitely *can't* ask Beth Foyle for those diaries. Because I can't think of very many people whose voice could be mistaken for yours. I've compiled a short list, and so far it's just Beth."

"This is a good point," I say, feeling stung by the idea that Beth could actually do something like this to me. "But also, this framing of me is almost comically bad. There's one other pairing that could not only pull it off, but would come up with something this theatrical in the first place."

"Ooh, my favorite cartoon snake, Saxon Gravesdown," Jenny says. "And his insidious wife, Elva."

"Exactly. If Peony Lane was suddenly looking for me, desperate to come clean about causing the death of Saxon's parents, Saxon could have got wind of the fact that she had a hand in how they died. That one event could be traced back to Saxon's whole downfall and the loss of his inheritance—it all started with the deaths of his parents, and it culminated with me solving Aunt Frances's murder."

"He could get revenge on the person who turned his whole life upside down, and then take you down in the process," says Jenny. "I don't know him very well, but this does look like his style."

"The other thing I know from past experience with Saxon is that he knows this house inside out." I shudder. "If there's one person who knows of a way into this house that won't be seen on the security cameras, it's Saxon Gravesdown."

CHAPTER

16

November 2

THE NEXT MORNING, JENNY AND I DECIDE TO WALK
to Castle Knoll for breakfast. My head is pounding from too
much red wine last night—and probably stress too. It's a
clear, sunny day, which I'm trying to appreciate, rather than
scowl at for making my eyes water and my hangover worse.
It's about a thirty-minute walk, cutting through the woodland trails on the Gravesdown estate and then following the
public footpaths that go over the main road to town and
across a farmer's field to pop out on the high street. There's a
shorter way to the far end of town, if you walk along the side
of the road and past the old collapsing pub, but I'm aiming us
toward food, and the best places are near the castle ruins.

"So," Jenny says, linking arms with me as we stroll down
the cobbled high street, "the only other time I've been to
Castle Knoll was for Frances's funeral, and that didn't in-
volve walking around this charming place. Introduce me to
the sights—where's the best brunch place? What do people
do for fun?"

"Brunch isn't really a thing here, Jenny—this isn't Islington," I say.

"So I can't have a Bloody Mary for some hair of the dog?" she asks. "No avocado toast with a view of a Sainsbury's car park?"

"I can offer you a cream tea with a view of the model village," I say. "The tiny pretend people paired with giant lawn games just might win you over."

"That sounds amazing—lead the way!" she says, and her enthusiasm is genuine.

I smile as I take us past a few tasteful art shops—local handmade pottery and watercolors mostly, but a nice change from the try-hard London galleries I've spent my life in, following Mum around during her various exhibitions and those of her friends. Jenny ducks into a shop that sells fossils and comes out with a bag of what is basically pick 'n' mix but with rocks.

"You get this paper bag, and you can fill it from a huge bucket of polished stones and crystals and stuff," she says, riffling through the bag as we walk.

"I know, Jen," I say, laughing. "I've been in there before." It feels nice to wander and enjoy the small things; I really don't do enough of this. A lot of people don't, really, unless you have a child dragging you onto a steam train or into a shop that sells kites.

I think of Jenny's comment last night, about how hard I've been avoiding relationships lately, and it stings a little because of how true it is.

But in avoiding the "charmers," as Mum always called my dad, I've found those guys who like to poke holes in my personality at every turn. In the past, I've dated such serious men—the ones who, when they tell me that my excitement over collecting stickers is infantile, I listen to. If I'm too excited over something simple, I'm not acting my age. If I'm too deep in my own thoughts, I'm not fun enough.

"You've been in there before? Did you get some crystal pick 'n' mix?" Jenny's voice punctures my thoughts.

"Crystal pick 'n' mix sounds like new slang for hard drugs, but Castle Knoll style," I say, and feel my mood lift again from its momentary dip.

"You've just invented a great new game," Jenny says. "Drugs or village souvenir? I'll go first: lemonade Punch and Judy," she says, and grins at me.

"You realize neither of us would ever be able to mix real drug slang into this game," I say. But then I add, "Rustic stick of rock."

We laugh and continue this to the tearooms. There, I show Jenny the model village, which is a replica of the village before the castle became a ruin. It's actually rather fascinating to look at, with the tall hill of the real castle ruin looming directly behind the walls of the tearoom gardens.

"You didn't lie—they have giant Jenga, giant Connect 4.... This is amazing," Jenny says, running around the dewy lawns of the model village garden and taking stock. "And then teeny-tiny people, and tiny houses!"

I leave Jenny to her enthusiasm while I order some cream teas and then sit at a slightly damp patio table and breathe in the crisp air. I realize my hangover is gone, and I feel like an elderly person as I think, A bit of fresh air does wonders.

I start as I hear the chime that indicates someone's tripped the motion sensor in my front-door camera, and my relief at the fresh air evaporates.

"It's just my delivery," Jenny says as she settles into the chair across from me.

"You . . . ordered something?" I ask, a little confused. I

wouldn't put it past Jenny to do some online shopping while she's here, especially since she definitely didn't bring the right footwear for tramping along the muddy footpaths of Castle Knoll.

"Yep, you'll thank me. Outfits with pockets." She grins.

I pinch the bridge of my nose, trying to contain the spiral of my thoughts.

"What?" Jenny asks. "You don't like pockets?"

"No, I love pockets, thanks, Jen. It's just . . . I'm getting so paranoid, I actually can't tell which of my theories are just fears now. That delivery alert rattled me, is all. Is this how Aunt Frances felt? How she lived her whole life?" My voice cracks a little as I speak, which surprises me.

Jenny reaches over and touches my arm. "You aren't your great aunt," she says gently. "Or maybe you've got some things in common, but it's the good stuff. I've read that diary too, remember? You're both a bit too clever for your own good, but I think with the right friends around, you can make sure your cleverness doesn't cause you to unravel."

I give Jenny a watery smile. "Thanks," I say. "I hope Aunt Frances had someone like you. Also, you need to move in with me now and be my anchor to reality. I can see how thinking that every aspect of daily life might relate to a crime can warp your sense of self."

"You do need some housemates, but as much as this town has charmed me, I belong in London," Jenny says. Her phone rings suddenly, and she gives me an apologetic smile. "It's my mum; I should take this."

While Jenny roams the tearoom gardens talking to her mum, I take a moment to watch the people passing by. The gardens are walled, but the patio I'm sitting on is raised enough that I can see over the sides. It's a nice way to people watch.

My eyes alight on an expensive SUV parked across the road next to the hardware shop. It belongs to Elva, the wife of Saxon Gravesdown, though it's not Elva who I see approaching the car; it's Saxon, leaving the shop in a sharply tailored light gray suit and a pink shirt that sets off the lighter streaks in his salt-and-pepper hair.

Saxon and I aren't on the best of terms, given the tricks pulled on both sides in a game that I ultimately won, but learning about how his family died has me thinking about him slightly differently. In one night, he lost both his parents and his grandfather. He was left to be raised by his uncle Ford, who inherited a huge estate that must have felt so empty with the absence of the rest of the family. I'm not warming to Saxon just because of his tragedy, but I'm starting to think of him somewhat differently. The man has a lot of secrets, and he's very good at hiding them. Aside from the interactions I had with him last summer, I actually know very little about him.

I pull my phone out and snap several pictures, a new habit of mine that is worryingly like Aunt Frances—I feel like the more information I have about those around me, the better off I am. If I take some photos that turn out to be useless, what's the harm?

But I know these won't be useless photos, because as soon as the SUV drives away, I swipe back to them and use the zoom function to see what it was that Saxon had clutched under his arm. From across the road, it looked like papers, but something nagged at me as I snapped the pictures—the slightly yellow color of them, and the stiffness of the stack.

And there it is—the label on the edge of the papers under his arm is distinctive, because it matches a neatly organized set. It's one of Great Aunt Frances's files.

I click on a few sharpening tools in my photo app to try to get the writing on the label to show up more clearly. It doesn't sharpen the whole thing, but the *G* followed by squiggles matches the *Gravesdown* I've seen on other files. After the comma, I can just about make out the first letter of the first name on the file. It's an *O.*

So that's why I couldn't find Olivia Gravesdown's file in Frances's collection—because Saxon took it. I wonder when he managed that. And why was he taking it into the hardware shop?

My thoughts are interrupted by Jenny coming back to the table. "My cousin in Southampton had her baby a bit early, and my mum is insisting I go straight to the hospital with some gifts and supplies from our family, since I'm relatively close by. Do you mind terribly if I abandon you for a little while and get the train to Southampton? You can come too if you like. Though it means shopping first, as Mum's given me a huge list of things to buy for her."

"I really don't mind," I say. "I was planning to head over to the police station anyway, and I imagine you'll have more fun shopping for your cousin than tagging along with me."

Jenny raises an eyebrow. "The police station, eh? Case-related, or a personal visit?"

I slap her lightly on the arm. "Case-related. I just saw Saxon and I think I need to pay him a visit, but the things I want to ask him might be a little out of my depth. I learned my lesson last summer. If I'm going to confront Saxon about anything, backup is essential."

"I love that the actual police are your backup," Jenny says. "But I'm glad you're being sensible. Because logically, if Peony Lane was right, and she really did cause that car crash, Saxon finding out all of a sudden would be the perfect motive for her murder."

"Exactly. And if he could do it in a way that would take me down in the process, all the better," I add.

"Well then, go and get your backup, and you've got to promise to fill me in on all the juicy details. And also tell me what you learn from Saxon." She has the gall to actually wink at me then.

I slap her on the arm again, harder this time. I don't want to admit that her teasing has me wondering more about Crane. Where does he live? What does he do in his spare time? Other than the fact that he's cool under pressure, is rather a stickler for the rules, and has an unnerving ability to observe me and draw correct conclusions about what he sees, I don't know much about him. And I don't like that he probably knows far more about me. When I'm around him, I tend to turn my personality up to eleven. Whether this is because I feel comfortable around him or because I'm lonely enough that I'm craving to be seen by someone, it's hard to say. Self-reflection-Annie doesn't tend to want to hang around with murder-solving-Annie.

As I make my way to the police station, I mentally recite Archie's fortune again.

The list you seek is the right one—the foil, the arrow, the rat, the sparrow.

I can think of a person who could match each of these things—the foil could be any of the Foyles, but I'm thinking it's Eric, because the arrow feels like Archie—he's the archer poised to shoot, the bringer of death according to the fortune. The sparrow could be Emily Sparrow, but is most likely Birdy.

And now I have a good candidate for who might be the rat.

CHAPTER
17

February 15, 1967

THE DAY AFTER ARCHIE SNEAKED UP TO MY BEDROOM,
Ford returned from London, saying his business there was con-
cluded. He invited me to dinner, and I asked if we might go to the
fancy restaurant at the Castle House Hotel. Rose was working
there, though not in the restaurant, and I felt a bit safer thinking
she'd be somewhere nearby. I hadn't told her I'd planned to break
things off with Ford—she'd be devastated to find out, given that
she wanted me to have this happily ever after where I became a
lady and we lived up at Gravesdown Hall together, me in the hall
and her with her fiancé in the flat above the fancy garages on the
estate.

"The house is much more private," Ford said as he drove the
small distance from my parents' house to the restaurant. This
had been what Archie had said too, but he'd meant it in a bad way.

"I just don't want you going there alone when you're going to
drop that kind of news," Archie had said sternly. Left unsaid was
his concern for my safety—Ford was a Gravesdown, after all.
And that family hurt people.

I rehearsed the scene in my head over and over and went back on my decision several times. Ford wasn't like his brother. Maybe they weren't even close before Edmund died; maybe Ford didn't really know what Edmund was up to.

But then Ford pulled up to my house in his sleek black Mercedes and didn't even ring the doorbell. He simply honked the horn to let me know he was waiting.

That alone made it easier. Archie would scale a tree at midnight just to share some theories on a mystery that had us both hooked, while Ford didn't want to walk the length of my drive.

I said a rather subdued hello, and he leaned over and kissed my cheek.

Something that I'm aware of about myself is that I lack the ability to control my facial expressions, no matter how hard I try. If someone is observant, they can watch every thought, emotion, and reaction flit across my features. This often causes one of two reactions in people. One, they praise me for my "honest demeanor" and mistake it for innocence. Or two, it makes people feel powerful because they can see right through me. But when people have been seeing right through you your entire life, you know that transparency isn't a weakness. It means it often never occurs to people to distrust you.

Ford is one of the only people I've met who reacts to me in a mixture of those two ways. Tonight, he could tell by my voice and my body language, and probably my expression, that my feelings toward him were cooling. Perhaps he saw that I'd come to a decision about our future.

I sensed him rally. He straightened up behind the wheel as he pulled into the hotel driveway and hurried out to open my door for me. He asked me about my day, about what I'd been doing with my time while he was away, and he managed to sound interested rather than interrogative. When he leaned back into the car to get me my handbag, I noticed a puff of smoke rise from beneath the lamppost near the back door of the hotel.

Archie Foyle was leaning against it in a weathered brown bomber jacket with sheepskin at the collar. He threw his cigarette on the ground and stamped it out under his shoe; then a woman stepped out from a battered VW and they turned and walked into the hotel together. She had short hair that was ash-blond and styled with too much Aqua Net. They weren't holding hands or anything, and I felt strangely relieved about that.

She turned around and met my eyes and gave me an almost sympathetic look. All this happened in a matter of seconds, but it was enough time for me to feel unsettled and to wonder who she was.

The inside of the restaurant had oak-paneled walls and crisp white tablecloths and was the sort of place that gives you things like too many forks and an amuse-bouche that is just cold soup in a small glass.

Ford looked right at home—though I expect his sharp jawline and the slight wave of his dark hair would be elegant even in a barn. He looked at me with keen eyes and said, "So then, Frances, I leave for a couple of weeks, and it seems absence did not make the heart grow fonder." One side of his face twitched, almost like he found that funny.

I looked over to where Archie and his date were being seated by the maître d'; Archie was right in my eyeline across the restaurant. The woman had her back to me, but whatever she was saying made Archie laugh. He didn't laugh politely; he laughed the way he always does—like he's three pints in and is in the middle of a noisy pub. Ford turned at the sound, and the two of them locked eyes across the room. I felt the temperature drop by several degrees.

"Friends of yours?" Ford asked, his voice betraying an under-current of anger.

"Vaguely," I said. I was careful to keep my allegiances to myself because I was curious about what Ford's problem with Archie could possibly be. Eric had been on the estate a lot when Edmund was alive, so I might understand Ford being angry at Eric, especially if he'd found out that Eric had been party to Peony Lane's vigilante justice against his brother. Maybe Archie was just guilty by association.

"Don't be fooled by his Robin Hood act," Ford said. He signaled to the waiter for the wine list, barely glanced at it, and rattled off the name of a wine that he presumably always drank when he came here.

"What does that mean?" I asked. Archie's laugh bubbled up across the room again, and my eyes darted to where he sat, one elbow on the white tablecloth, his faded dress shirt unbuttoned at the top. His bomber jacket was nowhere to be seen, but a dinner jacket belonging to the hotel was slung across the back of the chair he was sitting in. It was as if his goal was to pretend to follow the dress code but flout it at the same time. I was betting he knew half the staff here and that they probably enjoyed seeing him come in to dine when earlier he had been having a fag out the back with the kitchen porter. Robin Hood *actually* fitted him, now that Ford said it.

It fitted all of them—Archie, Eric, and Peony Lane. And maybe even Birdy, when I worked out how she was involved in all of this. They were some kind of coalition, taking down the rich and powerful when the normal channels of justice turned a blind eye. Even Archie's mystery police informant, passing him police records and case files, was being subversive. It made me wonder how divided the village was, how deep this network ran, and how widespread the anger toward the Gravesdowns truly was.

"It means that everything isn't what you think it is," Ford said. The waiter poured a taste of wine for him, and he spent ages sniffing it and swirling it in his glass before giving the nod of approval. Only then were both our glasses filled.

A sharp laugh escaped me because I was rather fed up. "You want to make this about class, when really it's about how utterly bored I am with your performances. True, I work at my family's bakery, and I ride my bicycle around the village and deliver bread to people while I'm still covered in flour. I'm eighteen years old and have never left England, I have no further education, and so on paper, I should really be impressed with you. And I have been, I won't deny that. But there are only so many times I can sip cocktails in your grand library and feel as though that's all I need in my life."

Ford put down his glass and gave me a long, appraising look. "Are you sure this is about me and my lifestyle suddenly being boring to you, and not about your conversations with the Foyle family?" His eyes flicked over to Archie, then back to me.

"Archie's harmless," I said.

"Oh, you think so?" He looked for a moment like he was going to say more, but he paused. "I don't want to see you hurt, Frances. And yet I have it on good authority that you've been digging into my family's recent tragedies."

I opened my mouth to protest, but he lifted a hand to cut me off. I felt my anger flare, and I wanted to shout, "How dare you spy on me!" and then storm out of the restaurant, but I didn't. Something in his face made me pause, and it wasn't any kind of sentimental feeling—with Archie and his date watching, I felt the claws of the mystery of the Gravesdown crash gripping me. I wanted information. I wanted Ford's side of this so I could compare it to what I knew.

But I couldn't compromise my own feelings just to get answers. A good investigator would have smiled warmly, tried to get Ford back to feeling comfortable, and gently pressed him for information—all while sprinkling the conversation with compliments or light-hearted repartee. I wanted to be a good investigator, but not if it meant being less of a good person. With everything we'd been through, Ford deserved the truth from me, not a false version of me that pandered to him to get what she wanted.

I squared my jaw and met his eyes. "Ford, I don't think a romantic relationship between us should continue any further." Even in my anger at being spied on, and at his arrogance, and at my realization of how little I'd been missing him lately, saying that felt terrible.

He blinked in surprise but quickly hid his feelings. He'd clearly sensed this was on my mind but probably doubted that I'd actually break up with him. "Very well," he said, his voice quiet.

"I understand if you want to cut our evening short," I said.

"No," he replied, and looked down at his hands, where he was restlessly turning the stem of the wineglass between two fingers. Other than that gesture, there was little sign that he was upset. But looking closely, I noticed his shoulders had hunched just a touch, and he was looking too focused on the reflections in his glass.

"Is this because of Archie Foyle?" he asked quietly.

"Not in a romantic way, no. It's just . . . I don't like secrets," I said. "After last summer, when I felt as though I was constantly the last to know things, I want to be around people who are open and honest." I reached across the table and laid a hand over his. "I know that even though you come from privilege, you haven't had an easy time in life. Losing your family the way you did—I can't imagine what that must be like. And I accept that really, their secrets are none of my business."

He didn't move his hand from underneath mine, but I felt his fingers pulse in a tiny flex, just once. It was like an involuntary reaction he was trying to hide when I mentioned his family.

He was quiet, so I continued. "But when I think about knowing you, there's so much more to who you are, isn't there? Things like your upbringing, your memories, what formed your character. I'm shut out of all of that."

As I said this, I realized I wasn't lying—I did feel a huge disparity between the way I knew Ford and the way I knew Archie. Ford kept so much to himself, like a tree where you only see the green and healthy bits, but belowground there's a whole root system that twists and snarls out to destinations unknown.

And if I'm to love someone, I want to know all of them. The roots, the debris, the broken branches. When Ford finally moved his hand out from under mine, he looked at me, and there was a moment of connection where he must have sensed this.

"I want to talk to you about my family and the things that I know," he said slowly.

I felt a small twinge of conscience as I realized that in my candor, I'd actually achieved more than I might have through flattery. Did this make me a better investigator, by following my instincts? Or a worse person, because I hadn't foreseen how I could manipulate the truth out of someone? But I hadn't lied—the many things about himself that Ford had hidden from me had truly been one of my reasons for no longer wanting to be romantically involved.

"I'd be grateful to hear your side of things," I said. "And I do understand that having your girlfriend researching your family in the library probably doesn't inspire much confidence."

He gave me a sad smile. "Well, if you've been asking around about my family's past, it wouldn't take you long to hear the most salacious bits of it. I assume you've heard about the crimes of my brother, Edmund?"

I nodded slowly, not daring to breathe too deeply in case it made him change his mind about sharing more.

Ford took a long drink of his wine. A small plate that held a quail's egg on a bed of some kind of foam was put in front of each *of us. The waiter announced all the flavors and cooking methods involved, but I wasn't listening. When he had moved out of earshot, Ford finally spoke. "Just before she died . . ." Ford said, his words coming out slowly, like he had to reach to the dusty corners of his mind and pull them out reluctantly. He took another drink of wine and continued, more quickly this time. "Just before she died, Olivia was approached by Peony Lane, who had put together a file of evidence and accounts of Edmund's crimes. Peony thought—quite rightly—that trying to go to the police about Edmund would be futile, because of how powerful my family's wealth and lawyers were. Are. Peony reasoned that the person who might know best how to take Edmund down was his wife. For the record, at the time I had no idea what my brother was doing; I only found out the day he died. Otherwise, I would have done everything in my power to put a stop to it."*

"When did you find out about the file?" I asked.

"The night of the crash. Peony Lane came to the house looking for Olivia, but she wasn't home. Olivia and I always had a good rapport—she was an interesting and intelligent woman. I told Peony that Olivia trusted me, and I would do even better than get the file to her: I'd help bring my brother to justice. It took a bit of persuading, but I think Peony saw that my outrage at my brother's crimes was genuine.

"So Peony gave me the file with everything she'd compiled on Edmund. Witness statements, signed affidavits, even some sedatives she'd found in Edmund's car as evidence. I can't think how she got those, but I didn't want to ask. I read through everything, and it made me want to burn the whole estate to the ground. My father was complicit, covering for Edmund's crimes. I felt like my family was rotten to the core, and I couldn't imagine what this would do to Olivia and to her young son, being brought up in such a place. I decided I would help her leave, if it came to that."

124

I gripped my napkin in my lap. "She must have been so scared," I said, "of what Edmund was capable of."

Ford nodded, and his jaw was tight.

"If Olivia knew about his crimes that night, she never would have got into that car willingly," he said. "I know that."

"Do you think she had a chance to learn the truth?" I asked.

"I'll never know for sure," he said sadly. "I told Peony I'd take the file to the police—we both felt that it would carry more weight if I was the one to accuse him. Otherwise, Edmund could just argue that his wife was trying to blacken his name in the event of their divorce, or that Peony was just someone with a vendetta against a powerful family."

My thoughts caught up to my emotions. "So you took the evidence to the police station?" I asked. "What happened?"

"The crash happened before I could get the file to the police, but I took it to them a few days later and left it with a member of staff I'd never seen before. When I went to follow up the next week, they said there was no record of it ever being received. And since the guilty parties were all dead, the police said the best thing to do would be to close the case. In Saxon's best interests, I agreed."

The waiter was back, and I waved my plate away relatively untouched. I noticed Ford hadn't eaten much of his food either.

"Why did you refuse any investigation into the crash itself?" I asked.

Ford didn't look at all surprised by my question. In fact, he seemed to have been expecting it. "That was another thing I did for Saxon's sake, and a bit for my own. My father and brother were dead; they couldn't hurt anyone any longer. Olivia was a victim of circumstance. I didn't want to prolong Saxon's grief and fuel village gossip by having them investigate what I thought at the time was drunk driving, and probably an argument about the end of Olivia and Edmund's marriage. So you see, Frances, you're investigating something that is long over. Let the dead rest in peace."

CHAPTER

18

THE WHEELS OF SAMANTHA'S OFFICE CHAIR SQUEAK as she sees me walk through the police station door. She reaches over to a drawer and quickly shuts something inside it.

I think of the calls she logged, someone posing as me saying that Peony Lane was harassing me. "Hello, Samantha," I say, keeping my voice neutral but my eyes fixed on hers. "There are some things I'd like to ask you, if you don't mind."

"I do mind," she says. "There's an ongoing investigation and your name has come up several times already. I can't discuss it with you." Samantha opens another drawer and pulls out a pill organizer. One of those plastic ones with little compartments for each day of the week. "I can't seem to find anything today," she mutters, opening more drawers. "My cardigan's gone missing, and I had a water bottle just now...."

"Here," I say, leaning over the large reception desk and picking up a bottle. "Is this it?" I hand it to her, and she swallows two large pills and gulps back a generous amount of water. She then looks at the bottle curiously and sighs. "This isn't mine, but oh well. It probably migrated here from one of the other desks."

This isn't going well. There's a very slim chance Samantha is going to tell me anything now. She hated Aunt Frances, and by extension now seems to hate me. I'd try for flattery, telling her that she clearly knows the ins and outs of the whole station, but it won't work on her. The best way to get her talking is to make her defensive. People who think they're the glue that holds together an entire office hate being accused of substandard work.

"Can I just ask you one question—a hypothetical one," I add hastily. "Let's say I was working on this desk, and someone called in with a complaint about harassment. What would I do to verify their identity? Just ask their name and assume they're being truthful?"

"Excuse me," Samantha says, her eyes narrowing at me as she sees where this is going. "The way I do my job is none of your concern!"

"Oh, okay. So someone could call up and if the phone number *looks* legitimate, why even bother getting any more verification that they are who they say they are? I mean, if I were a kid and wanted to make some prank calls, I know where I'd start," I say, watching the color rise in her cheeks.

"Why does it even matter to you that complaints were made about Peony Lane stalking you? They were correct! The security footage on your estate confirms it!" she says.

"So you *knew* that caller wasn't me!" I say, watching her expression carefully. "Where's the PC who came to check up on me? I'd like to talk to her."

"She was transferred," Samantha says, not breaking eye contact.

"How convenient," I reply. We stare each other down

for several more seconds, but my eyes wander to the wall adjacent to her desk. I've never really looked at it, probably because it's lined with photos of all the members of the Castle Knoll Police Department going back decades. Several of the photos are even in black and white, but my eyes land on a faded color photo from 1987. I take a few steps closer to it, because I want to know who was working in this station when Aunt Frances's paranoia about being murdered was in full swing—by then she had been collecting everyone's secrets for a couple of decades.

The photo only has four men in it, standing solemnly with their hands clasped lightly in front of them. Their names are across the bottom of the frame, and one stands out immediately. I wouldn't have recognized him from his photo, but there in the middle is the name Tobias Marks. I blink to double-check, but it has to be him—the new chief inspector, Toby Marks, got his start here, in Castle Knoll. He only looks about twenty in the photo, and I'd place him in his mid-to-late fifties now. I suppose it makes sense that he'd want to shift to a quieter role back where he started, with a view to retirement in a few years.

"Detective Crane isn't here." Samantha's voice cuts through my thoughts. "He's a busy man; he can't spend all his time waiting for you to come and say hello."

"I never said I was coming to see him," I tell her. I mean, I absolutely was, but there's no way I'm admitting that now. As I stand there in a rather tepid stalemate with Samantha, it occurs to me that there's something Jenny and I should have done much earlier. When the detective removed Peony Lane's file from Aunt Frances's library, we should have checked the files of anyone even remotely connected to both Peony Lane and the Gravesdown family at the time of the crash.

"Did I hear my name?" Crane's distinctive baritone floats

from behind me, and I turn to see him standing in the police station doorway.

I've had enough of Samantha, I decide. "Yeah, I need you," I say, and in one swift motion I tug him by the arm back out the door and into the car park.

He resists a little, but still walks with me. "As nice as it is to be needed . . ." He pauses and gives me a pointed glance. "I'm in the middle of my workday. You assume I don't have things to do, Annie."

I bite my lip and wrestle with the sheepish feeling that's suddenly hit me. I realize I'm still holding on to his arm, and I let go hastily. "I'm sorry," I say, and I mean it. "I have a horrible tendency to drag you around like some kind of detecting accessory, don't I?"

He doesn't reply, but the thoughtful look on his face makes me feel worse. Deep down I was hoping for some kind of rebuttal, a reassuring *Don't worry, you don't do that.* Silence means the opposite. I may have won a point for self-awareness, but these kinds of moments sting.

"Okay, can I try again?" I ask gently.

Crane gives me a solemn nod, but I see the edges of his mouth soften, like there's a smile a few breaths away if I can just grab on to it.

"I've had several thoughts about Peony Lane and the crash that killed the Gravesdowns," I continue. "And I wanted to do some investigating to see if I can verify anything. I'd like it if you came with me to talk to Saxon Gravesdown, because I saw him earlier in town carrying Olivia Gravesdown's file—the one from Aunt Frances's archives."

Crane's brow creases. "How did he get that?"

"That's a good question," I say. "And one well worth asking, since we're also looking for someone who got into the house to kill Peony Lane while the doors were all locked."

Crane reaches a hand into his pocket, and I hear the jingle of car keys, but he doesn't take them out. His other hand scratches his jawline lightly, in that way that bearded men all seem to share, apparently communicating deep thought—or in Crane's case, indecision.

"Really, I should be saying, 'Thank you for your helpful information, Miss Adams; the Castle Knoll Police Force will look into it,' and send you on your way," he replies.

My hands find my own pockets, and I look down at my shoes only to remember I'm still in wellies. My confidence drains a bit further as I realize that these boots make me feel more like a small child looking for puddles than a fashionable writer who has recently relocated to her inherited estate. "Is . . . is that what you're saying?" I ask.

Another car pulls into the station car park, and we both turn to see Chief Inspector Marks hurry from it toward the station. Before he goes inside, Marks looks straight at Crane and his expression darkens. Crane's smile finally makes an appearance. But it's not a wholesome one; it's got a slightly sinister edge that twists across his face. It's not a look I've seen on him much, and I'm intrigued.

"No," Crane says, not taking his eyes from Marks. "Let's go." He pulls his keys from his pocket and gestures toward his car, in a way that telegraphs that he's happy to go anywhere with me. Marks shoots a glare back in reply, but Crane only seems energized by Marks's obvious disapproval.

When we're pulling out of the car park, I turn in my seat and take in the look of responsible concentration on his face and the careful attention he's paying to the speed limit. "Not that I'm upset at getting what I wanted," I say, "but am I correct in assuming that I was just used as fuel in an argument between you and your new boss?"

A muscle in Crane's jaw tightens, and I notice his foot tips the accelerator up a bit as we round a bend. "Marks has an issue with my level of comfort with 'the locals,' as he calls everyone in Castle Knoll."

"I just recognized him in a photo on the wall of the station," I say. "He's local too, right?"

Crane nods ruefully. "He likes to forget that not only did I grow up here, but he did too. He had bigger aspirations than the Castle Knoll Police Department and transferred to London at the first opportunity. I can't think why he wanted to come back here. I've heard he made a big show of being better than Castle Knoll when he left. Meanwhile, no one around will talk to him or give him the information he needs when he's out trying to do my job—which he does, by the way." Crane takes his eyes off the road for a second to give me a meaningful look.

"He meddles in your investigations?" I ask.

Crane nods. "When he's in a good mood he tries to treat me like a pet project, but there's always a patronizing edge to it. I'd say it was a good old-fashioned power struggle, but something about his actions seems . . . personal somehow." Crane takes a hand off the wheel and rubs the back of his neck, looking lost for a moment. When he puts his hand back, his thumb taps the leather lightly, like he's jittery.

"Personal how?" I ask. It's a rare opportunity to prod into Crane's life—we're always on good terms, but there's been a constant current of professionalism running through all our interactions. On the odd occasion when that slips and we start to veer into more private territory, one or both of us grasps that professionalism again like it's a life raft.

Crane lets out a long breath. "He's brought up details of my past cases," he says. "In some of my earlier cases there were some small things I missed, but never anything that mattered in terms of an arrest or a conviction. Just odd things that show he's scrutinizing my history."

"That still sounds like a power play," I offer. "He wants someone to pick at in the office, and you don't offer a lot of material for that, so he's gone digging."

"I suppose. I don't know, it's an instinct thing." He looks at me again, and there's a little more warmth in his glance. "I know you understand—you've got the same instincts."

I did not expect this compliment at all, nor the way I want to let his words etch themselves onto my skin like a tattoo. I shake my head lightly in the hope that my ridiculous inner monologue will pipe down.

"Well, what do your instincts tell you?" I ask.

But our conversation comes to a halt when Crane pulls into a long drive paved with herringbone bricks. The impressive white house at the end of it looks crisp and immaculate in the same way as Saxon's haircut, and I sense we've arrived. I give Crane an inquisitive look in the hope that he'll share more, but his expression shutters, indicating this conversation is over.

"Oh—something interesting you might want to know but that you didn't hear from me," Crane says, "is that I was able to get some witness statements that tell us more about Peony Lane's movements before you met her in the woods." His open expression makes me feel like he's giving me this information less because he thinks I can use it and more as a small gift. Like a cat leaving a dead bird on your doorstep, Crane is telling me about the movements of a murdered woman to feed this new unofficial partnership. I don't hide the pleased look that I can feel lighting up my face.

"Anything that might shed light on the strange things she

said? Her whole 'I have things to do, and Frances taught me about cheating fate' thing?" I ask.

"I'm not sure, but on the morning she was killed, several cars driving into Castle Knoll saw her walking along the pavement heading toward town. But she never made it into town, because not long after, another person driving said they saw her going back the other way. She must have changed her mind, turned around, and headed in the opposite direction, where she eventually met you."

"Huh," I say, turning the information over in my mind. "That is interesting." I have no idea how it's going to help me solve her murder, but I take it for the small token it is and tuck it away in my thoughts for later.

SAXON ANSWERS THE door, and if he's surprised to see us, he hides it well. But that's Saxon—he has that easy charm that comes from growing up with the world at your fingertips. However, he is also deceptively clever—something he hides behind a shallow veneer.

There has been an uneasy peace between Saxon and me ever since I beat him out of his inheritance last summer by solving Aunt Frances's murder. Saxon played the game well. A bit too well, actually—well enough to get himself into his own crop of trouble. I had more than a little hand in that, and the fact that he seems to have forgiven me for it makes me all the more suspicious of him. He's the type to play the long game, because he was raised by two of the best strategists around—his uncle Ford Gravesdown and Frances.

"Annie, Detective Crane." Saxon nods to us each in turn. "I'd ask why I've got the pleasure of your company unannounced, but I already know the answer to that."

Crane raises an eyebrow. "Do you now?"

Saxon ignores Crane and fixes his stare solely at me. "I've been wondering when I'd be questioned over the death of Peony Lane," he says. He turns back to Crane. "Though I'm surprised to see *you* here."

I'm ready to jump to Crane's defense, but he leans against the doorframe and gives Saxon a sardonic smile. "Making my competence as a detective into a punch line isn't going to rattle me, Saxon—my ego isn't that fragile." He continues to lean, and he's considerably taller than Saxon, so it gives the impression he's waiting for Saxon to give ground. I'm actually rather impressed when Saxon steps back from the door and into his hallway, inviting us in.

"I'd offer you tea," Saxon says, not looking behind him as he walks deeper into his home, "but we've run out."

I'd be reluctant to drink anything Saxon offers me anyway, so I just shrug. He leads us into a sitting room with high ceilings and windows so large they put the diamond-latticed ones at Gravesdown Hall to shame. Plush white carpets run wall to wall, with white sofas and armchairs to match. It's like being inside a snow globe—one I want to upend, even if it would only cause the illusion of chaos.

"I don't have a lot of time, so we can skip any pleasantries," Saxon says, picking at an invisible thread in the cushion next to him as he settles on the sofa.

Crane takes the armchair across from Saxon, and I settle into its twin opposite.

"Let's start with your mother—Olivia Gravesdown," I say, trying to keep my voice a bit gentle. This is about the crash that killed his parents, after all. And Saxon was a child when his whole world was turned upside down; that has to make a mark on a person.

The look Saxon gives me is shrewd, and a little angry. "I

thought the murder currently being investigated was that of Peony Lane," he says.

"It is," Crane cuts in. "But I'd like you to answer Annie's questions about some details from a past event concerning your mother, if you don't mind. You know the one we mean." Crane's tone is quiet but earnest, and I'm rather in awe of how he communicates this feeling of *you're needed, you can help* in so few words.

Saxon clears his throat, clearly uncomfortable, but says nothing.

"I know you have her file," I continue. "The one Frances kept in her investigation room—which implies that you've been in my house."

"I got that file on the day of the funeral," Saxon interrupts. "When the house was open and everyone was coming and going. I haven't been sneaking around since, so you can swallow those accusations right now."

"Fine," I say. "But Peony Lane mentioned your mother's name to me the morning she was killed. That doesn't feel insignificant."

Saxon stands abruptly and crosses the room to the white bookshelves that line one wall. In one quick movement he pulls at a thin folder tucked between some books, and Aunt Frances's yellowed file slips into his hand. He returns to his seat, opens the file with his features carefully neutral, and pulls out the crash photo—the one of the crumpled car, with the addition of drawn-on outlines indicating where each body was found.

"You want to talk about the crash that killed my parents? Fine. But first you need to give me a very good reason, *Annie*, as to why you're here digging up the ghosts of my parents. And one that's better than 'Peony Lane told me to.'" His expression stays neutral, but his jaw is clenched so tightly that it's making all of his words sound compressed, like they're being squeezed out under the strain of barely contained emotion. It's the closest I've ever seen to Saxon losing his temper, and I'm feeling justified in my decision to ask Crane along.

I swallow and compose my thoughts for a second before speaking. "Peony Lane's prediction was the catalyst for the terms of Frances's will being dictated the way they were. One might argue that she's the reason you lost everything."

"Or," Saxon says, his voice gathering the slight growl of the anger he's trying to dampen, "one might argue that *you're* the reason I lost everything."

I work hard not to react. If Saxon notices the way my fingers flex on the arm of the chair, or how I'm fighting not to look to Crane for reassurance, he doesn't show it.

"But there's a bigger link between Peony Lane and your mother," I say slowly. "One you might not know about. It seems Peony cut the brake cable that caused the crash. And if that's true, then Peony Lane was more than just the catalyst for the games Frances laid out in her will; she was responsible for changing your whole future. If that crash had never happened, your life would have been drastically different."

Saxon scoffs, but the angry edge is there in his posture, and he's still holding the crash photo up. "Before you run away with your *investigation*"—he spits the last word out like it's something poisonous he's been desperate to get out of his mouth—"I have an alibi for the morning Peony was killed. I stayed overnight in the Castle House Hotel, for—" A perfectly timed thump sounds on the ceiling just above us, and I imagine Elva up there listening in and wanting to make herself known by whatever means she can. Saxon sighs. "I stayed at the hotel for reasons that don't concern you. I was down at breakfast in the restaurant most of the morning; I had a book with me and I was taking my time before deciding to come home. Most of the staff there can verify this.

"I didn't kill Peony Lane," he continues. "But I'm not sad that she's dead." He gives me a level stare and holds the crash photo even closer to me. Finally I reach out and take it. "The brake cable was never cut—even Frances figured that out, from the tire marks in the road." I blink at the photo for a moment. He's right, of course—I can see the marks from someone slamming the brakes hard.

"I'll tell you a few things for free," Saxon says. "Because I'd like to see what you do with them. The crash that killed my parents was never investigated, except by Frances, years after the fact. This file contains key things she worked out— namely, that a newly repaired car had scratches around the lock at the boot, while all the damage from the crash was to the front. Additionally, the rear passenger door was open, and my mother's body was in the road. Also in this file are Frances's theories that my mother caused the crash, survived, and it was she who grabbed the keys and caused the scratches to the boot, trying to open it and get something out. But Frances never found out what Olivia was so desperate to retrieve." Saxon's expression twists, and the knowledge that passes over his face shows me just how deeply I've underestimated him.

"This is a puzzle you've been trying to solve for years," I say. "Isn't it?"

"It is. But I have a different theory from Frances's." He nods at the photo. "You're astute, Annie, but you lack the ability to think like a Gravesdown. I know we've had our differences," he says, as one corner of his mouth twitches upward in a smirk, "but I'm going to teach you a lesson in how to unravel the motives of the truly corrupted rich and powerful. And I'll only tell you what I know if you can answer me correctly. Are you ready? *What's the one thing you could have in a car boot that would cause you to speed away so quickly you lose control of your car?* The kind of thing you wouldn't want *anyone* to find?"

I'm at a loss. It could be anything—money, drugs, evidence incriminating a Gravesdown in all kinds of crimes. But then I notice there's a slight shine in Saxon's eyes, and it's not a glint of satisfaction or the smugness that comes from playing a good chess move. It was only there for a fraction of a moment, but his eyes watered just a touch when he asked me that last question. It's *emotion*—it's the thorn of a loss so old that it calcified in his childhood heart and has been carried through to adulthood. It's tucked away tightly, but it's there.

"What's the one thing someone would hide in a boot that they wouldn't want discovered?" I repeat, my expression soft and my own chest tightening just a bit with a sympathy I never thought I'd feel for Saxon Gravesdown.

"A body," I say finally.

Saxon nods, and it's solemn, but understanding passes between us. "I believe that my mother didn't die in that crash. She was already dead when the car hit that tree. She was dead before it even left the drive."

CHAPTER

19

THE KEYS TO THE BENTLEY—INCLUDING THE ONE TO the boot—were never found," Saxon says, and his voice holds a finality that indicates this conversation is over. He hands me Olivia's file like a prize I've won before ushering Crane and me out the door.

"You know what this means, don't you?" I say. Crane is taking the curves of the road a little faster than usual, and I'm looking at the file in my lap, trying to piece together how this car crash played out, to try to understand how this might relate to Peony Lane's recent murder. Periodically, I have to glance up out of my window at the hedges as they whip by, in order to stave off carsickness. "Olivia's body didn't get in the road simply because the boot popped open, and Edmund and Harry were killed on impact."

"How then?" Crane asks, keeping his eyes on the road.

I feel my mind working at double speed, keeping time with the blur of the scenery outside the window. "There was a fourth person in the car," I say. "That's the only way to explain it!"

"That's . . . that's actually plausible," Crane says, sounding slightly surprised. "It would explain the fact that the rear door was open—that is, if Saxon's theory is right, and Olivia was killed elsewhere and her body locked in the boot. It would mean that the additional passenger not only survived the crash but would know *all* the missing pieces to this story."

"Exactly," I say. "What if Peony Lane recently found out the identity of that fourth person? And someone killed her to make sure she never revealed that information?"

The car crawls up the bright white gravel drive to Gravesdown Hall, and when Crane parks, I'm pleased that he gets out of the car and walks up to the house with me. The thought of him just sitting in the car while it idles, sending me off toward my door so he can drive off with the least inconvenience to himself, is something that I'm glad I don't have to worry about.

"I'm curious about your security," Crane says when we reach the large front door. He glances at the camera above my head. "Especially if Peony Lane made several unnoticed visits to your house. I'd like to know why she didn't just ring your bell and come and talk to you. Especially since she was so open with you on the morning she died."

We're still standing in front of the carved wooden doors of Gravesdown Hall, and I rummage in my backpack for my keys. We're both quiet, thinking. I notice several delivery boxes stacked behind the three-foot stone vase near the door but make no move to pick them up just yet.

Crane is looking up at the camera again, moving around to see if it tracks him as he goes. It doesn't, but I already knew it wouldn't, because I was the one who chose it. "You wanted to ask about my security system?" I say.

"If you don't mind showing me the live feed," Crane says,

"I'd be interested. Especially given that we now know that Saxon has been in and out of your home."

I pull my phone from my pocket and notice the battery is dangerously low. I open the app for the front-door camera to see which angles it catches us from and see a live stream of the backs of our heads. The camera is set into the overhang of the roof, facing the front door from a height.

"Though it's important to note that Saxon could have had that file for weeks," I say. "Months, even. During Aunt Frances's funeral, lots of people were all over the estate, and caterers and friends and family were in and out of the house constantly. I didn't miss the file because I didn't know it mattered. It never occurred to me to keep track of all those files, in case anything ever went missing."

Crane nods, but he reaches over and gently lifts my phone from my fingers. "Why did you get a camera like this, instead of one of the more popular doorbell cams?" Crane asks.

"Something dumb about wiring," I say. "Apparently I could have had one, but I'd be changing the batteries in it constantly. This one"—I point to the camera above and slightly behind us—"was one that could be wired in through the roof somehow."

"Well, I'm not a fan of it," he says, his brown eyes looking at the feed with laser focus. "Look." He points to the view of us on my phone and then the real-life view of the doors.

"Okay . . ." I say, unsure why he disapproves. "It covers the whole front door, so that's good."

"No, Annie, look closer," Crane says. The app is draining the battery faster than usual, and I'm down to about 3 percent. "This view cuts off the entire second door."

"Oh, that door doesn't open," I say, leaning to look at the phone over his shoulder. "Or it does, but not unless the other door gets opened first."

"And you don't think that matters?" he asks, giving me a cynical look.

I huff but resist the urge to roll my eyes. "What I'm saying is, no one would need to bother opening the second door, because you'd already have the main door open." To demonstrate, I unlock the front door on the right by using the two keys it needs—the skeleton key for the original lock and the new key for the modern dead bolt. It swings open, and I run a finger along the edge of the second door to find the flat metal piece I'm looking for. My finger slips into the indentation, and I flip up the release for the other door.

Crane takes my phone but angles it so I can see the feed as well. The doors are twice as wide as a standard door—taller, too, due to the age and style of this house. You can't see the edge of the left door on the camera feed at all. It swings open as I flip the latch, and the only change on the camera feed is the quality of the light that reflects off us. A thin beam of light illuminates one side of my hair, due to the window at the end of the hallway being suddenly more exposed.

"Look, here." I point to the change in the light. "I guess that's one way to see if someone opened the second door, but I don't see why they would."

"I've already gone through the security footage you provided on the day of the murder," Crane says, "and it only shows Beth making her deli delivery. In that footage, Beth doesn't step into the house when she opens the door, but this revelation about the angle of the camera and the second door changes things. We need to look at it again."

I sigh. He's right, and I wish I'd thought of that detail. I navigate on my phone to where the footage from each day is stored in folders in the cloud, but my phone freezes, and then the screen goes black. "The battery doesn't last long on this phone—I need an upgrade," I say by way of apology.

"I've got to get back to the station anyway," Crane says, but he doesn't move. "I'll look at the copies of the footage I've got on my computer there."

"I don't want it to be Beth and Archie," I say, and my stomach does a worried lurch, not appreciating the cream tea from earlier.

"I know," Crane says, and he brushes a knuckle against mine, just for a moment. It's reassuring, as if he's saying, *This may be part of the job, but I know there are times it doesn't feel great.* "And there's a good chance it wasn't," he adds. "If the murder of Olivia Gravesdown is connected to the death of Peony Lane . . . Archie was only a teenager when that crash happened."

"Yeah, but being a teenager doesn't mean you aren't a killer," I say.

Crane bites his bottom lip and nods at the ground. "You're getting better at not letting your feelings about the people around you cloud your suspicions of them. Frances would be proud."

As he walks back toward the gravel drive, I say quietly, "That's what I'm afraid of."

THE LIBRARY IS starting to gather a thin layer of dust, and I wonder for a moment why the cleaning service I employ haven't been polishing the furniture in here. It would be my luck if they weren't just aware of the death that happened in this library but were superstitious about it too.

I pass by the big writing desk at the center of the space and pull the brass chain on the glass desk lamp there. The cheerful green glow of it reminds me of old university libraries, or parlors with Chesterfield sofas the color of conkers where Victorian lawyers would sit smoking cigars. I continue past the two large sets of windows, latticed in dark metal and smothered with the red Virginia creeper that covers the house, to the little wooden door in the far wall.

Inside, I pull the cord that hangs from the ceiling, and a bare lightbulb flickers to life. The room is small—it was probably once a broom cupboard or a document room of some sort—and windowless. It's whitewashed, but the walls are still covered in the remnants of Great Aunt Frances's life's work—preventing her own murder.

Sadly, she didn't succeed in that, but she at least lived nearly sixty years before it came to pass. When the dust settled on her murder case, along with the cold case of Emily Sparrow from 1966, I debated taking down the old murder boards Aunt Frances had made.

But it seemed wrong to meddle with her Post-its and old photos, the red string joining the theories and motives of people who had come in and out of her life over the years.

But the problem I face now is that so much of this house is left untouched as an homage to Aunt Frances that I don't know where I fit into it. It hits me then, with the lightbulb still swinging on its chain, making the shadows of the filing cabinets shift with it, that I actually don't feel like I fit here at all. I might be the heir she wanted, in that I solved her case and another she couldn't, but I don't want to live life as her professional successor.

But then, what kind of life *do* I want to live? I do love the puzzle of things, of figuring out what's really under the surface of people's actions, lies, and stories. But I'm scared of being swallowed up by the force of Frances's personality in this house. It permeates the walls, the air—even the light feels like some part of her history and not any piece of my present or future.

I have deep affection for her, and profound respect, just

from the documents I encountered when I was trying to solve her murder. But she wasn't a perfect person. She fixated, she worried, she feared. And sometimes when I'm alone in this house, I feel like that same path is the only one I have.

I'm going to grow old before my time, becoming ever more afraid of the people around me. Because the more secrets you uncover about people, the less you trust anyone. It's like that old saying: Shine a light on something and you're going to get a lot of shadows.

I run a finger along the top of the filing cabinets, thinking aloud. "You must have loved being alive, though, to fear your own murder to such a degree. Or was it just the unfairness of it all? I mean, none of us know how much time we've got, but feeling sure that someone's going to cut that time short on purpose?" I pause, wondering if it's going to help me or hurt me to try to think more like Frances. Ultimately, the way she saw the world got her killed. "I wish I knew more about the rest of your life," I say. "What kept you going that *wasn't* all this? Or was there *anything* more to your life?"

I take the keys for the filing cabinets from their hiding place in the little ceramic cat I've put on the shelf. It's one of the few things from my room in Chelsea that I've put in the main house. Before I moved here, it lived in my bedroom my entire life, and it's rather ugly when you really look at it. It's got a painted yellow collar that is actually the spot where it splits in two—its head hinges back to reveal a hollow inside you can use as a little box. I don't know why I wanted it in here, hiding the filing cabinet keys; maybe it's just that small sense of me being the keeper of these archives now.

These files are hard to navigate unless you already know the things Aunt Frances discovered. Her files are listed alphabetically, and the main headings are not organized by people's names but by secret. They start with tabs like *Arson* and *Assault* and go all the way through to *Wrongful Death*. Only within each subject are the individual files then listed by the names of the people harboring those secrets.

I start at the *A*'s, because there's no point in trying to guess which secrets Archie, Eric, Peony Lane, and Birdy each had. If I'm lucky, maybe I'll find them all in the same file.

On a whim I check the *M* drawer to see if there really is a file for murder, and I was right—there isn't even a tab for that subject.

Archie, Eric, Peony Lane, Birdy . . . I say the list in my head over and over as my fingers flit across names in manila folders with surname first and first name following. As I'm looking, the line from Archie's fortune slides through my mind, a connection I almost can't grasp because it's spider-silk thin.

The list you seek is the right one—the foil, the arrow, the rat, the sparrow.

The skin on my arms crawls, and I rub my hands up and down them to stave off the feeling. Earlier, I thought Saxon was the rat, but what if it's someone else? Someone who was older at the time of the crash, and potentially involved? The fourth person in the car . . . slinking away after depositing Olivia's body in the road, making it look like she was thrown from the car and killed that way. So if Archie is the arrow, and Eric is the foil—not just because of his surname, but because he contrasts with Archie in some way . . . and Birdy is the sparrow, who does that leave?

Peony Lane . . . and Ford, possibly? But I can't think why either of them would be considered a rat.

I want to pay closer attention to Archie's fortune, especially since Peony Lane had it in her hand when she died. Since she was the one who told it in the first place, she'd know it by heart, right? I think back to our conversation in the woods and her telling me, *I have a fortune to tell you, but you aren't going to want it.*

I jumped straight to the conclusion that the fortune she had was mine. But she never actually said that.

And then she came straight to the house, with Archie's fortune in her hand. It has to be important, even if Archie and Beth claim not to believe it.

So I try my best to decode it, starting with thinking about who the rat might be.

I try the *B*'s, for *Betrayal*, and it's where I find Eric's and Birdy's files together.

Both are empty. I swear under my breath. It's a clever way to make it look like the files are still complete, at a glance. I utter a string of insults to past-Annie, berating her for waiting so long to change where the keys to the files were hidden.

I check every drawer alphabetically until I get to the very end of the files. It's here that I find Archie's file, in no category at all. It seems to be empty, but I put my hand inside it anyway. My fingers flutter against two thin slips of paper: One is the handwritten address of Peony Lane; the other is a torn-out page from a notebook, lined. I recognize the paper as being the same type as in the diaries Aunt Frances used.

My hand shakes a little as I see that it's a short letter, written in Aunt Frances's careful, looping handwriting.

Archie,

Your secrets don't belong in here. I don't need to write them down to recall them—I know them all by heart.

Yours,
Frances

Because Saxon had his mother's file, my first thought was that while he was stealing Olivia's file, he took the contents of several others as well. But now I'm not so sure. From this note, it's clear that Aunt Frances thought differently—she expected Archie to be the one to come here digging.

Why?

CHAPTER

20

THE AIR IN THAT FANCY RESTAURANT WAS SUDDENLY
*stifling, so I excused myself to the ladies' because I needed a mo-
ment to breathe and clear my head. I wanted to splash water on
my face and stare meaningfully in the mirror, like distressed but
elegant women do in films, but I had powdered my face and put
on a bit of blusher and mascara, and it seemed a horrible waste
to ruin that.*

*Instead I simply leaned forward over the sink and looked
deeply into my own eyes, like I might see some answers there. My
eyes looked spring green tonight, lightened by the dress I had on,
and I'd put my hair up in a French roll—it took me several tries to
get it right, but I was tired of asking Mother to do it for me; I felt
far too old for that. She still tried to have a hand in what I wore—*
Don't wear the red, Frances. Redheads should never wear
red. Green is best—*and she had annoyingly good advice on
that. My freckles were fading for lack of sun, and the powder I'd
put on made me look almost porcelain. If I didn't know me, I'd
think I was the type of woman who, if pushed, would break like a
china doll.*

I had the strangest vision suddenly. I imagined Archie standing in the mirror behind me, leaning slightly against my back, one hand on the marble surface of the sink, the other around my waist. I could feel his stubble as he nestled his chin into the crook of my neck from behind me, smiling at our reflections in the mirror. I could smell his stale cigarettes, but underneath that was an almost spicy, earthy scent—the smell of someone who spent hours outside, doing whatever they wanted. It was the smell of recklessness, and freedom.

And then Archie shifted, and it was Ford there, wrapped behind me in the same position. But his posture was more Ford as he tucked his chin toward my face. His jaw was smooth, and he turned his face into mine so that I could feel every contour of it—the softness of his lips, the arch his nose made against my cheekbone, the flutter of his eyelashes as his eyelid closed against my temple.

My mind was trying on men like I'd try on shoes in a department store, which wasn't like me at all.

Ford was being very reasonable about my decision to stop seeing him—surprisingly so. He had a history of being a bit of a society playboy—yet another reason we didn't fit—and I suspected that being left wasn't something that happened to him often. Possibly ever. The Ford I knew was a planner, liked to win, and also liked a good game. So he was either bored with me anyway or entirely confident he could win me over in the end.

And why on earth had my mind put Archie in that position? I'd never thought of Archie that way—a year ago he'd been Rose's boyfriend, and that just makes a man shift into being a rather neutral sort of person. When you know your best friend has been involved with someone, you don't think about how surprisingly strong their hands are or the genuineness of their smile, no matter how long it's been since their relationship ended.

When I blinked, the men in my mind were gone, but I wasn't alone.

Archie's date had entered the ladies' and was a few feet behind me, watching.

"Whatever he tells you about me," she said, "you mustn't believe it."

Confused, I turned away from the mirror finally, facing her.

"Whatever who tells me? I don't even know who you are— why would I be talking about you with anyone?" I asked.

The woman smirked but didn't say anything. She was a few years older than me, and her Twiggy style was less effective up close. It looked more like a costume or a disguise. Her heavy cat-eye makeup was an attempt to hide the tired look in her eyes, and I noticed how thick her foundation was—it had smeared a little to reveal a mottled green patch under her right eye.

She saw me glance at it, and even though my eyes rested there for only a second, her mouth twisted into a sarcastic smile.

"Observant, aren't you? Archie said you were good like that. I'm glad to see he was right." Before I could interject, she continued. "Don't worry, this wasn't him." She touched her eye lightly, then opened the small handbag she was carrying and started digging around in it. Finally, she pulled out a small scrap of paper and handed it to me. "Archie said you wanted this."

I unfolded the paper. "This is . . . Peony Lane's address?"

The woman nodded.

"What did you mean, when you first spoke to me just now? You said, 'Whatever he tells you about me, you mustn't believe it.'"

She took a couple of steps toward me, and I noticed she was a little shaky. Not swaying from drink, but unsteady in a way that made me think her nerves were rattling around inside her like loose change.

"My boyfriend and I are investigating some things Ford

Gravesdown got up to, around the time of the Gravesdown crash. On the one hand, he could have been the only good egg in his whole family. But on the other . . . there are some things about that night that don't add up. I'm only telling you this because you're a friend of Archie's," she added hastily. Voices were rising in the hallway outside the ladies', and I suspected one of them to be Ford's. I just hoped the other wasn't Archie's.

"Ford spoke of an evidence file," I said quickly. "Something Peony Lane brought him to incriminate his brother, Edmund." I hoped mentioning this would spur her into sharing more about that file.

"It exists," she said, her face becoming carefully neutral. "But all these players—Olivia, Peony, Eric, and Ford, even Birdy Sparrow—they were playing a different game from the one you think they were. For at least one of them, this whole thing was only ever about the money."

The door opened to the ladies', and the face of a young man I vaguely recognized peeked in. He ignored me, looking directly at the woman. "Samantha, we need to go—things are getting heated and I think we've got what we came for."

When he pushed the door open a bit wider to let her out, I noticed his constable's uniform and I remembered where I'd seen him. He was the officer who'd come to collect me when I was brought in for questioning the previous summer, when Emily disappeared. He hadn't been in charge of her case, but he had been involved in looking for her.

"All right," the woman said, and she gave me a sad smile as she passed me. I followed her out and came face-to-face with a thunderous-looking Ford. But Ford's expression wasn't directed at me; it was all for the young police officer.

The long corridor we were standing in had a door at the end of it, which opened to the car park outside. It was propped open, revealing a police car idling there, its headlights illuminating fat raindrops that had started falling. Someone was in the passenger seat of the car, but they were hidden in shadow.

"This conversation isn't over, Constable," Ford said to the young man. "You can't detain someone for a case that isn't open!"

"I'm not detaining anyone," the constable said. "I asked Eric if he'd be willing to come and chat with me about various things, and he accepted. If I was detaining him, he'd be locked in the back!"

Ford simply grunted, then took several long strides down the corridor and marched straight outside to the police car. He flung open the passenger door and stood there expectantly. Eventually, Eric emerged.

Ford dug into his pocket and pulled out a set of keys. "Here," he said, handing them to Eric. "You can drive my car back to the Dead Witch. I'll ring for my driver to collect me."

Eric only nodded, took the set of keys, and walked off into the dark without sparing a glance for any of the rest of us.

The constable and Samantha were watching Ford with narrowed eyes, and for a moment it was like there was an electric current strung between the three of them—the woman looking daggers at Ford, the young police officer watching her with an inscrutable expression, and Ford staring at him as if he could peel back all his layers and expose his secrets. Finally the constable and Samantha turned down the corridor and got into the police car to drive away.

Ford turned to me. "I'll walk you home," he said.

"Oh, really, that's not necessary," I replied, trying not to sound as baffled as I was. Why on earth did Ford care what happened to Eric Foyle?

"No, it is," Ford continued. "I can't leave you to walk home in the dark, getting rained on. I've got an umbrella—here . . ." He gestured back toward our table, and I walked that way because I needed to fetch my coat.

When we got to the table, the bill had been paid already, and a waiter was hovering with our coats. I glanced to where Archie had been sitting, but the table was empty.

So I found myself sharing an umbrella with Ford, walking along the dark lanes back toward my house. When I shivered, he reached inside his wool overcoat and pulled out a silver flask.

"It's the same single malt I've poured for you up at the house," he said idly. "It'll warm you up."

I undid the cap and gingerly took a sip, recognizing the peaty notes of the familiar scotch. It had never been a drink I particularly liked, but I found this sip felt prematurely nostalgic—I was saying good-bye to a future with Ford and all these luxurious things. Whether I appreciated expensive drinks or not, it had been an adventure in its own way, I supposed.

I rubbed my finger over an engraving on the front of the flask, and after I'd replaced the cap I tilted it to see if I could catch enough light to read it by.

"Ah," Ford said, taking the flask back gently. "It simply says my full name, with a Latin phrase my father was fond of."

"What's the phrase?" I asked.

"Fraternitas omnia vincit," Ford quoted. "It means 'Brotherhood conquers all.' Which was sadly never the case in my family. My father had a similar flask made for my brother."

I tried to keep my mind away from the crash scene photo Archie had shown me, but I could easily imagine Edmund's silver flask being tossed about in the wreckage of the Bentley. It wasn't in the photo itself, nor listed in the gossipy article in the Gazette as being found in the wreckage, so I wondered what had happened to it.

When we got to my door, I tried to muster a sincere good-bye, but it was rather hollow. I couldn't stop thinking about brotherhood, after what Ford had said. And about Archie and Eric.

I bit my lip, remembering all the things I'd learned recently about Eric Foyle. His long history working for the Gravesdowns— and then, just now, Ford's familiarity with Eric and how easily Ford had ordered him out of the police car.

Eric Foyle was a police informant, I realized. And Ford had just put a stop to it.

CHAPTER

21

March 5, 1967

WHAT'S THIS POSTCODE?" ARCHIE SAID AS HE SQUINTED *at the paper. "Does that say Cornwall?"*

"No, that's the village name, Crownell—Samantha's hand-writing is just messy," I said. It was midday, and we were in the kitchen at my parents' bakery. It was Sunday, so the whole place was closed, but Archie and I wanted somewhere private to talk through all our theories. When Mother told me she'd pay me ex-tra to check all the mousetraps, it seemed the perfect chance to make a little spare money while also having the privacy I craved. Everywhere in the village has ears—the Dead Witch, with Eric Foyle behind the bar, the library, the tearooms . . . Everyone knows my family and my connection to Ford Gravesdown.

Or, I should say, my former connection. I was conscious that the more I was seen with Archie, the faster gossip would spread. As soon as I had the thought, though, I was ashamed of it: Why should being seen with Archie feel like a step down from Ford Gravesdown? They were very different people, of course, but that's part of why I felt relaxed in the empty bakery with Archie. I could be myself.

Which was why I was going to ask Archie several candid questions, and not let up until I got honest answers.

"So do you want to take a drive to Crownell?" Archie asked. "I've got an old banger I've fixed up—it's nothing special, but it runs. I think Crownell is about an hour away."

"I do, but I want to talk first," I said. I walked around the large countertops in the kitchen to a cupboard next to the industrial refrigerator. "Here," I said, taking out several paper bags. "We keep the previous day's bread in here, pastries, cakes . . . anything that doesn't sell. What employees don't take home, we feed to the pigs or throw away. But this will just be from yesterday, so it should all still be edible."

Archie's eyes lit up, and he started digging into the various bags. He pulled out several Eccles cakes, an iced bun, and some broken biscuits and started eating like he hadn't had food in days. When he noticed me watching him, he shrugged. "The food at the Dead Witch is all the same," he said. "And the deal I have is sort of like this." He gestured at the leftover pastries. "I eat when the kitchens close, just from whatever's left."

"I'm curious, Archie," I said, choosing my words cautiously. "If Eric works at the Dead Witch and you live in one of the rooms above, I assume you see quite a lot of each other. You told me you rarely spoke to him."

"I don't," he said, chewing. "I mean, I don't see much of him; we manage to avoid each other easily. I know when he's on the bar or in the kitchen. If we spot each other, we go the other way."

"What happened between you two?" I asked. Archie had hopped up to sit on the countertop while he ate, and I tried to jump up next to him. When I missed the counter the first time, I felt Archie's hands swiftly grab my waist and pull me upward. My

momentum plus Archie's extra lift meant I landed firmly next to him, and he moved one arm to the countertop behind me so that it wasn't encircling my waist. The other arm he kept in his lap, but our proximity to each other suddenly felt like a new, exciting thing. It was different from how I felt near Ford—Ford was this slow burn of careful conversation and long glances. But Archie felt electric, sitting there next to me. He was the petrol spark of wild ideas, easy smiles, and, if you invited them, looks that were far less polite but illicitly tempting. Since turning away from Ford and his well-ordered intentions, my mind had become rather untethered. It was going to places that were experimental, strange, and extremely alluring. I had caught the scent of the more wicked side of freedom, and it already had me enthralled.

I'd asked Archie a question, but I'd already forgotten what it was. He clearly sensed some change in me, because he was looking at me in a way that was curious, but tinged with something else. Our friendship was newly formed but rather intense—we'd spent all our spare time together over the previous few weeks, talking through theories, secrets, and strategies for unraveling my fortune and outsmarting my fate. He never once questioned my growing fixation on my fortune, or why uncovering the secrets of those around me seemed to calm my restless mind. And I was glad of that, because I often felt bad about my burgeoning obsession. Because what kind of person feels better when they learn about the dark deeds of others?

Then again, my dogged attempts to uncover the truth behind the Gravesdown crash were also benefiting Archie, if Ford Gravesdown was to be somehow implicated. So why would he question them?

"You want to know why Eric and I don't speak?" he repeated, and brushed a loose strand of hair away from my forehead. I felt my lips part involuntarily in response, and then I gained control over my expression and nodded.

"It's actually rather simple," he continued. "After our father left with Ford's first wife and we got evicted from the farmhouse, we had one last chance to get some cash to get back on our feet. We had something valuable to sell, and Eric was in charge of doing that. Everything was riding on that money, but instead of just selling it like we'd planned, Eric tried to double our money by betting it in a high-stakes poker game, which he lost."

"That's . . ." I tried to make sense of what exactly that was. Foolish? Almost laughably so? "Wait—you're telling me there are high-stakes poker games being run in Castle Knoll? Archie, that's ridiculous."

"You're thinking of some kind of gambling syndicate," he said, and laughed. "I like the way your twisted mind works, Frances, I really do." He reached out and gently rested his index finger under my chin, setting his thumb in the indent just under my bottom lip. He kept his hand there for a moment but dropped it when the rest of his story made his expression cloud over. "But it was just Ford, playing games. Eric had something Ford wanted, and rather than just buy the damn thing, Ford swept Eric up into playing for something bigger. And of course, Eric lost."

"So now you hate both Eric and Ford," I said.

Archie turned and rummaged in another paper bag and pulled out his second Eccles cake. His expression turned playful, which lately I've noticed is the only mask he hides behind in any convincing way. "Ford more than Eric, really. Because Ford saw Eric's weaknesses and manipulated them to his advantage. But in my opinion, the best revenge is simply to expose the black heart of something. Given the right circumstances, I know the Gravesdown rot will be aired out, and things will settle into their right places again."

"But in the meantime, you have to live above the pub, with a fractured relationship with your brother, and fester in those feelings," I said. "That can't be good for you, Archie."

Archie simply shrugged. "Well, at least I have more pleasurable pursuits to keep me occupied," he said, and he reached across my lap, leaning close in a typically exaggerated Archie sort of way—to get to the paper bag of custard tarts that was sitting next to me. When he sat back upright with one of them in his hand, he looked meaningfully at me and quoted something I knew I'd read but couldn't name. "There are glances of hatred that stab and raise no cry of murder," he said, and bit into the custard tart.

"Where is that quote from?" I asked.

"You need to spend more time in the library," he said, then continued to chew quietly, one corner of his mouth pulled up in a smirk.

"Are you trying to say that you can be angry at something but not have it dictate your actions?" I prodded.

He gave me a meaningful look. "It's just something I think we should both try to remember."

Then he dusted off his fingers, hopped down, and sauntered toward the back door to the kitchen. "It's George Eliot," he said, turning back to me. "I think it's about keeping secrets. Now, let's go and find my car. We could both use a bit of excitement, and I've got the perfect idea where to find it."

CHAPTER

22

THE FACT THAT ARCHIE HAS SEVERAL OF AUNT FRAN-ces's diaries is still gnawing at me, so I decide to pay him another visit. I have a portable charging brick for my phone, so I throw that in my backpack and it charges as I drive the little black BMW to Foyle Farms.

When I turn down the long road that leads to Archie's farm, I can't tell if Archie is at home or not, because there are so many cars around. It's impossible to remember which one he's driving these days. I notice several additional old cars since my visit the day before, all looking rusted beyond repair.

The sun from earlier has been sucked up behind a layer of thick gray cloud, leaving the autumn light flat and weak. The house looks a bit sadder this way, more tired and faded. Foyle Farms has two large barns—one is used by Beth's wife, Mi-yuki, as her vet clinic, and the other has now been kitted out so that Archie can work on his cars in there. As I walk between the cars abandoned outside, I start to feel uneasy. It's like a car graveyard, and since murder is on my mind, every scuff and scrape they bear starts to look violent.

As I walk past one of the tarpaulins, my heart nearly stops. There's a triangle of metal peeking out from one side, and what's left of the paint on it is a muted, rusty purple. I check my surroundings for signs of anyone nearby, and then quickly lift the back of the tarpaulin to view more of what's under there. As I expose the boot of the car, my suspicions are confirmed.

It's the wreck of the Gravesdown Bentley. It has to be—it's a Bentley from that era, in that unique color, and when I circle around to the front of it, I can tell by its shape that the front has been crushed by a heavy impact while the boot remains intact.

My phone only managed to gain about 5 percent battery on the drive up, and I call Crane quickly before my battery dies again. Even though I'm hoping Archie didn't kill Peony Lane, I need to function on the assumption that he might have. A text pings from Jenny, letting me know she's made it back to Gravesdown Hall after visiting her cousin in Southampton.

"Annie, is everything okay?" Crane asks. His voice is echoey, and I can tell he's in the car. "Are you still at home?"

"No, I'm at Foyle Farms," I say. I explain about the wrecked Bentley, and Crane quickly agrees to a detour.

"I've reopened that file," he says. "So this is definitely of interest. But I also have some things to run by you, regarding that security footage."

When I hang up, I'm bending down, trying to peer under the tarpaulin, when I hear the crunch of footsteps in leaves.

"Annie?" I turn and see Beth and feel a bit relieved. "Grandad just ducked away somewhere," she says, "if you were coming to talk to him. I don't know where he's off to, but maybe you could come back later?"

"I'm happy to wait," I say. "I have some car questions. Do

you know anything about this one?" I try to keep my voice casual, and I think I mostly manage it.

"I'm afraid I don't, but my uncle Eric is in the garage—he's been tinkering a bit with Grandad on these things." She turns toward the garage and calls out to him.

Eric Foyle comes out of the garage in mechanic's coveralls, and I recognize him from the police station yesterday, when I saw him dropping off Samantha. "Hello, I know you," he says. He smiles and extends a hand. "I don't think we've formally met, but I saw you yesterday, at the station."

"Yeah, I'm Annie," I say, shaking his hand. "It's good to meet you, especially if you're working with Archie. I'm the main investor in his car restoration business. Not that I'm checking up on you all or anything," I add hastily. Eric's got a firm grip, and his hands aren't nearly as rough as Archie's. Like Peony Lane, he looks to be in excellent shape for someone who is probably in his late seventies. I notice his slicked-back white hair is immaculately combed again, and he's short and stocky but gives the impression of someone who has been strong his whole life. He takes off his glasses and lets them hang on the fabric cord around his neck.

"Oh, you can check up on us all you like," Eric says, and his expression is a little mischievous. "If you're financing the business, you might as well see what your money's being used for." He winks, and though it's friendly, I don't like that he's made me feel as though I'm his boss all of a sudden. Archie never gives that impression, but I suppose I've known him longer, since before I started investing in his work.

"Annie wanted to know about this car," Beth says, gesturing to the Bentley.

"Oh, that one's a bad business," Eric says, and he lifts half the tarpaulin up. It exposes the rear part of the car again, and the weathered purple paint gives the car a sickly tinge in

163

the weak light. There are scratches on the boot, rusted but distinctive, near the lock. "It only arrived yesterday, but I've already told Archie he needs to clear it away; there's no restoring this one. Not with its haunted history." Eric's expression is pinched as he looks at the wreck, and more than a little sad. "This is the Gravesdown car, see. It killed three people." He shudders, and replaces the tarpaulin.

"How did Archie come by it, if you don't mind my asking? It seems like a rather strange and morbid thing to bring to his garage," I say.

"You'll have to ask him, and I can't think why he'd want it. My best guess is that it's a mystery he never solved. He and that Frances of his got into playing investigators when they were young. They were, what, nineteen maybe? They teamed up with my old girlfriend, Ellen, God rest her soul—she's Peony Lane, you know, or was—and Samantha, and they were going to expose the whole corrupted history of the Gravesdowns."

"And did they?" I ask.

Eric lets out a long sigh and rubs the back of his neck. It's something I've seen Archie do, and I start to see a small resemblance between the brothers. "They certainly let some secrets out, but learned a few new ones in the process," he says cryptically.

Just then, Crane's car pulls up in front of the farmhouse. He parks it and gives us all a nod of acknowledgment as he navigates his way around the various pieces of machinery to where we're standing. "Annie, Beth." Crane nods to each of us. "Eric, it's been a while." He extends a hand and the two men shake. "Is Archie not here?"

"He's at the auto auction in Little Dimber," Eric says.

"Do you mind showing me this car?" Crane asks.

"Not at all," Eric says, and he pulls the tarpaulin back farther.

I turn to Beth. "I wanted to ask you about something. Can we go inside for a minute?"

"Of course," she says. "I don't like looking at that car anyway; it gives me the creeps."

"I don't blame you," I say. "Thanks, Eric, it was nice to meet you."

Eric gives me a small wave of dismissal, his eyes not leaving the wreck. He's talking with Crane, walking him around the car, as Beth and I head into the farmhouse.

Inside the farmhouse, my eyes immediately go to the bookshelf, and I feel a jolt of alarm when I see that the diaries aren't there anymore. Archie's keeping secrets—that much is clear now.

"Beth, when I was here the other day, I noticed that your grandad had some journals on this shelf," I say, and walk over to it. "He was pretty cagey about them, and I'm wondering whether you know why."

Beth is quiet, but she doesn't look upset or annoyed with me for bringing it up.

"They're Aunt Frances's, aren't they?" I prod. "It's just, I think there might be some important things in there that could help us work out who killed Peony Lane."

"They are Frances's," Beth says. "And if Grandad doesn't want you reading them, it won't be because he's hiding anything bad. It'll just be something personal or embarrassing, probably."

"Beth, if he's hiding something that might shed light on what happened to Peony Lane, I might be able to help make it right."

"He didn't kill her," Beth says levelly.

"I'm not saying that," I tell her carefully. "But is there any way you can get those diaries back for me? Do you know where your grandad moved them to? Technically those journals belong to me now, and I think we both know that Aunt Frances would want me to have them. Especially if they'll help me solve a new case."

Beth shakes her head.

"Aunt Frances wrote those diaries for a reason; you have to see that," I plead.

This seems to have some effect on her. She rubs her temple and looks at me. "You're right about that," she says cautiously. She sighs, tapping a finger on the table in front of her like she's weighing something up in her mind. "Just give me a day, okay? I need to think about it and do some looking around."

I feel confident that Beth and Archie didn't kill Peony Lane and aren't trying to frame me for her murder. If there was something in those diaries that implicated nineteen-year-old Archie in any kind of crime, he'd have destroyed them or hidden them better.

Eric comes through the back door then, and wipes his muddy boots on the mat before sitting down at the kitchen table.

"The detective says he's ready to take you back to Gravesdown Hall," Eric says. "But before you go, I did think of something about Peony Lane that you might be interested in knowing."

"Oh?"

"She was in Edmund Gravesdown's pocket for years before he died," he says, his voice hard.

"Edmund? I thought she hated him. Don't you mean Ford? I could see Aunt Frances wanting to keep Peony Lane close, maybe even on a retainer," I say.

"I'm positive it was Edmund—he paid her quite a lot of money for something, up until he was killed. Some say it was to keep his wife's nose out of his business—Olivia, she liked fortunes, and she always wanted to be entertained. She was a strange one, Olivia Gravesdown, God rest her soul. Anyway, I don't think Peony Lane told their fortunes so much as made their bad business go away."

"What? How do you mean? But then why would she vandalize Edmund's car, and why would he let her get arrested if that was the case?"

Beth is looking at us both curiously, but she doesn't say anything.

"I don't know, but my best guess is to cover up something else. I was there that day, the day Peony vandalized that car. I helped, even." Eric smooths a hand across his hair. "I thought I knew Peony well, but I was wrong. I think she and Edmund were in on something, something they did together, and that vandalism was planned to throw anyone who got curious later off the scent."

"How? Eric, I'd like to know more about that day, if you can tell me." I pull my phone out of my pocket and open up the recorder, but Eric shoos it away. The low-battery warning pops up again, and I close it down.

"I don't know anything more. I'm just saying, that week, things weren't right around the Gravesdown estate. Frances, Archie, and Samantha sniffed around later, and whatever sleight of hand Edmund pulled before he died, to wipe his whole rotten family's secrets away—well, it worked."

"Eric, I can tell you know more than you're saying. I have a theory about the crash— Do you mind if I—"

He cuts me off. "People have had theories for years; just leave it alone. It's old ghosts, and the detective is stirring them all up again." Eric's voice is rising, and I can see the color rising in his neck. He's getting angry. All these people clearly meant something to him. I just wish I knew what. "I don't like it," he continues. "Let the dead rest. That's all I'll say about it."

"You'd better go, Annie. The detective's waiting," Beth says. "I'll be in touch," she tells me meaningfully.

"Please," is all I say back, as I head out the door.

Outside, Crane is still looking at the wrecked Bentley. He's wearing latex gloves and has some clear plastic bags in one hand.

"Find anything?" I ask.

He looks up, startled. "I'm going to have this towed—I want a forensic team working on it. I really want to get into the boot, but it's locked. The key is obviously long gone, but I don't want to force it open and destroy some fragile evidence that's decades old."

I nod, and we stare at the boot in silence for a moment, like it's a coffin at a funeral and we're waiting for it to be lowered into the ground. "I just had an interesting conversation with Eric Foyle," I say eventually. "I think there's a possibility that Peony Lane didn't have the best moral compass."

"What do you mean? You think she was the additional passenger in the car? That she walked away from that crash years ago, and dragged Olivia's body into the road to make it look like she died in the crash?"

"It would make sense as to why someone killed Peony," I say. "If someone who cared about Olivia found out about it recently, her murder could have been revenge that was sixty years in the making."

"I know he has an alibi, but I'm still not letting Saxon Gravesdown off the hook," Crane says. "His wife has been known to cover for him in the past—who's to say she hasn't done it again?"

Crane tries the boot, but it doesn't budge. He actually gets more forceful than I expected and shoves his weight against the back of it, rocking the car slightly.

The bare wheel rims are resting on spare tires, keeping it level and off the ground, and when Crane pushes against it with a bit of force, the wreck bounces a little.

It's small, but I hear a *thud* from inside the boot.

I feel the color drain from my face as a wave of foreboding washes over me. The electric pulse of adrenaline stings my skin as I hear Crane say, "Stand back, I'm not going to wait for a forensic team. I'm going to pry this open."

There's a crowbar resting against another old car, and Crane forces it into the rusted seam where the boot meets the bumper. The sound of wrenching metal fills my ears, then the boot swings open.

Crane is already on his phone when I let out a scream.

Nestled inside is Samantha, and she is very clearly dead.

CHAPTER
23

BETH RUNS OUT OF THE HOUSE AT THE SOUND OF MY scream, with Eric slightly behind her. I back away from the open boot, so that the body inside is obscured from my view, but I can't get the image of poor crumpled-up Samantha out of my mind.

"Stay back, please," Crane calls to Beth and Eric. "Annie," he says, turning to me, his voice slightly quieter. "Can you please go and stand near the house? This is a crime scene now, and I need you all out of the way."

I nod, my head swimming.

Beth links arms with me when I come and stand next to her, and Eric comes to my other side. He keeps his hands in his pockets as he watches Crane examining the contents of the car.

"What's in there, Annie?" Eric asks. "With the detective acting like that, it can't be something good."

"No," I say, and swallow hard, knowing that what I'm about to say is likely to distress him. "It isn't. It's . . . Samantha. From the police station."

Eric looks at his shoes and nods over and over, like the movement of his head will help him process that information. "Oh, Sammy," he whispers. "What did you do?"

Beth is quiet, still watching Crane as he examines the body in the boot.

"You knew Samantha well, didn't you?" I ask Eric.

"Yeah, I did," he says. His voice is gravelly now, and when he draws in a breath, it's more of a wheeze. Sirens wail in the background, and soon several police cars come down the long drive. We watch the lights continue to pulse after the noise is turned off, the whole scene bathed in alternating flashes of blue and red. It makes the purple of the wrecked Bentley look like a rusted bruise, and I think if anything connected to the Gravesdown estate could be haunted, it's that car. Not the library, where Frances died, or the solarium, where we found Peony Lane. But this car? Just looking at it, it feels like it's cursed.

Beth has been whispering to Eric, rubbing his arm in comforting circles as he tries to catch his breath. But suddenly she looks up and follows my line of sight to where Crane is examining the body in the boot, talking to the other investigators who have just arrived.

Then her eyes dart to the periphery of the scene, to a figure in the shadows. Beth's open expression closes down then, and hardens, a vibrant living thing suddenly preserved in ice.

"I'm going to head back to Gravesdown Hall," I say slowly. "They aren't going to tell us anything, and I'm better off out of the way." I wander a couple of paces away and dial Jenny's number. She picks up on the second ring.

"I've got my murder-solving hat back on," she says quickly, when I tell her about the body in the boot. "I'll have another riffle through Frances's files, in case there's something we missed."

"Thank you," I say. "I think we need to double our efforts now, and look into the connection between Samantha and Peony Lane." When I hang up, I notice Eric just within earshot, and his eyes meet mine for a moment. They're clear and rather watery, but still a striking blue. He blinks at me, and he looks almost hopeful.

"You're going to look into Samantha's death too?" he asks. "I don't want them pinning this on us, and it'd be easy for them to do."

"I think Samantha was somehow wrapped up in what happened to Peony Lane," I say. "So I'll do everything I can to find out the truth." I pause, watching the police taking photos. "Did either of you see or hear anything out of the ordinary? Samantha's body couldn't have been in the boot of that car for very long. I only saw her this morning."

"I've been at the deli," Beth says. "When I got back here for lunch, everything was quiet. I think Grandad must have already left with the tow truck."

"I was in town," Eric says. "I always drive Samantha to work, and we were going to have lunch, but she called and canceled on me at the last minute. Said she had someone else to see. Now I'm thinking that whoever that was probably killed her." He sniffs, and his voice wobbles as he says, "I should call her daughter. I know her family well, and they should hear this from a friend, rather than the police." Eric heads back into the house, and Beth and I watch the police in silence for a few minutes.

"I don't like that new chief inspector," Beth says eventually.

Beth's eyes find the figure on the periphery of the property again, and I squint to see that the shadow she was glaring at is Toby Marks. He's talking on the phone, with a takeaway cup in his other hand; then he ends his call and walks over to

Crane, and the words they exchange are quick and perfunctory.

"Me either," I say.

Crane heads our way, taking off his latex gloves and turning them inside out in the process. He stuffs them into the pocket of his wool coat, his expression a mixture of sadness and frustration.

"Annie," he says when he gets close enough. "If you're on your way home, I'd like to come with you. There's something at the Gravesdown estate that I want to look into. With your cooperation, of course," he adds hastily.

I don't want to admit that I'm feeling a little shaky still, after seeing Samantha's body, and the idea of driving back with Crane's steady presence is more than a bit reassuring. "Of course," I say.

He follows me to the black BMW, tapping messages out on his phone.

"Has the chief inspector taken over the crime scene now?" I ask, as we start down the long drive.

He shifts in his seat slightly. "He's not *taking over*; he's just doing his job."

"Or he's doing *your* job?" I counter, and then realize it's really not my place to try to fight his work battles alongside him.

Crane doesn't answer, so I focus on the rush of changing leaves that's creating a collage as I drive, keeping my expression carefully neutral.

Finally Crane speaks again, changing the subject. "How are you feeling, Annie? You tend to have issues with blood and things like that."

"I'm okay," I say. "There wasn't any blood, and I'm getting oddly better at tapping into that detached feeling when I see a dead body." I pause and remember that Crane knew

Samantha too. They must have worked in the police station together for years. "Are . . . are *you* okay?" I ask, my voice a little softer. "I mean . . ."

"Thanks for asking," he says, before I can say anything more. "I'll be fine. I've known Samantha for a long time, so it's sad and shocking to have her turn up like that. I can't imagine she'd be a threat to anyone, but people kill for all sorts of reasons." In my peripheral vision I see him chew a fingernail, and I realize that he's actually not that okay.

Just as I'm trying to think of the right thing to say, I notice something on the roundabout sign up ahead that I've never paid attention to before. I've never had a need to, really—it's just a list of neighboring towns with their distances mentioned.

But in the middle of the towns listed is the village of Crownell. I think immediately of the address scribbled in Aunt Frances's files: Peony Lane, 95 Mayfly Lane, Crownell. Without really thinking about it, I pass the roundabout exit to Gravesdown Hall and take the Crownell exit instead.

"What are you doing?" Crane asks, leaning forward. "Do you need to turn around?"

"Detour," I say, following the next sign. "There's somewhere I want to check out."

I hear Crane make a noise in this throat, halfway between a scoff and a sigh. "I should've known you'd head that way eventually. I suppose I should be grateful you're doing this on my watch," he says. "But I wasn't lying when I said I need to look into something at Gravesdown Hall. Just promise me we'll get there eventually."

"You know where we're headed?" I ask.

"Annie, I'm part of the investigation into Peony Lane's murder. We obviously went to her house," he says flatly. He sounds amused rather than upset.

"So you have the keys?" I ask hopefully. "And you don't object to me poking around?"

"I do have access and technically I object. You and Jenny are still on our list of suspects for Peony Lane's murder. If it gets out that I've let you into her residence to riffle through her things and look for clues, I'll be in serious trouble."

"You said *technically* you object," I say, and give him a quick smile before turning my eyes back to the road. "Chief Inspector Marks has just swanned in and taken over your crime scene. He's left you with avenues of investigation that have already been trodden—like Peony Lane's house. What else are you supposed to do but circle back and double-check that you didn't miss anything on first inspection?"

He lets a small laugh escape but stifles it quickly.

"And so what if your diligent double-checking *happened* to be most convenient when I was with you?" I continue.

We pass a sign that says WELCOME TO CROWNELL, and I slow down to see the names of the streets. Mayfly Lane is right off the main road, and I take a sharp right turn in order not to miss it. I focus on the house numbers, finally seeing a very normal-looking terrace with a cheerful 95 on the front, the number painted in yellow and glazed onto a navy ceramic tile. There's a pink splodge on the tile as well, which I suspect is an artist's hasty rendition of a peony.

I park in the drive, turn off the car, and give Crane a level look. "Given our history of working well together—" I start to say, but his laugh cuts me off, short and sarcastic.

He turns toward me and rests one arm on the back of my seat. "By *working well together*, do you mean that you recklessly put yourself in danger, instead of coming to me with your plans, and then I have to help you out of whatever mess you've found yourself in?"

"Come on," I say. "You'd have done the same in my place!

175

It was either keep you in the dark or lose my entire inheritance. Anyway, my point is that you *know* that Jenny and I didn't kill Peony Lane, or Samantha, and that we aren't involved in whatever else is going on. And Peony Lane was *extremely* interested in my house in the days leading up to her death. She didn't want to talk to me; she was there for some other reason."

"Frances's files," Crane says. "That was what I wanted to look into back at Gravesdown Hall. There are other files relating to Peony Lane that are of interest."

"Well, they're probably gone," I say. "I checked a whole list of people, and someone got to those files before me and cleaned them out. And I'm guessing it was either Peony Lane or her killer."

"Annie, there's nothing inside Peony Lane's house of any significance," Crane says.

I sigh, wondering how to break down the wall that is Detective Rowan Crane. I turn to face him fully, so that my shoulders are square to his. The old leather of the BMW seat creaks as I twist in it, and I unlatch my seat belt so that I can move properly. He keeps his hand on the back of my seat, but his attention zeroes in on me like I'm a word search and he's scanning for relevant letters. I'm just another puzzle to solve. For some reason that irks me. I think of Frances's green diary—her and Ford, always trying to win a game they couldn't stop playing.

"Rowan," I say slowly, and his first name is strange in my mouth. It's the first time I've called him that, and his eyes widen a fraction at my use of it. "I think we can both agree that I'm going to find my way inside that house, whether I have permission to or not. Either I can do it under your watchful eye—being open about what I'm looking for and what I find, because we're not in competition for anything now—or I can come back here and snoop around secretly and keep my findings to myself."

Crane looks at the front door.

"There's no security doorbell," I say. "And the windows of the neighboring houses are all dark. No one has to know you let me in." The silence stretches out between us. "And given how Marks is treating you, I think it's important for you to remember that you're still in control of a lot of things. Even if they're littler things, I have no doubt that you'll make them matter."

He lets out a long breath and closes his eyes for a moment. When he looks up, his expression is resigned. "Fine," he says, opening the passenger door. "But as we're looking around, you fill me in on *everything* you've been thinking that you might not have shared with me yet. Theories, file discoveries—I want to know every direction you're considering."

"Agreed," I say, and grin at him.

"What?" he asks. "What's that smile for?"

"I just think it's high time that you started bending the rules," I say. "This is all in pursuit of the truth, you know, and bending the rules is perfectly fine in these sorts of situations."

"It's more that you made a decent case for me to keep an eye on you. You have a history of making foolhardy decisions when you come up against too many roadblocks."

"You say foolhardy, I say tenacious."

"However you label it, I figure you're better off coming in with me to see that Peony Lane simply has a house full of crystals and incense, and quite a lot of junk. And then your curiosity will be sated, and you'll leave this place alone."

From his pocket he takes a special set of keys, like something a locksmith might use, and inserts a thin metal piece into the Yale lock on the front door. The lock clicks, and the door swings open.

When I turn on the lights, it's like stepping into a kaleidoscope, because everywhere new that my eyes rest, I see a completely different picture.

We're in a small sitting room, piled so high with interesting boxes, books, suitcases, and fabrics that I can hardly even see the deep burgundy walls. Plants take up just about every surface, trailing and bending, and some have already started to wilt and turn brown from lack of water. Of everything in the little sitting room, they make me feel the saddest. I think it's because I know that Peony Lane died in the solarium surrounded by shrubs and trees, and now I'm faced with her own plants suffering for the lack of her.

To ease the tension building in my neck and shoulders, I start telling Crane about the theories I have, and how my biggest question is how someone might be getting into Gravesdown Hall.

"You seem very sure that this car crash is linked to Peony Lane's murder," Crane says.

"And you aren't? I mean, she told me to look into it right before she was killed, and then the wreck of that crash turned up on Archie Foyle's land, with a fresh body in it." I walk over to a set of shelves and run my finger along the spines of the books there. Peony has a very similar selection to the one Aunt Frances kept in her little murder room—minus some of the darker titles. There are plant identification books, and books on star charts and tarot, ley lines and Celtic history.

Archie's fortune runs through my head again, and I feel my whole body tune in to the vibration of it. I'm not generally a person who gets plugged into esoteric things, but this place feels like the source of all the uncanny things these fortunes have stirred up—it's Peony Lane's private sanctum, and looking around it makes me feel like a ship's captain on the edge of discovering a new continent.

My fingers stop on a book—*The Migration Patterns of English Birds.* My heart stutters as I pull it from the shelf. *Migration*: My brain trips on the word. I flip to the first chapter and start to read. *Migration is the art of moving with the seasons, an act of survival that is both beautiful and circular. Indeed, spring is often marked in our minds by the return of birdsong, signaling that the seasonal pattern of leaving and returning has been completed once more.*

"The bird returns . . ." I whisper. I flip through the chapters, not knowing what I'm looking for, but this book doesn't just hold information on bird migration—it holds slips of paper as well. Envelopes with names on them fall into my fingers with each chapter, and my hand shakes as one with my own name on it falls into my palm.

"What's that?" Crane asks, looking over my shoulder.

"If I had to guess," I say, "it would be fortunes she wanted to tell but hadn't been able to yet." I take the envelopes and pile them up—there aren't many, a handful maybe—and pocket them when Crane is looking the other way.

Just as I'm about to close the book, I realize something stiff is wedged in between the pages near the back, in a chapter on sparrows—which is not long at all, because according to this book, sparrows don't migrate.

It's a curious fact, and I wonder if it fits in with *the bird returns.* Perhaps that part of Archie's fortune doesn't concern Birdy at all. Or maybe I'm reaching to fit the fortune to every new thought or event I come across.

The piece of paper in this chapter is a certificate of some kind. I pull it free from the other pages and my breath catches when I read what it is.

"It's . . . it's a marriage certificate," I say, and Crane hovers closer to me, scanning the writing and the date listed. The ink on the year is smudged, but the rest is clear.

"I . . ." His brow furrows, and he seems to be in just as much of a state of disbelief as I am. "This marriage was never made public," Crane says. "And it can't have lasted long at all, but . . . given their whole history, how could no one have known about this?"

"And what happened?" I say, my voice breathy. We both stare at the names for a moment, not able to really believe what we're seeing.

Because apparently on March 6, in some year that I can only guess was around 1967, Archibald Lester Foyle married Frances Jane Adams.

And for some reason, the only person with proof that this marriage ever happened was Peony Lane.

CHAPTER
24

ARCHIE'S CAR WAS QUITE SURPRISING. MUCH LIKE AR-
chie himself, it was unassuming to look at and a little rough
around the edges, but strangely interesting inside. He must have
kept half his life in there, because the back seat had a battered
suitcase that was so overfull that it didn't close, and a collection
of various-sized boxes stacked in between blankets and loose
pieces of clothing.

"Don't mind all the clothes," Archie said, waving a hand at
the back seat as we buckled ourselves in up front. "They're clean
and I use them to cushion the boxes so they don't rattle around
when I'm driving. I know it looks messy, but it's actually very organized back there."

"What is all that stuff, if you don't mind me asking?" I tried to
keep my eyes on the road, where rain was battering the windscreen and the single working windscreen wiper was having a
hard job keeping the view clear. Luckily it was the one on Archie's
side, so he could see something of the road.

"Mostly things from the farmhouse that I didn't want rotting away in there," he said. "But there are some other things too. Those big boxes are all full of records, and I pop up at car boot sales around the area and buy and sell them every weekend. I can make a bit of money that way."

"I meant to ask how you were supporting yourself," I said. "Just with car boot sales?"

"Well . . ." He looked a little embarrassed and shook some of the remaining droplets of rain from his wet curls. "I know you spent time with Walt and Emily and their friends, so I'm sure you know about my little side business too."

I felt my eyes narrow slightly. "You mean that you've been selling marijuana around the village."

"Hey," Archie said, his voice a little defensive. "If you're going to judge, just do it on your own time, okay? And don't look in the glove compartment." He smirked as he squinted through the curtain of water coming down over the windscreen.

I suddenly wondered if I was being uptight. I'd felt stifled by Ford, hadn't I? Feeling like I had to walk around the village dressed in the coat he chose for me, going for cocktails, and playing chess in his library.

Defiantly, I pressed the metal disk that released the door to the glove compartment. A clear plastic bag of weed tumbled out into my lap, and I picked it up and held it in the air between us.

Archie laughed, and it was a sound that was becoming so familiar to me now. Like you'd caught him in the middle of the best day of his life, or like joy was just another layer of clothing he had on. I wanted it to encircle me too, and I wanted that careless freedom it promised.

"I had an idea for some excitement," he said. "But getting high before knocking on Peony Lane's door wasn't it."

"That's funny," I said. "I didn't even think to ask where we were heading." I laughed lightly to myself, because I realized I'd just got into Archie's car and wrapped myself up immediately in the mystery of his boxes and belongings. "I suppose that's a sign that I just wanted to go anywhere."

"Well, I hope you like Southampton, because I've just missed the turnoff for Crownell," he said, and his grin was so wide that it seemed to tug his posture upward. Archie was a child on a fairground ride, leaning forward, believing he could make the ride go that little bit faster just by moving his body.

"I've only ever been to Southampton for the department stores," I said. "With my mother. And it's just occurred to me that I'm outraged by that fact." I shifted in my seat to look at him. He was wearing a thin blue jumper underneath a battered black leather jacket, and everything about his appearance had a rumpled secondhand feel to it. He was the opposite of a department store. And I couldn't tell exactly what was happening to me, but I did know that my heart sped up thinking about the odd adventure that was Archie Foyle.

"Well," he said, and turned to me for a moment, his eyes full of the promise of so many things in that small fraction of time that they were off the road. "You should have said so earlier! Southampton holds all kinds of excitements—where should I take you first?"

"Surprise me, Archie," I said. "There are so many things I haven't done. I've never smoked weed, I've never been to a concert, I haven't hitchhiked or slept rough or been to France or—"

Archie's laugh cut me off. "Let's start with some food, okay?" He reached over and tugged my earlobe, and the gesture was both new and familiar at the same time. And I realized that was the appeal of us—me and Archie. All the things about Castle Knoll that were part of me were part of him too, but there was a freedom he managed in the middle of all of it that I craved. And with him I could have both—I wanted both. The sense of home *in the heart of the tumbling castle ruin, the pubs and rolling hills and familiar faces. But also the knowledge that you could leave at any time, to live a bigger life in a bigger town, even just for a day. Or maybe a week. Or a lifetime.*

I wanted that. I wanted Archie.

CHAPTER
25

I DON'T KNOW WHAT TO SAY, OTHER THAN . . . THAT was an unexpected turn," Jenny says. She hands the marriage certificate back to Crane, who takes it gingerly, as if it's an injured baby bird.

Evening is falling at Gravesdown Hall, and Jenny, Detective Crane, and I are sitting on the floor in the main library, the fire roaring again. When you have a fireplace like this, every evening it's unlit feels like an unfinished sentence.

Crane went back to the police station for a few hours after we returned from Peony Lane's house. When he came back to Gravesdown Hall, he and I looked through the file Saxon gave me on Olivia Gravesdown, finding a frustratingly small amount of information there, while Jenny made dinner for us all.

Jenny's comment hangs in the air as we sit staring at the flames, our empty bowls pushed out of the way of the many pieces of paper scattered on the carpet. There's something about the library that makes you want to sit on the floor rather than any of the armchairs or sofas. For me, it's the feeling of being in among the pieces of evidence spread around, while also defying the grand formality this room seems to ask of a person.

The envelopes with people's names on them—the ones I suspect are fortunes Peony Lane never got to tell—are still in my coat, which hangs by the front door. I don't want Crane to know that I took them—if he saw me do it, he didn't challenge me, so I'm not going to give him a reminder. Instead, I decide it's time to let him know about the missing diaries, so I relay the full extent of the conversation I had when I first visited Archie, just before Jenny and I found Peony Lane's body.

"I want that yellow diary," I say to Crane when I finish. "I want all the diaries he has, of course, but that one in particular. I think he's holding on to it because there's something in there that implicates him. If he and Frances were actually close enough to get married, even for a short time, I'm betting Archie knows a lot more about the secrets that were in these files than he's letting on."

"But, Annie," Jenny says gently, "now that we know they were married, it seems even more likely that Archie's keeping those diaries to himself because he's embarrassed about what's inside them. Maybe Frances wrote about . . . I don't know, something more intimate that he doesn't want to see the light of day."

I bite my lip, considering this. "Or he just has them for sentimental reasons, and there's nothing in there that will help solve Peony Lane's and Samantha's murders. The key to solving the murders could just have been in the files alone."

Crane has been quiet for so long that when he speaks it's like a hammer falling. And his words are just as direct. "I think that's probably the most likely scenario. Because Frances was a collector of secrets, not a solver of crimes."

We let his words hang in the air for a moment, because he's right, and it bears remembering.

"Poor Archie," Jenny says. "It makes so many details make sense now—like how Ford never gave him his farm back while he was alive. Ford must have never trusted Archie, and he was only allowed back onto the estate when he wasn't a threat to their marriage."

"And then Archie brought her flowers every morning," I say. "Until the day she died." My eyes are getting surprisingly misty, and as I blink to try to clear them, I notice Crane watching me carefully. "Anyway." I sniff and try to get my mind back onto a logical track of thinking. Managing my emotions isn't my strong suit, something I suppose I get from Mum. "I'm still convinced that somewhere, buried in their quick burn of a romance, is the key to what happened to Peony Lane. Whether Frances wrote about it in that diary or not. Because I just know that Peony Lane having that marriage certificate isn't a coincidence."

"Is there any other evidence of their relationship?" Crane asks. "Around the house here, I mean?"

"Not that I've ever seen," I say. "But . . . when you had another police officer retrieve Peony Lane's file from Frances's collection, I noticed a plastic bag stapled to it. What was in there?"

Crane pulls out his phone and starts to flip through pictures. "That, it turns out, was Olivia Gravesdown's wedding ring."

"Wait, in Peony Lane's file? How come Frances was in possession of it?" Jenny asks.

I hold out my hand for Crane's phone, and he carefully puts it in my palm. I zoom in on the photo, examining what I can see of the ring. "Do you have any other pictures of this ring?" I ask.

"It's all in evidence," Crane says. "This was something I snapped for my own personal reference, so it's strictly off the record. But it's a custom-made gold engagement ring, with a ruby set between two smaller diamonds."

"A ruby," I say, thinking. "There were smaller rubies dotted on that dagger, but there were settings in the handle for two larger stones. Do you think her ring was made from one of the missing ones?"

"It's not impossible," Crane says. "Though the ruby in the ring is much smaller. The main question would then be, why? The Gravesdown family had so much money they could have bid for the Crown Jewels. Why recycle a ruby from that dagger for an engagement ring?"

My phone chimes, and I look at the security camera alert that's just flashed up on the screen. "Another badger," I say as I play back the footage from only seconds before.

"That reminds me," Crane says, reaching for my phone. "I rechecked your front-door camera footage from the day Peony Lane was killed. Our theory about the double door was right."

"What's that?" Jenny asks.

"Crane and I were talking about ways someone could get into the house but not be seen on any of the cameras," I say. "The simplest explanation is that someone was let in through the second double door, here." I scroll on my phone to where I saved the file from that day, and open up the footage of Beth coming to make her delivery. "The camera is angled so sharply that you can't see the other front door." I push play, and the footage shows Beth ringing the bell, her tan mac and spotty umbrella distinctive in the grainy footage. She's got a basket of cheese, bread, and chutney from her deli in her other hand. Twenty seconds go by, then she reaches into her pocket, takes out a key, and opens the front door. The hallway table that holds post and a small vase of flowers becomes visible because it's just inside the door. I see her set the basket down inside, but . . . I tap pause. "Is she still holding the keys?" I ask.

"It's hard to tell," Crane says, hovering over my shoulder. One of his hands is resting on the carpet just behind my back, careful not to touch me but close enough that I feel the casualness between us crack slightly, giving way to something slightly more charged. Jenny is watching us both with a rather smug expression.

"There." I point. "The light on Beth shifts." I pause again. "That's the light from the far end of the hallway, throwing a stripe across Beth as the second door is opened."

"Exactly. Which means Beth let someone else in that day," Crane says, frowning. "And here . . ." He reaches with the hand that he's not leaning on and presses play on the phone in my hand. For a second I can smell his aftershave, and I have to work hard to keep my thoughts from running away with me. Finding out about Frances's rather active love life has made me realize how stagnant my own is, and I feel strange about that suddenly. Crane points to the frozen frame. "She intentionally locked them back in the house. Any ideas who that could be?" When I don't answer, he continues. "I've watched that footage countless times, and there aren't any telling shadows or partial images of the other person in the frame at any point."

"I'm thinking of the missing files, and the murder," I say. "I think the most likely people Beth would have let in are Archie, Peony Lane, and Samantha. Archie was back at his farm in time for me to visit him on my walk into town—I did stop and write in a notebook for an hour after I met Peony Lane in the woods—and Beth popped in at the farmhouse not long after I arrived. It's possible that Peony Lane walked straight to Gravesdown Hall after she met me, and Beth was there and let her in for some reason. . . . But it seems really unlikely, and oddly coincidental, that she would arrive just when Beth happened to be there. I think it's more likely that Peony Lane got in some other way, and Beth let her killer in."

"That's a good point," Crane says. "Though Beth could have let in more than one person. But that means that after the body was discovered and the murder made public, Beth would know who killed Peony Lane, and she's protecting them."

"Which points back to Archie again," I say, my voice flat.

"The files are the most obvious reason he'd be sneaking inside," Jenny offers. "But he wouldn't need any accomplices for that, other than using Beth to let him in."

"It might all come back to the history of that group of friends," Crane says. "Archie, Eric, Samantha, Birdy, and Peony Lane."

"*The foil, the arrow, the rat, the sparrow,*" I murmur. "It's another reason why getting that diary is essential. Aunt Frances may not have worked out who killed Olivia Gravesdown, but some of the secrets about the relationships between those people are the key to finding out."

Crane's eyes fall on the notes strewn across the carpet in front of us. "Archie hasn't been seen since we found Samantha's body earlier," he says. We're all quiet for a moment, and I jump when the fire makes a sudden *pop*. "The police have been looking for him, but curiously, he's nowhere to be found."

"What if he's not the killer, but he's in danger? Because of what he knows?" Jenny offers.

My phone buzzes, and I see Mum's name flash across the screen. I groan, thinking about the family drama on the periphery of all this. My finger hovers over the decline button, but then I remember something. I decide to take the call. But before I do, I turn to Jenny.

"You said Mum was being visited by Birdy Sparrow the last time you saw her?" I ask Jenny quickly. She nods, and I click accept. I don't move to another room—I have questions to ask that are decidedly case-related, and having Jenny and Crane here makes me feel grounded.

"Mum, hi," I say cautiously.

"Hi, Annie," she says, and the forced breeziness in her voice seems doubly strong this time. I'm immediately on alert, and I realize I should have checked in with her much sooner. Guilt claws at me, but I don't have time to wrestle with it, because Mum keeps talking. "I just wanted to check back about that file I mentioned," she says. Her voice isn't casual at all anymore, it's urgent, and I'm now sure that something isn't right. "The one about Peony Lane? I'd really like it for my research—this new set of paintings is just . . . troublesome, and I'd love some more facts about her. I think it could be inspiring . . ." She's babbling, and so I try to take control of the conversation, to see what's really going on.

"Mum, answer me honestly—is everything all right? You don't sound like you, and I'm worried."

Mum sighs, and her voice settles a little. "I'm fine, honestly. It's mainly just stress, with this new collection I'm supposed to be creating."

"Peony Lane is a very specific character to dig into for research, though," I say. My heartbeat slows a tiny bit, but I'm still on edge. "Why her?"

"Oh, just something Birdy said, when she was up here last. She said there's a really pretty ring in that file, and that it's got some real history. This new series is going to be darker, more visceral, and I could use the ring to bring the images to life. Rubies, blood, those kinds of things." Mum laughs. "You'll hate it, I have to say."

How does Birdy know that there's a ring in that file? I think.

"Is Birdy still there with you?" I ask.

"Oh no, she's gone back home to Castle Knoll," Mum says. "She only came up to London for lunch."

"But Birdy doesn't live in Castle Knoll," I say. "She lives in Brighton. I remember, from when I contacted her to tell her about solving Emily's case."

There's a long pause on the other end of the line. "No, I'm sure she's always been in Castle Knoll," Mum says. "She just likes to keep a low profile. She ran away for a time years ago, but she came back not long after Emily disappeared and her parents left. She said she always wants to be near Castle Knoll."

I think of that line, in the book on birds that Peony Lane had. *Sparrows don't migrate.* It feels like it's in direct contradiction to *The bird returns.* It strikes me that you can cause a lot of trouble in a town where everyone thinks you're gone but you never really left.

"So Birdy wanted you to get that file," I say. "Just because of the ring?"

"Oh, I think it was more that she liked the idea of me having it here, of it inspiring my art."

I'd say Mum was naive, but she just doesn't think like I do. "I think it's less that she wanted you to have it," I say slowly, "and more that she wanted that file *out* of Castle Knoll."

"What does that mean?" Mum asks. "Annie, is something strange going on in Castle Knoll? Is Jenny still staying? I don't like the idea of you alone in that huge house . . ."

"There's just been a weird string of coincidences lately, that's all," I tell her. "With you asking about Peony Lane."

Mum is quiet for a minute. "What coincidences? What aren't you telling me?"

I bite my lip. *The bird returns.* I can't find a way to explain to Mum that I've started fixating on fortunes, the same way Aunt Frances did. That Peony Lane is constantly on my mind, and I'm wondering if Birdy's return to Castle Knoll after her brief time away wasn't what that fortune meant. What if she returned to Gravesdown Hall to kill Peony Lane, after she'd been here once before, decades ago? What if Birdy returned to kill Peony Lane because years ago, she and Peony killed Olivia together, and suddenly Peony wanted to confess, putting them both in jeopardy?

"I'll check in with you tomorrow, okay?" I say. "I promise."

"All right," Mum says, but she doesn't sound reassured. "Please be careful, Annie."

"Jenny's still here," I say. "And everything's fine." I don't mention Crane, who is politely studying the fire. Telling Mum about even the smallest whiff of a police presence completely contradicts what I've just said to her. Everything isn't fine, everything is going sideways, and I feel like my life here at Gravesdown Hall is just a pantomime of the one Aunt Frances led. This house is a target, with all these files at its heart. Maybe I should just take them all out and put them on a big bonfire and invite the whole village so they can watch their secrets burn.

CHAPTER
26

THE RAIN STARTED TO LET UP AS WE DROVE INTO *Southampton, and Archie seemed alive with ideas of things we could do. But he took extra pleasure in not telling me a single one, which I pretended to find aggravating but found all the more alluring. He navigated busy roundabouts and took shortcuts down back streets like this was his second home.*

Finally he found a place to park the car, wedged into a line of others on a random street that was surprisingly busy for a Sunday. He reached over me and pounded the glove compartment with a fist, causing the little door to open again. He pulled out the bag of weed that I'd carefully stowed back in there for the remainder of our drive, and opened it to reveal several smaller weed-filled bags inside.

"Directly behind your seat you'll find my portable radio," he said. "I can't get much on it in Castle Knoll, but we'll get a clear signal here." Archie was smoothing out a small square of paper, presumably to roll us a joint, and my nerves started to properly crackle.

I wasn't going to back down; I meant what I'd said—I was craving surprises and new things. I was eighteen years old, still living at home and working in my family's bakery. As I rummaged in the pile of things behind the seat, I realized I had the potential to change my entire life. My whole way of doing things could just be turned on its head. The threat of my fortune was getting smaller the larger my horizon stretched.

Perhaps if I stretched it as far as I could, my fortune would blow away on the wind, taking my belief in it with it.

I settled back into my seat with the radio, which was just a little taller than a loaf of bread. Archie had rolled us a joint using the dashboard of the car, and he was quick and efficient at it. He shuffled over next to me and handed me the unlit joint so he could fiddle with the radio knobs until some music came through.

The middle of "Mellow Yellow" by Donovan filled the car, and Archie took the joint back from me and placed it between his lips, sparking the lighter with one hand and cupping the other around the end of the joint until it caught. He took a drag of it, held the smoke in his lungs for a second, and then exhaled slowly. He handed it to me but tucked a finger under my chin and looked into my eyes with a small smile before I could inhale.

"Don't go too hard with that, since you've never had any before," he said. "No one needs to be sick today. We've got things to do."

I inhaled neatly, the way I'd seen Emily and Walt do, and tried my hardest not to cough. I actually managed it, but possibly because not much of the smoke went into my lungs. When Archie passed it to me a second time, I overcompensated, and the dryness of it all hit my throat and had me spluttering.

Archie didn't laugh, which I appreciated. The radio DJ's voice floated around the car as the song ended; I didn't take in any of the words, but the lilt of his voice felt like a rowing boat close to shore, where the waves are small and the water so clear you can see the bottom. I laughed at my own thoughts then and caught Archie watching me carefully.

"It's the perfect time for a walk," he said. "I've parked here because there's a secret little market round the corner—random tat mostly, but it's one of the places I get my LPs. Lots of artists meet up there; it's interesting."

He led me through a little alleyway into a courtyard that felt like the back of his car—piled high with things that at first seemed random, but when you looked closely you could tell they held the stories of a lifetime. Tables were erected in crooked rows, many with records that people flipped through and bartered for; others had reproductions of famous artists' works that I'd seen in the papers—Andy Warhol, mostly, but there were other artists represented, with original work in bold colors and confusing styles.

As it got busier, Archie slung his arm across my shoulders to keep me near, and we spent what felt like hours laughing and digging through boxes of secondhand books, wind chimes made of seashells, and postcards of naked women mixed in with scenes of London and the seaside. It was like someone had taken a box of lost things and shaken it until some of them broke, then put a lid back on it knowing that when no one was looking, they'd reassemble themselves in more beautiful ways. Or was that just how my mind felt after the joint?

Archie eventually led me to a food stall where he ordered a mountain of things I'd never tried before. We gorged on Indian food, and I felt almost ready to confess every emotion I was having right as I was having it. But I managed the most important one, as the sun started to go down and evening crept in around us.

"I don't want to go home," I said.

"Okay," Archie said. "We'll stay out." He smiled at me, and I leaned in toward him. He pulled me closer, and my hands found his shoulders. He tilted his forehead so that it met mine.

"Good," I said. "But I want to stay out for days, Archie. I don't want a distracting afternoon. I want . . ." My words faltered as his nose brushed mine. His mouth was hovering a breath's distance away, but he didn't close the gap. He was waiting for what I had to say.

"I want to step away from my fate, and I want to live my life."

He kissed me then, and Archie Foyle kisses like he laughs—like he's finally got to the chorus of his favorite song, like he's in flight, like he's in love.

CHAPTER
27

I LIKE THE FOYLES—ALL OF THEM—BUT THEY AREN'T looking good at the moment," Crane says. We're still sitting on the floor in front of the fire, and he stretches his legs out in front of him, leaning back on his elbows. Jenny has disappeared upstairs to phone her mum—she's one of those people who talk to their mums regularly and still somehow manage to fill hours with conversation. Not for the first time, I wonder what that's like.

A storm is building outside, and the wind is starting to rattle the glass in the big windows, giving an ominous feel to our evening. The night is slipping by in a haze of theories and firelight, but I feel like there's a connection Crane and I are trying to grasp that keeps slipping away. "I'd like to work out what the Foyles aren't telling us," he continues. "If Beth let someone into your house on the morning of the murder, I want to know who it was, and why she did it. Because I agree with you—the most likely scenario is that more than one person entered the house that morning, and when whatever they came here to do went wrong, Peony Lane was the casualty."

"That file on Peony Lane," I say. "Who has it now?"

Crane's expression clouds over. "Marks does, at the station. Why do you ask?"

I don't answer the question; instead I ask another one. "Have you had a close look at it?"

"No, Marks is reviewing it, then he'll consult the rest of us when he's got something. Annie, what are you thinking?"

"Birdy was visiting Mum a few days ago, and I think she's got Mum fixated on Peony Lane in order to get that file out of this house. On the morning she was killed, Peony Lane approached me and told me expressly to go and look in Olivia Gravesdown's file. At the same time, Beth made a delivery and let someone into this house for a reason."

"To get that file? But they'd have to know where the keys were. And you told me you changed where they were hidden—you don't keep them where Frances always used to, right?"

"Yeah," I say. "To find the keys, you'd have to know about the little ceramic cat, which means you'd have to know something about me and where I like to hide things."

"But also—someone got into the files, and they took files that *weren't* Peony Lane's. You said that other files were missing, right? And that you're pretty sure Archie didn't have a file?" Crane asks.

"Her note in that file seemed very personal, and I think what she said must have been the truth—she knew all his secrets by heart." I feel a strange tightening in my chest then, and I wonder what secrets Archie's been keeping from us all. I don't want to enlist Crane to take that yellow diary from him by force, but he probably could. If Archie is the main suspect in the murders of both Peony Lane and Samantha, I imagine his whole farm will be thoroughly searched.

Crane closes his eyes, and in the firelight he looks like he could be thinking, or simply choosing a moment to be quiet.

Eventually his eyes snap open and it's like his mental to-do list has suddenly lit up inside his mind.

"I need to be going," he says, standing. "It's getting late, and I've still got paperwork to finish."

"Of course," I say. I reluctantly walk him to the door, and when he turns to leave he gives me a long look. The rain is battering the gravel drive now, and the wind is blowing so hard it's hitting it at an angle.

"I'll get Peony Lane's file from the chief inspector," Crane says, his expression taking on a steely edge. "If you're right and the key to all this is somewhere in that file, I may even bend a few rules to get it." His face is still serious, but there's a glint in his eyes, and I feel my own expression shift as an appreciative smile spreads across my lips.

"I'm going to pay a visit to Birdy Sparrow as soon as I can," I say. When his eyebrows shoot up a little, I add, "This is me putting this on the agenda in case you want to come, since we seem to have unofficially teamed up to solve this."

He laughs lightly, nodding. "I'll check back in soon, then," he says, then he winks, so lightly and quickly that it could have just been a smile going rogue, and dashes through the rain in the dark to his car.

WHEN I LOCK the door, I place my back against it and close my eyes for a moment, listening to the bones of the house creaking. With a house as old and large as Gravesdown Hall, strange noises are constant. It's taken me weeks to stop running around checking every window when I hear the slightest groan of a tree branch against a pane somewhere, or rattling every doorknob to make sure the locks hold.

But my heart lurches when I hear a sudden slam from the back of the house. The wind has clearly caught something.

The noise happens again, louder this time, and I take a few feeble steps down the hall. "Jenny?" I call out. I don't hear any reply, but then the stone walls and oak-paneled hallways of this house mean someone could literally be screaming on the second floor and downstairs you'd hear nothing.

This is ridiculous. I stride the length of the hall with the false purpose of a child who is trying too hard to be brave when faced with a dark wardrobe or a gap under the bed. Perhaps the trellis that climbs the side of the house has been pried loose and is being smacked into the wall by the wind. The slam sounds again, louder this time, because it's definitely coming from the back of the house. The trellis, then. Though the only way that trellis would come loose is if it had more weight on it than the feeble roses that decorate it. It would only come loose if someone climbed it.

I debate turning around and running up the stairs to check that Jenny's okay, mentally calculating which windows that trellis might grant access to.

Instead I rush through the kitchen but stop at the edge of the step down into the solarium. The space is dark, the rain lashing against the glass of its ceiling and walls, and the plants inside have taken on an inky blackness against an already shadowy interior.

But as the slam echoes through the solarium, I finally see what's causing it. The back door of the solarium is open, swinging wildly with each gust of wind. I step carefully into the room, my bare feet feeling strange against the tiled path. It's a foolhardy thing to do, but maybe the wind caught the door after it wasn't closed properly? I try not to think about how heavy those doors are, and how implausible this theory is.

And I don't want to be the person who has gone so far into Frances's mindset that she can't close a creaky door in an old house. When I finally reach the back door, I catch the metal handle, feeling the paint come off in flakes with the rainwater. I pull it closed, and it takes a minute for me to get the door to land back properly in the frame. I blame the police for this—all their coming in and out; slamming this old door has bent it a bit.

"Annie!" Jenny's voice cuts through the sound of the lashing rain, causing me to jump. "Where's the light in here?"

I take a minute to steady myself, but I don't take my eyes off the door. I slide the bolt into the lock, though I have to stand on tiptoe and force it a little. "The switch is in a weird place," I call back. "It's one of those 1930s metal toggle things, but the only lighting in here is from spotlights in the floor. Here, I'll find it." I carefully feel my way along the glass of one wall until I get to a cast-iron support midway along, where the light switch is. I flick it, and warm light floods the solarium, but the spotlights at the base of the palms and tree ferns also add drama and shadows.

"You okay?" Jenny asks, joining me. "Where's Crane?"

"He left," I say, waving my hand lightly at the comment like it's so meaningless it could float away. It's not meaningless, but I'm focused on the problem of this door, thinking about Peony Lane and why she was in the solarium, and who found her here. "And this door was hanging open," I add. I turn abruptly and face her. "There's something we're missing about this crime scene," I say.

Jenny crosses her arms. "You think? I mean, aside from how multiple people entered the house undetected, and how someone walked *right past us* and stuck a knife into an already dead body—she was already dead when that knife went in, right?"

"Crane confirmed that, and he confirmed that she died in the house, rather than being killed elsewhere and dumped here," I say. "But I think these doors are the key to people coming and going on that day."

"We've already established that if they're locked, these doors can't be opened from the outside without breaking in," Jenny says. "Because they lock using the dead bolt from the inside."

"Yes, but we've been so fixated on how someone got in that we haven't thought about how whoever Beth let inside through the front door must have come *out* a different way. After Beth's arrival, the footage of that door shows only police coming and going. Jen, what if Beth let the killer in, and they were trying to sneak out the back, and they encountered Peony Lane because she was already here? What if they let her in, even?"

"Wait, what?" Jenny crosses her arms and examines the solarium doors like they might start talking at any moment and give up their secrets.

"Given the time stamp on the footage of the front-door cam, the person Beth let inside wasn't Peony Lane—Peony was talking to me on the footpath leading to the estate at that time. So it had to be someone else, and my main suspect right now is Birdy, because of how determined she's been to get hold of that file. Plus, something I've been wondering about is not only how Peony Lane got inside, but why she was in the solarium, of all places."

Jenny nods along, picking up the thread. "She would have approached the house through the wooded paths, which is consistent with where you saw her last," Jenny says. "And when she got to the solarium, she saw her old friend Birdy through the glass, and Birdy opened the back door and let her in."

"If it was Birdy and Peony Lane who killed Olivia together all those years ago—let's say they came to Olivia for help with taking Edmund down for his crimes, and she refused or threatened them, so they retaliated with murder—and Peony was the one to recently get an attack of conscience, Birdy might have been willing to do whatever it took to keep those secrets buried."

"You moving in to Gravesdown Hall and getting friendly with the local detective, solving previous murders . . ." Jenny bites her lip. "It could be enough to make them both nervous, but react to those nerves in different ways. One wanting to let the secret out, the other wanting to hide the truth forever."

I nod. "Birdy keeps a really low profile around Castle Knoll," I say. "I didn't even know she lived here until my mum told me today, and no one in town ever mentioned it. We have two main priorities now—find Birdy Sparrow, and get that diary from Archie, by any means necessary."

CHAPTER

28

I DIDN'T LEAVE THE HOUSE WITH MUCH MONEY THAT *day; I hadn't been planning to run after my life at such a pace that I might catch up with it. But Archie was popular at that market, selling weed and chatting to people who approached him and called him by name. He made quite a lot that afternoon, buying and selling things. Trips to his car were made, records brought out and traded—he even had trinkets of his own to sell. He produced a battered wooden jewelry box from under the driver's seat, which turned out to contain a jumble of old jewelry. Some of it looked like things my grandma would wear, long out of fashion, but among the twisted necklace chains and broken watches were some interesting brooches and a thin gold bracelet I rather liked.*

"One of my regular clients paid me in concert tickets today," Archie said as we walked toward the seafront. *"There's something on that's hard to get into, and I think it will make an excellent first gig for you." I felt my face light up, and he kissed me again— after that first kiss, we couldn't seem to stop; it was a new form of*

communication between us and we could get so many thoughts across that way.

I called my parents from a phone box and told them I needed a last-minute holiday. I couldn't let them worry—not after Emily had disappeared and punctured the bubble of safety that the parents of Castle Knoll had lived in for so long. Mother was taken aback, but I made a strong case for my independence and told her I was only in Southampton with friends. I didn't mention Archie—everyone in Castle Knoll knew the Foyles, and Mother still thought I was seeing Ford. I felt dishonest, not being open about Archie, when the taste of him was in my mouth and the smell of him was on the folds of my clothes in secret places. I told myself it was just that I wanted to keep him for myself for a little while, and not let anyone else's judgment cloud my emotions.

We shared another joint in the dark by the seafront, ate fish and chips, and found ourselves in a crowded concert venue wrapped in the noise of electric guitars. I was mesmerized by how the vibrations of the music rattled my bones and filled me up, and we danced and drank and kissed, and then stumbled back to a hotel in the early hours.

Archie slept next to me but insisted that he wouldn't touch me beyond the kisses we'd already shared. "Please?" I slurred into his ear, but he just smoothed back my hair and kissed my forehead.

"In the morning, when our heads are clear, I have important things to say to you. Good things, but serious ones. Because I'm not your temporary adventure, Frances," he said, and kissed me so lightly I could feel his vulnerability laid plain. The softness in him, he was showing it to me—and I wanted to take it carefully and show him how much I'd treasure it.

I watched him drift off, and I brought my yellow diary out of my bag and scribbled these things down as if I might unravel if I slept without emptying them from my mind. They were too heady to sleep with, like perfume that intoxicates but dulls the rest of your senses if you inhale it too deeply.

THE NEXT MORNING, *true to his word, Archie woke me gently and looked at me with a mixture of yearning and surprise. I noticed he'd brought the wooden jewelry box back to the hotel with us, and he'd untangled the many necklaces and bracelets. He'd separated out the thin gold bracelet he'd caught me eyeing, and it was waiting for me on the bedside table. He gingerly unclasped it and refastened it around my wrist, kissing the underside of it— the place just below the palm where you check someone's heartbeat. It took him a few tries to do up the clasp, partially because he had something else in his hand, something small that he was keeping hidden. He looked at me again, and I couldn't decipher the meaning of it. His hair was slightly disheveled, and he'd taken his shirt off to sleep—for some reason that gesture of closeness and familiarity pushed my imagination into a thousand new rooms. My mind was setting up a home with him, and it was safe and kind and inviting. No whispers of murder could sneak through the cracks; it was a life I wanted to immerse myself in and I knew that if I wanted to, it was a future I could choose.*

"What?" *I asked, smiling.* "What's that look for?"

"How badly do you want this, Frances? Me and you?" *he asked.* "Because I don't want to be just a phase you go through before you go back to a serious life with Ford. I want to do everything right with you—the adventures and the bit that comes after. After the hangovers clear and the sun comes up and all the concert venues are just empty rooms with litter and spilled drinks. I want to look at your face in the middle of a gray day when the party's over and know—and I do know this, Frances—that life is still beautiful and good because I love you."*

I leaned forward and kissed him, putting everything I felt—and a few thoughts that surprised me, those deeper, more urgent things—into that kiss. "I love you too," I whispered when we broke apart.

His face was so bright that his smile was like a crack in the sun. He wound his fingers between mine—his right hand to my left—and as he did, the small thing he'd been holding emerged and looped around my ring finger.

It was an engagement ring, gold and ornate, and my breath caught when I looked at it. "It's so beautiful," I said. "Where did you get it?"

He slid the ring fully down my finger, and when it nestled right where it needed to be, it felt so intimate that I wanted all of him always, starting right then.

"Family heirloom," he said, and his eyes locked on mine. "Marry me, Frances. Will you? I don't care how sudden this is, it feels right."

My face hurt from smiling so hard, and I kissed him before I could get the words out. "Yes," I managed between breaths as my heart sped up and he kissed me harder. "Yes, Archie, I'll marry you."

We made love and Archie was the slow, considerate partner I'd been craving for that first time, and then again later he showed me how passion built and flowed between us, and I felt completely and utterly happy.

With my head on his chest in that hotel room in Southampton, I twisted the engagement ring he'd given me, admiring how it was the perfect size for me. The ruby set in the center caught the light through the window, and it was a little scratched and seemed slightly worn, but much like Archie himself, the light revealed a deep and complex hidden center.

We went straight to the registry office before lunch, and I didn't even care that our marriage was witnessed by strangers, taking less than ten minutes to be completed. I signed my name on the certificate, feeling lightened by the idea that this could be the last time I'd sign Frances Jane Adams. I am filling up the rest of this page with my new signature, Frances Foyle. I can't stop smiling watching my left hand write that name, with my ring gleaming there as a symbol of my new life.

CHAPTER
29

WE CAN'T EXACTLY GO CHARGING OFF INTO A STORMY
night looking for Birdy," Jenny says. "So what now?"

The wind is still howling outside, but we've secured the
solarium doors, as well as several windows that were rattling.

"I don't know," I say, scanning the various papers and files
we've littered the library with. They're mostly only tangen-
tially related to Peony Lane, but poring over the files of random people who work at Castle Knoll Police Station or the
coffee shops Peony Lane might have frequented just feels
like spinning our wheels. "What other loose ends do we have
that we might be able to make progress on just from what's
here?"

Jenny's eyes dart around the library, bouncing from various trinkets on the shelves to the antiques locked away in
glass cabinets.

"What about that knife? The one found in Peony's back?"
Jenny says. "Wasn't that originally part of the Gravesdowns'
antiques collection?"

"Jenny, you're a star," I breathe, my pulse picking up as I realize we might have more information on that knife to hand than we realized. "I can't believe I didn't think of this before, but there's a whole inventory of these antiques, for insurance purposes." I cross to the large desk in the center of the library and heave open one of the drawers, then I riffle through stacks of papers until I finally uncover a box file with the words *Insurance Inventories* written down the side in large black letters.

"I mean, I don't think you can blame yourself for not thinking, I know, I should check the Gravesdown estate's antiques inventory!" Jenny says.

"Still," I say, "the best place to find out the history of that knife would be here—especially if it was ever declared stolen. Whoever stuck it in Peony's back had a reason, especially because she was already dead when they did it. It was a statement of some kind, a reminder of the past. It had to be." I leaf through photographs clipped to papers announcing the origin, value, and other details of endless items contained in this house. My forehead creases as I learn that objects I haven't paid much attention to but have probably been abusing, thinking they were ordinary and insignificant, are actually extremely valuable. "Remind me to stop using that velvet chaise as a step stool to reach the higher bookshelves," I mutter, as my eyes water at the value of it.

"Wait." Jenny pauses and reaches over my hand to something midway through the stack of papers. "It's the ring."

"Oh my God," I say, scanning the documents the photo is attached to. "Look, the dagger is clipped into this stack too—they *are* related. But . . . wow, that's weird."

"Ownership contested . . . what does that mean?" Jenny says.

"These are legal documents," I say, pulling out more pages concerning the ring and the knife. "And police reports. Look—the history of that ruby ring is really bizarre."

Jenny and I sit in silence as we read through the pages. Finally she says, "But would someone commit murder just for this? Over a ring?"

"Here's an explanation of the historical feud over the ring," I say, pulling a yellowed typed page from the pile. "The dagger is actually a French letter opener, made in 1840. It features a pair of uncut rubies that were bought at auction, and the lady of the house commissioned the letter opener to showcase them, along with a collection of smaller rubies the family already owned. But that's the least interesting thing about it . . ." I turn the typed page over, skimming through a description of the style of the hilt and details about the jeweler who designed the settings. "Here, look—the origin of the feud. This typed note is dated 1970."

In 1900, Alexander Gravesdown brought his valet, Owen Foyle, before the court to claim that a ruby had been pried from a dagger on display in the library at Gravesdown Hall. Alexander claimed that in order to hide his theft, Owen Foyle had the ruby cut down and fitted into a ring, which he gave to his wife, Henrietta. Owen claimed the ruby ring had been in the Foyle family long before the Gravesdowns came into possession of the dagger.

The ruby ring was the focus of a court case between the Foyles and the Gravesdowns, which was only resolved when Owen agreed to surrender the ring in order to keep his family employed by the Gravesdown family, and living on Gravesdown land.

Subsequent generations of Foyles have tried to sue for the return of the ring, but none have been successful.

"This is all very interesting, Annie, but what exactly does it tell us?" Jenny says.

"Something very significant," I say. "If the rough-cut ruby that was found in the road at the crash scene was one of the ones missing from the handle of the dagger, it means that the dagger was in the car that night."

"Oh my God, and that means—"

"Exactly," I say. "If my theory is correct, and there was a fourth person in the back of the car, someone who survived the crash and walked away—or who survived the crash, opened the boot to remove Olivia's body, and then ran . . ."

"Then the fourth person in the car was likely to be the one who had the dagger," Jenny says.

"Yeah," I say. "The two cases—the Gravesdown crash and Peony's recent murder, as well as Samantha's—definitely seem to be intertwined. We're close to figuring out how, but there are still some pieces missing."

JENNY AND I decide to haul some spare mattresses down to the library and lock ourselves in for the night. Everywhere else feels too open—I couldn't get hold of the cleaners to ask for their keys back, so that set of keys is still out in the world. And I was so distracted by Samantha's body turning up on Archie's farm that I didn't think to ask Beth to return her set.

Beth. The thought of her letting someone into the house,

in such a specific way as to be completely undetected—it was an act of betrayal. And she'd stood next to me, comforting her uncle as we watched the police dealing with Samantha's body. A body found on *her* farm.

"This feels very sleepover-ish," Jenny says, piling quilts over herself. We've put the mattresses on the floor near the fire, and it does feel cozy.

"I can't tell if this reminds me of being thirteen and sleeping in your sitting room and watching scary movies, or of being at uni and us crashing on people's sofas at two A.M. because we missed the last tube home," I say.

"The perfect mix of both, I think," Jenny says. She lies on her stomach with her arms folded under her chin and looks at me thoughtfully. "There's something I wanted to ask you."

I yawn and prop my fist against my temple. "Go for it, but just be warned that my mind is rapidly emptying of most normal thoughts because I'm so sleepy. You'll either get too honest an answer, or one that's bonkers because it's part of a lucid dream."

"Fair. Okay, so . . . don't hate me, but why do you seem like you're actively avoiding your family and your writing these days?"

"What? I'm not, I'm just tied up with other things."

Jenny gives me a cynical look. "A year ago, you were so excited about the drafts you were working on that you sent them out before you'd even edited them. Now you scribble in a few notebooks, but when's the last time you finished something? And actually, on that note—we both went to the same art school; I *know* what it looks like when you're plugged into something creative. When was the last time you picked up a camera? I bet no one in Castle Knoll even knows you studied photography. Did you even bring your equipment here?"

"I have it upstairs—I'm setting up my own office," I say

214

carefully. "But, Jenny, just because you have a career that fits your talents so perfectly doesn't mean it works that way for everyone. Loads of people go to uni and then never use their degrees again. And we've had this conversation before. I just . . . didn't know what to study, so I studied that." I'm waking up a bit, defensiveness acting like caffeine in my system.

Jenny's talent comes so naturally, and she's never had a problem with focus, so she can get really impatient watching other people flounder. Our biggest fights have always been about exactly that—she can't understand what it's like to feel lost and float between things, and I can't understand what it's like to be driven toward the same goal your whole life.

"So, is writing just going to be another photography course?" she asks.

I feel my lips pull into a tight line. "I love both, and I don't think you see how related the two are. My brain feels the same when I look at a setting and find a story in it. Then I adjust the features on my camera to shift the light and the focus to bring out some parts of that story and let other parts fade into the background. I can look at that same scene with a notebook in my hand and create a reason why there's a lonely person on a bench or why the bins are overflowing. There are interesting things everywhere, and I *do* have enough ambition to be the person who puts a spotlight on them."

"Then why aren't you?" Jenny asks. She's got the fiery look she wears when she's totally convinced she's delivering harsh truths for the sake of personal growth, and it makes me feel annoyed and contrary at the same time. I don't like anyone trying to control me—Frances and I have that in common.

"Who says I'm not? This real-life murder solving is another version of that! Or, it's a version of it that uses the skills

I already have, while giving me new ones in the process." My voice is starting to rise, and I can tell Jenny and I are heading into another one of our *What does Annie do with her life?* arguments. I clench my jaw because I'm ready to fight my corner.

"Annie, I don't like you rotting away in this huge house, slowly morphing into your great aunt," she says, her voice even. She's trying to lower the tension by being the calm one, which just makes me want to be louder.

"What do you want me to do, then, Jenny? I could sell the place and move to a tropical island. I'd sit on the beach and feel just as lost there as I do here. If I didn't have this house and I was still living with Mum, I'd be doing *the exact same thing*. I have enough sense to know that I can't outrun myself."

"I'm not telling you to do that," she says.

"Then what are you telling me? Why the third degree about my ambition, and turning into Aunt Frances?"

"I don't know," Jenny says, getting flustered. "I just never thought you were the kind of person who'd want to live a life that's *this isolated*! Find a boyfriend, consider a future and a family, and pursue a life's work! You're going to be eighty on your own here one day, and have nothing to show for it except for one murder that you solved!"

"Two murders," I cut in, my voice a mumble. "I solved two murders last summer."

"You see! This is what I'm talking about! Turn those cases into compelling books, write screenplays, do a whole photo essay exhibition, I don't care! I just don't like to see you doing nothing but fixating on clues and theories about who killed who. Because, Annie, one of those fortunes you got from Peony Lane's house has *your name on it*, and ever since you told me about that stack of envelopes I've been wanting to throw them in the fire!"

"Okay, I'm not going to—" I stop, suddenly listening.

"What is it?" Jenny sits up and drops her voice to a whisper.

We hear a floorboard creak, and someone tries to stifle a cough.

"Someone's in the house," I mouth to her.

We exchange a look, and I reach toward the rack that holds the fire tools, grabbing a long cast-iron poker. We stand up as quietly as we can, and as an afterthought, Jenny grabs the long-handled fire brush. It would be comical, her standing there in designer silk pajamas, brandishing what's essentially a miniature broom as if it's a sword, but the doorknob to the library starts to rattle. Then we hear the jangle of keys and the scrape of metal as a key is inserted in the lock.

"Beth," I mouth to Jenny, and she nods back at me.

We hurry across the room to put ourselves right to the side of the door, so that when it opens, we can get behind Beth and confront her once she's in the room.

The door swings open, and I lower my poker slightly when it's Archie, not Beth, who steps into the library. He takes in the mattresses and blankets near the fire and realizes he's not alone. He turns and puts both hands up in the air when he sees Jenny and me holding our fireplace weapons. Neither of his hands is empty—one holds Beth's set of keys, and the other holds one of Aunt Frances's files. I notice, by the thickness of it, and the ring in the plastic bag stapled to the front of it, that it's Peony Lane's.

"Archie, what the hell are you doing here?" I ask. I lower my poker fully, as I don't feel threatened by Archie in the slightest. "And where did you get that file? Do you know the police are looking for you? A body was found on your farm!"

"I know," he says, and lowers his hands. "I put it there."

CHAPTER
30

March 16, 1967

WE SPENT THREE AMAZING DAYS AND NIGHTS IN SOUTH-
ampton, filling our time with each other.

"We could move here," Archie said. "You know your family's
trade, you could teach me how to bake bread, and we could open
our own little shop. We could turn our backs on Castle Knoll and
start afresh together."

We were in his car, driving back from the cinema. My mind
was still half in the film—Elizabeth Taylor and Richard Burton
in The Taming of the Shrew—*but Archie's words about open-*
ing a bakery pulled the rest of my focus to the present.

"A bakery isn't starting afresh," I said. "Not for me. It would
just be . . . having the life I had before, just somewhere else."

Archie shrugged, then reached over and tugged my earlobe
affectionately, his eyes still on the road. This time I thought about
the gesture a little more, and I couldn't decide whether or not it
carried a hint of condescension. I squeezed my eyes shut and tried
to block out my need to investigate the motive behind every touch
he gave me. That was a Frances I was trying to shed—the girl

who saw everything, even the friendly things, as mysteries containing secrets. "I understand," Archie said.

"What about London?" I offered. "You could get a stall in one of the markets there, selling records and odds and ends. We'll rent a flat and make friends and have people round for parties. Maybe I could find a course to take. I never thought about university before, but the idea appeals to me more and more."

Archie's relaxed expression became more focused, and I saw the start of worry pinching the corners of his eyes. "London just feels . . . I don't know, too big and too loud for me."

I realized then that we'd driven out of Southampton, and we were heading back toward Castle Knoll. I thought back to this morning, before we'd left for the cinema. Archie had collected everything from the hotel room and returned the key to the front desk, but I'd been too lost in the euphoria of the previous few days to think much of it.

The car was quiet for a bit, and I chewed a fingernail, thinking. "Archie," I said eventually. "What about your original motives . . . your need to expose the Gravesdown family's secrets? Have you given up on that, or is it still something you feel you have to do?"

Archie looked over at me, then his eyes snapped back to the road. "That farmhouse is mine by right," he said. "Well, mine and Eric's. But it can be ours, Frances, yours and mine. We can buy the farmland and the house from the Gravesdowns and separate those two properties forever. I'll have the money to do it, soon. It's a large house with lots of land—it deserves a family like the one we'll have."

The one we'll have. I felt something twist in my stomach, because I hadn't considered babies. When you're a woman, people talk to you your whole life in terms of when you'll have children, never if. God forbid they let you make up your own mind and keep your future out of their business.

My future—I saw the sign for Crownell approaching, and I

felt my worldview shrink again. I'd told Archie I wanted to live my life, and I'd meant it.

Archie was still talking about the life we were going to have, but I'd stopped hearing the words as my concerns for my future took over. He seemed to have it all mapped out, confident it was the right path to take.

"How long have you been thinking about this?" I asked. My head was starting to hurt, because I was grasping at too many futures at once. I clung to the affection I had for Archie—that was real, at least; I truly did love him.

Archie flushed, keeping his eyes on the road. "I mean . . ." He rubbed the back of his neck with one hand, then gripped the wheel again. Finally he glanced at me, and he looked sheepish, but his look was so enamored at the same time that I felt the unease in my stomach turn to warmth. "I've loved you for a long time, Frances," he said. His eyes were back on the road as he spoke, but the feeling in his voice told me all I needed to know. "Do you remember, a couple of months ago when we first saw each other in the library, and you made a joke about how I couldn't start seeing you just to get to Rose?"

"I remember something about that, yes," I said, not liking the thought of him and Rose together.

"Well, the reality of it was the other way around—I only went out with Rose to get to know you. You were with John, but I knew he was going behind your back."

I threw my hands in the air. "Did everyone in the village know this but me?"

Archie pulled the car over gently, to a grassy spot on the side of the road just before the roundabout that announced its exits like a series of bad choices—Crownell, Castle Knoll, Gravesdown Hall, and another to the motorway, where other destinations held bigger towns but not bigger problems.

He turned in his seat and looked at me carefully. "I promise,

John cheating was something I caught wind of accidentally. I don't think it was an open secret, and I wanted to tell you, but I didn't know you well back then. Anyway, I used to come to the bakery, and I don't think you noticed me all that much, but you were always this light behind the counter."

"I only ever remember a handful of conversations with you, Archie," I said. "I'm sorry if I should have been paying better attention."

"We only did have a handful of conversations, and I knew at the time that they meant more to me than they did to you. It's never bothered me. I just knew I'd need time to win you over."

We looked at each other, and the silence stretched out. "This investigation into the crash, and Ford . . ."

Archie looked conflicted, then resigned. "Would you like it better if I stressed that my intentions have always been good? Heart in the right place and all that?"

"Are you telling me that you've only been prodding at these secrets, this vendetta against Ford, because of . . . me?" I couldn't put the facts and his motives together—I didn't want to. It was Ford who played games, not Archie.

"All the questions and details and things that I came to you with, those are true. Do I think Ford has dark secrets that should be exposed? Of course I do! But I never had the guts to go after him until I saw you looking into Peony Lane. I knew there was common ground, and please don't be angry with me, Frances—I saw a chance, and I took it. Two birds, one stone. That sort of thing."

"Please don't mention birds," I said, my head really throbbing now. I rubbed my temples to try to sift through my recent choices, then I looked up at the roundabout ahead, at the different signs and destinations. "Actually, no—let's face these birds. Take me to Crownell," I said fiercely. "Please."

Archie let a second pass, and then another, just looking at me.

221

I think he expected me to explode at him, to question his motives and whether he was being truthful.

And I was angry, but I was angry with Peony Lane, and my fortune, and my own mind. I'd tried to turn off my belief in all this, to recklessly pursue joy and all the good things you should experience when you're young and in love. But my fate was like this many-tentacled thing, always reaching out and pulling me back into itself.

Archie started the car, and we drove the short distance to Peony Lane's house in silence. There was a light on in her sitting room, but I could only see a crack of it because she had her curtains drawn.

We rang the bell, and it took several minutes for someone to answer, but when the door opened, the woman's face peeking out wasn't Peony Lane's.

"Birdy?" Archie said, blinking in surprise. "What are you doing here?"

The woman was blond, and once Archie said her name, I recognized the similarities between her and her sister, Emily. My heart started racing and I linked arms with Archie, my other hand reaching across my chest to grip his biceps for that extra sense of security. As I did so, my ring caught the light and Birdy gasped.

"Archie?" she said, her features twisting from shock to anger. "Archie, what did you do?"

CHAPTER

31

ARCHIE FOYLE, I HAVE *SO* MANY QUESTIONS TO ASK you," I say, sounding a bit like he's my child and I'm giving him a telling-off. "Like who *exactly* have you been murdering, why are you in my house at two A.M., and what the hell is the story behind the marriage certificate that Crane and I found at Peony Lane's house?"

Shock registers on Archie's face, but interestingly, it's only when I mention the marriage certificate. Murder and breaking into Gravesdown Hall don't seem to qualify as things he's ashamed of.

"I know what it looks like," Archie says, the words rushing out. "But just let me explain. Here . . ." He holds the file out to me, and I take it gingerly. "I was just coming in because I wanted to put this back. I didn't think you'd be down here; I thought I could slip in and out and you wouldn't notice."

"Was it you that Beth let in the other day, then? The day Peony Lane was killed?" I ask, still holding the poker in one hand. If Archie killed Samantha, he very likely killed Peony Lane, too. But he seems so relaxed in the way he's talking about all this that he must be either innocent of both crimes or a complete sociopath. I'm very much hoping it's the former.

"Beth? Letting someone in the house? No, I don't think Beth would do that, and it certainly wasn't me. I was at the farm all morning; I didn't kill Peony. You even came to see me—you can vouch for me, Annie."

"By our estimation, you could have entered the house after I left on my walk, killed her, and got back to your farm just as I was arriving. It would have been tight, but possible," I say. "We've already confirmed that someone planted that dagger after Peony was already dead, so her murder could be a separate incident."

"I promise, it wasn't me," he says, and he seems sincere.

"What about Samantha? You just told us you put her body in the boot," Jenny says.

"That's why I needed to get the file back here," Archie says. "Please, can I sit down? My heart's going a mile a minute. I've got to catch my breath after the fright you just gave me. I'm not young; I can't just get startled and calm right down." He doesn't wait for my response but moves farther into the library and settles himself in one of the armchairs near the fire. He has to shuffle awkwardly between the mattresses on the floor to get there, but he goes for a specific chair, as if this is his house and he's got a favorite one.

Jenny and I stay standing but move closer. "I'm going to need those keys, by the way," I say, holding my hand out for them.

Archie shrugs and tosses the keys lightly in my direction, and I have to stoop to catch them before they land in the mountain of quilts on the floor. When they land in my palm, they're heavy and there are more of them than there should be. Plus there's a key ring on them I don't recognize—a vintage-looking enamel and metal one that I think has an eagle on it, with a faded Stars and Stripes underneath. It looks like an old souvenir from America.

"Whose keys are these? They aren't the ones I gave to Beth," I say.

"They were in Samantha's handbag, along with that file," Archie says, and his eyes dart toward the room where the files are kept. "And I'll say it again—no, I didn't kill her. I was in the garage working on one of the cars, and I heard her call to me. She had the tarpaulin off that wreck—the Gravesdown Bentley—"

"Yeah, why do you have that?" Jenny cuts in.

"That wreck was a mystery that Frances and I tried to solve and didn't quite manage. We thought we had, but . . ." He pauses, and a faraway look passes over his face. "We could never locate the wreckage of the car, and when I found out it had been walled up inside that derelict pub all these years, well, I knew I had to bring it to the farm and try to work out what happened the night of the crash and why the car was hidden there of all places."

"Go back to how Samantha got into the boot of that car," Jenny prods.

Archie looks pained for a moment, then takes a deep breath. "Samantha wanted this." He pats the pockets of the oversized wool coat he's wearing and pulls out the yellow diary. "When she called me out of the garage, she was holding the file and said she knew I had Frances's diaries. She said she'd trade the file for the yellow diary. I wasn't going to give it to her but I went inside to get it all the same. I wanted to know why she thought that file would be so valuable. I didn't know what was in it. I thought it was just all the information Frances and I had found out about Peony Lane years ago. But I wanted to wave the diary in front of her, see if it might get her talking."

225

I look at the diary hungrily, and Archie pauses and notices my gaze. His expression hardens and he puts the diary back in his coat pocket, then continues. "When I came back, Samantha was on the ground, her eyes wide open and foam coming out of her mouth. She wasn't breathing or moving—she'd clearly been poisoned. The contents of her handbag had all spilled out when she fell, and that pill organizer she always used was on the ground next to these keys."

"You think someone swapped out one of her pills?" I ask.

"Her eyesight wasn't great, so yes, I think that's exactly what happened. Someone decided to poison her, and whoever it was did it at the police station. All they'd need was access to her desk. Anyway, Eric was inside with Beth, and I just couldn't have them getting involved with all of this. So many past ghosts, you know."

"Yeah, I'd really like to know about those past ghosts, Archie, if you don't mind," I say, my voice level.

He pats his pocket absently, like he's wanting to make sure the diary is still there. "It's nothing that can help this whole mess," he says, and when he looks at me his eyes have such pain in them that I shrink back from him.

"That's not a good enough reason to hide Samantha's body," Jenny says. "Beth and Eric were there when we opened the boot, and they were sad, but it wasn't like their worlds ended. You could have left her out in the open and called the police."

"And where were you at that point? When Crane and I opened the boot?" I add.

Archie gives me a hard look. "Believe me or don't. But I'm trying to help. That file"—he points to the papers in my hand—"it's got some information in it, but not a lot. Not enough to figure out who might want Peony dead. I think Samantha thought that the diary had some deeper insights

226

into Peony's life, given Frances's past fixation on her, and that's why Samantha wanted it."

"So it sounds like both of those items together might reveal something," Jenny says.

We're quiet, but I continue to give Archie a meaningful look, putting every telepathic thought I can into willing him to give me the diary.

"Ellen—I mean Peony," Archie says, "recently she'd started talking a bit about a fortune coming close to its conclusion. An old one, she said. She was in the Dead Witch the night before she died, saying she wanted to hurry something along. She'd had a bit to drink, but she said Frances taught her a little about messing with fate. Peony really did think she'd killed the Gravesdowns. Her reasoning for all that is in this yellow diary."

Archie stands and pulls the yellow diary from his pocket. "Take this," he says, handing me the diary. "If there are secrets to be found out if the two are read together—the file and the diary—then maybe they need to be set free. Maybe it's time."

Then he walks stiffly around the mattresses and out of the library without looking back at us. We hear the boom of the front door slamming a moment later, and I look at the object in my hand. It's unassuming, and rather tattered—more so than the green diary I have from Frances's previous year.

Its pages don't sit quite flat, and the leather of the cover is worn. It's clear that Archie's read it countless times.

CHAPTER

32

ARCHIE, HOW DO YOU KNOW EMILY'S OLDER SISTER?" I asked as my thoughts started to shuffle together frantically. "Is Emily here?" I asked. "Do you know where she is?"

Birdy gave me a long look, and I watched sadness color her features. "I remember you, just a little. You were a friend of Emily's," she said quietly. When I nodded, she continued. "She's not here, and I don't know where she is. But I'm glad someone still cares."

Our eyes met, and an understanding passed between us then. The town might have forgotten about Emily, but we hadn't.

Birdy looked over at Archie again, and the look she gave him was shrewd. "Why is Olivia Gravesdown's wedding ring on this girl's finger?" she asked him harshly.

My fingers flexed as if I'd grabbed an electric wire. I pulled my hand away from Archie and looked at the stone on my ring finger. My horror at it grew—something that only moments before had been a symbol of this new life I was stepping into, of love and a future without murder, was actually a symbol of death. Archie had blatantly given me the most key piece of evidence from the very murder we'd been investigating, all while vowing to love me forever.

I swallowed hard, my throat suddenly stinging. "Did you know? Did you know that's what this was? Olivia's ring?" I asked, the tremble in my voice making me sound years younger. It was a thin slice of hope to cling to in that moment, that he might not have known about the ring's history. Was it possible he'd simply come by the ring innocently? Maybe he found it, or bought it from one of those market stalls he frequented.

But his face said it all. His eyes watered, and he reached for me. I drew back, shock hitting me so hard I struggled to stay upright. "Why?" I whispered. "Why would you put this ring"—I twisted it on my finger until it came off and I held it up between us like it was a dart I could throw at him—"on my finger, knowing where it came from?"

"Come inside," Birdy said, her voice low and urgent. "You're making a scene. I don't want the neighbors prying any more than they already do."

We stepped into the small sitting room, but the mood among the three of us was tense, and none of us sat down on the small sofas there.

"There's more to that ring than you realize," Archie said, and he reached for me again, but I pulled away. "I promise, it really does belong to me—to you now. I just haven't had time to explain. Let me tell you about it and then if you still don't want it, we can buy a matching pair of wedding bands. Something simple, but nice and new."

"There's nothing you can tell me about this ring that won't make it feel cursed!" I said, my voice gathering all the heat that had been building in my chest. The room was silent then, save for the ticking of the clock on the mantelpiece, suddenly loud and rather ominous.

"What else are you keeping from me?" I whispered finally. I

hated the suspicion that was filling me back up; it was a familiar feeling that I'd been running from these past few days. It made me feel drained, rotten, and doomed. The suspicious Frances was someone I'd seen growing from the betrayals of her friends the previous year, who was festering and worrying and losing pieces of what made life feel joyful.

It was then that another voice sounded from behind the settee where I was sitting. Peony Lane had emerged from one of the rooms down the hall and had been standing there taking in the whole scene, silently.

"You'd better tell your new wife everything, Archie, or this marriage is headed for divorce before the week's even out," Peony Lane said, crossing her arms.

Seeing her for the first time since she'd told me my fortune at the fair was a shock, not least because she wasn't dressed in her over-the-top fortune-teller's garb. She wore smart polyester trousers and a simple white blouse and wouldn't have been out of place working in an office somewhere. Perhaps this was what she did when she wasn't telling fortunes.

I blinked at her, realizing that this woman had a whole life that had nothing to do with my fate—mine was only one future among scores of predictions she'd made. In between all that, she was a person who did the mundane things we all do.

I remembered then that she and Eric Foyle had stood up against Edmund Gravesdown the only way they knew how. This was the woman who Ford told me had compiled a whole evidence file on his brother and had come up with a proper plan to take him down for good. The file that had signed affidavits from Edmund's victims, even samples of the drugs he'd used to incapacitate women, with details on where they'd been found and when.

I have to admit, I admired her organization and her careful planning to take down an evil man.

Archie opened his mouth and shut it a few times, like a fish floundering for air. When he didn't say anything, Peony Lane crossed the room to a desk and rummaged in a drawer for a moment. Finally she pulled out an envelope. Archie's name was written clearly across the front of it, and she handed it to him. "I wrote this for you."

Archie opened the envelope and scanned the writing on the paper inside. He scoffed, then put it in his pocket. "I don't believe in this fortune nonsense," he said.

I felt small then, and all those times Archie had sat patiently, taking me seriously as I talked about my fate and my worries over what was to come . . . felt so flimsy now. Tears shook me finally, and once I started crying I couldn't stop. I felt like my hope was being cruelly, casually shredded to pieces.

"Was it all an act? Did you ever care about me, or did you see me as some kind of means to an end? You planted those seeds of doubt about Ford, you . . ." I rounded on him, fighting to find the words for just how betrayed I felt. And how scared I was. Because if I couldn't trust my own heart, if I couldn't trust my own ability to feel love and be loved, who could I trust?

"Frances, please, it's not like that!" Archie pulled me close to him, but I pushed at his chest, fresh tears staining the front of the coat he hadn't taken off. "I love you, and I've never lied to you. We'll get through this, you and I. If you want, we can sell that ring."

"You said you've never lied to me, but you have! This argument you had with Eric? A high-stakes poker game, with Ford fleecing him? That never happened, did it? Did it!" I shouted at him, and Birdy winced from the armchair where she was perched, but once I started letting myself be loud, I wasn't going to stop. "Your argument with Eric—it was the other way around! He refuses to talk to you because you were the one who 'lost' this valuable item," I screamed, my voice shrill and desperate.

"What makes you more unhappy, Frances? The fact that I

stole from the Gravesdowns, or the fact that I stole from my brother?" Archie's posture settled, and I regarded the change in his expression from contrite to calm with dawning horror.

"Who are you, Archie Foyle? And what the hell have you done?" I whispered.

"Perhaps Peony can share where she's hidden a very significant knife," Archie said, looking at Peony as if I hadn't spoken.

I felt a shock of ice through my veins at the mention of a knife. In the back of my mind, an image of that ruby-handled dagger Emily had talked about was becoming even clearer. The red stone in Olivia's wedding ring (I could never think of it as mine now), the ruby in the dagger . . . were they just insidious clues in the mystery of how Archie had defrauded the Gravesdowns? Or was he a part of their whole tragedy somehow?

"All of you are going to tell me everything," I said heavily. "Right now."

CHAPTER

33

November 3

OF COURSE WE STAY UP ALL NIGHT READING THE DI-
ary. It doesn't occur to me to write down the feelings I have
as I read, but my fingers are shaking with emotion and lack
of sleep as I flip through the pages. By the time dawn breaks
I feel numb with confusion and outrage on behalf of the
players on the page. Heartbreaks that aren't my own and
wounds that have decades of dust on them are brought to
life as if they are fresh and uniquely mine.

I understood every choice Frances made and why she'd
made it, but the one thing I don't understand when I get to
the end of her diary is what really happened the night of the
crash.

So then Jenny and I take the file apart and examine every
scrap of paper in it, and every scribbled note Frances made.
We add more logs to the fire, make coffee, breakfast on leftovers, and pace the library sharing theories.

Peony Lane's file is confusing because it doesn't contain
notes about her life or who she was as a person. Instead,

inside the file bearing her name holds the evidence against Edmund Gravesdown that Peony Lane had delivered to Ford all those years ago. The file that was supposed to have stayed with the police, the crimes within investigated, and the evidence used to expose Edmund—albeit posthumously—as the criminal he was.

We both agree that this is significant, but we can't place exactly how.

Finally we sleep, and the morning passes us by that way.

When we emerge again it's early afternoon, and my mind feels hazy in a way that reminds me of something halfway between jet lag and a fever.

"We've been coming at this all wrong," I say, chewing one of the stale croissants we found in the cupboard.

"How do you mean?" Jenny replies, pouring us both mugs of coffee.

"There's a big question we're forgetting to ask, which is, *Why now?* Last summer, a set of events occurred that meant that finally, after all these years, someone murdered Frances."

Jenny nods. "Ah, I see what you mean. So what changed very recently, enough that Peony Lane suddenly became a target for someone who was connected to her past?"

We're quiet for a moment, thinking. "Something that stands out to me," I say eventually, "is that the pub collapsed, exposing that the Gravesdown wreck had been hiding in there all this time. It fits Archie's fortune—*It begins with a secret revealed . . .*"

"But we're talking about Peony Lane," Jenny says. "That fortune bothers me, actually. The fact that Peony Lane had it in her hand when she died—what if we're applying it wrong? Or to the wrong person, maybe?"

"That's an interesting thought," I say. "I wonder if Peony

Lane had a revelation when that pub collapsed and exposed the wreck. What if, all those years ago, a fortune came to her that she couldn't quite place?" I say, picking up my mug of coffee and pacing the library.

"What do you mean?" Jenny asks, watching.

"One of the last things Peony said to me was, 'Frances taught me a thing or two about cheating fate.' And when she died, she was holding Archie's fortune, with the word *MINE* scrawled across it." I stop pacing and look at the fire, and my eyes lose focus for a moment. The flames blur in smudges of amber and yellow light, then snap back into sharp relief along with my thoughts. "In Frances's diary, Peony Lane hands Archie a written fortune, but she never directly states that it's his. What if she suspected it could be hers *or* his but didn't know which?"

Jenny nods slowly. "And when the pub collapsed, she realized and finally claimed it, writing *MINE* across it. But then she'd have wanted to go straight to Archie, to tell him."

"What if she did? She mentioned Foyle Farms to me in the woods, told me there was something there I should get. And that phrase in the fortune . . . *You cannot cast the shadow of a shape that's not your own* . . . I think there's more to that. Frances's account in the diary has me thinking that the whole group of friends were lying to protect one another, had been for years, and some physical evidence on that wrecked Bentley was going to expose the one who was actually a murderer."

"How?"

"I don't know, but I need to have another look at that wreck and hopefully discover something new," I say.

Jenny sighs and absently shuffles some of the papers she's laid out in front of her. "Let's focus on the puzzle of all these papers and how it might be solved with that diary. You think Frances knew who killed Olivia Gravesdown, but she just . . . let them walk around free all this time? Never bringing the killer to justice? That doesn't sound like her," Jenny says.

"On the surface, no, it doesn't seem like something she would do. But look, these pieces of evidence—they're mostly to do with Edmund Gravesdown's crimes. He was a horrific predator, but . . . Ford's story in Frances's diary, about how Olivia was compiling all this to bring her husband down and stop him for good . . ."

I reach over the pile of papers, picking up a signed witness statement from one of Edmund's victims. Reading it makes my hand shake and my stomach boil with anger, but the final twist is that the woman said she was visited later by a member of the Gravesdown family, who threatened her into silence.

"This statement doesn't say which member of the Gravesdown family this was," I say, pointing to the words on the page. "What if . . . what if we all had it wrong, and we assumed Olivia would be outraged by her husband's crimes but in reality . . ."

Jenny's voice drops to a horrified whisper. "She was complicit."

I nod, swallowing hard. "There are only two reasons I can think of for Frances to know who committed a murder and not to expose them. One is if the victim was someone Frances felt probably deserved it."

"I mean, does anyone deserve that, though? All that 'eye for an eye' stuff is just—"

"I'm only saying that from Frances's hypothetical perspective; this isn't a philosophical conversation about the nature of justice," I say, pinching the bridge of my nose. I stand up and add two more logs to the fire, staring at them and willing them to catch. "The other reason I can think of for Frances to protect a murderer is if it was someone she loved. And . . ." I take a deep breath, inhaling the scent of the dry oak logs as the embers finally catch them. "I think in this case, it was possibly both."

"You mean . . ."

"That the person who killed Olivia was either Archie or Ford. And somewhere between the diary and the file, there's concrete proof of it. Frances may have protected the killer, but she was fastidious in her secret gathering—she wouldn't want the information to die with her, not if it still might matter one day."

"Well, it looks like she was right—it matters now."

CHAPTER

34

ADDENDUM, ADDED JUNE 10, 1970. THE FORTUNE SAYS,
"You cannot cast the shadow of a shape that's not your own," but
in these lines I have made every effort to try. Because it is I who
hold the pen, and the shadow in this story was never mine to be-
gin with.—Frances Adams Gravesdown

THE ONLY PLACE for Archie to sit was on the same small settee
as me, but I moved slightly to put a few inches between us. I still
held the ruby ring in my hand, refusing to put it on again but not
ready to cast it away.

Birdy was opposite us, and I finally took a breath and really
looked at her. She had some of Emily's features—the blond hair,
for one—but there were some striking differences too. She was
about four years older than me, in her early twenties, and seemed
more contained than Emily. More beaten down by the world too,
possibly, which I suppose made sense, if she'd run away from
home several years earlier. All this time we'd thought she was
somewhere far away, but she'd only flown to the next town.

Her clothes were faded but clean, and didn't fit her well—she looked as if she'd filled them out properly at one point but had grown thin against her will. Like with each thing life had taken from her, a physical piece of her had gone too. Or maybe I was projecting my ideas, because she seemed a little like a ghost. It was like an almost-Emily was watching me, her eyes less calculating but just as clever.

"The first thing you need to know," Peony Lane said, as she moved to sit next to Birdy, "is that all three of those Gravesdowns deserved it. Whatever you might think about justice and doing the official right thing, Olivia, Edmund, and Harry Gravesdown were untouchable as far as the law was concerned."

"Did you kill them?" I asked plainly. I didn't know who I was asking, really. For all I knew, they'd all killed the Gravesdowns together.

"You should hear this from him," Birdy said, and jutted her chin toward Archie. "Your husband." Hearing her refer to him as my husband did something odd to me. I felt like a coin was flipping in my mind. My affection for Archie still didn't waver; it was something real and I almost hated that it was so rooted within me. But now my choices over the previous few days looked less like a strong woman taking control of her future and more like a scared girl trying on a new life only to find out that it doesn't fit.

I looked at Archie and schooled my features into a careful challenge. "You knew about all this?" I hissed. "And you were, what? Playacting with me in our 'investigation' into this crash, when all along you knew so much more than you let on?" My voice was rising again, tears constricting my throat and making my words sound shaky and strange. "Archie, were you there?!"

He looked at his knees and quickly wiped the corner of his eye. He looked young, too, in that moment. It was like my coin flip took both of us when it turned. Archie wasn't the cavalier man who'd do anything to please me; he was a boy who'd lost his family and his home and was consumed by revenge. Consumed enough to lie to me, to keep secrets from me, all for a twisted goal that had been brewing inside him for years.

And it looked like he was on his way to getting it—his revenge—though I still doubted Ford was going to topple, like the single domino left standing in a row of crooked people. Ford wasn't his family; for all the other mistakes he'd made, he wasn't a criminal. That I knew of.

"Eric had been working for Edmund Gravesdown for about two years, as his valet. At first, it seemed like a cushy job. He was paid well and got some great perks that people don't normally give their valets. He was bought nice clothes, given books and expensive bottles of wine—even a gold watch.

"But the longer Eric worked for Edmund, the more withdrawn he became. I'd ask him about his work, and he'd snap at me to stay out of it. When I'd ride my bicycle up to the estate to give him a message or say hello in passing, he'd shoo me off like I was a rat begging for scraps. Finally, after one particularly bad day, Eric got drunk and confessed that his job didn't just consist of valet duties. I'll stress here that Eric didn't know the extent of Edmund's crimes at that point, but it was Eric's job to deliver bribes to the police, or rough up a bartender if he'd been caught saying things that were too close to the truth. But one day, someone at the police station came to him with information he couldn't ignore."

"Samantha," I said, my voice almost a whisper. "She's your police informant, isn't she?"

"Yes. It was Samantha who saw the extent of the injustice. She saw victims fail to be heard, get told horrible things about themselves or their lives. She was told to destroy evidence, refuse calls, and take bribes. But she didn't—or, at least, she fought back in the only way she knew how. By keeping things she was told to get rid of, by taking statements and playing detective herself.

Soon, her friend Ellen—Peony Lane—learned some of the things that were happening, and she joined the fight in her own way."

"Did you know all this then, as it was happening?" I asked.

Archie shook his head. "Other than what Eric told me that night he got drunk, no. I just knew they were ganging up against the Gravesdowns and needed to be stealthy about it. I was sixteen, bored, and feeling like I wanted in. Eric had this life that I desired—he had so many pretty girlfriends." Archie looked at Birdy, who rolled her eyes. "He was with Ellen, then they split and he found Birdy Sparrow. Eric was like a tornado of adventure for whoever he was with, and I wanted to be that too."

I felt my jaw clench. "Like with me?" The words were out of my mouth before I could stop them, but I had to know. "Are you just trying to echo something you watched Eric do, so you can live out some boyhood fantasy?"

Archie reached for my hand and I was slow to pull it away, so when his warm fingers wrapped around mine I froze with the jolt of his affection. "No." He whispered the word into the back of my hand as he pulled it to his lips. He kissed it, and though I felt my heart twist with the beginnings of a grief that I could already tell was going to rend me in two, I couldn't pull away. "And you know that, Frances. And I'm going to be here, fighting for you, getting us through this. I'm steady, underneath it all."

Tears pricked my eyes again, and I sniffed them back. I tried to focus on the story at hand, even if I knew that pulling my own feelings out of the moment was just lying to myself.

"You best just tell her what you did," Peony said. "Get it out of the way and out in the open." She was watching us with a stern expression, like she was already tired of our drama.

"I went up to see Eric one evening, and Olivia was the only one home," Archie began. "I was going to turn back around, but she invited me inside. I'd never been inside Gravesdown Hall, and Olivia was being so nice—I didn't think there was anything *untoward about her; I thought the evil in the family was just the men. The reality of it was that I was bait, someone to threaten Eric with, and I'd walked right into her hands. Eric had already started to refuse to do some of the things they were asking him to do, and the family were getting worried he was going to talk. Worse still, they'd seen Ford with Samantha, and the rift in the family was growing worse by the day. If anyone was going to take the family down, it was going to be the youngest son. And if Eric and Samantha gave Ford the information he needed, well . . . Ford might as well have had an army."*

"I don't understand how Olivia was going to use you as bait," I said.

"Olivia gave me some brandy and biscuits, and then Edmund and Harry arrived. They were arguing, but they stopped once they saw me standing there with Olivia. I started to realize I'd walked into a hornet's nest when she snaked an arm around my shoulders, cooing in that syrupy voice she had about how nice it was to have another Foyle boy in the house. I tried to move away, but her hand clamped on my arm so hard I had bruises in the shape of her fingertips the next day.

"Edmund grinned at me and I swear it was like I was a fox about to be given a head start before the hounds were set loose. I remember everything he said like it was yesterday.

"'Well then,' Edmund said. 'It's a perfect time to show him the car. Let's all drive you home—we can visit your brother.' This look passed between all three of them, and I knew then that Eric had refused them something, or had been caught betraying them in some way. And I knew that I was about to be used to convince him to fall back in line.

"Olivia finally let go of my shoulder, and the three Gravesdowns moved as one toward the door. There was a moment, a few seconds maybe, where they huddled together to whisper some secret or plan. We were in the library, and I was near the writing

desk, where this ruby-handled dagger was just sitting, being used as a letter opener. I took a chance and swiped it, sticking it inside the waistband of my trousers. If I was going to be forced into their car, I was going in armed."

"So he took the knife out of self-preservation," Birdy said, her face softening a bit. "And let's none of us forget that you were still only sixteen."

The ghost of a smile crossed Archie's face. "Foyle years are like dog years. Sixteen as a Foyle is like forty for everyone else."

Birdy laughed then, but it was a sad sort of laugh. Like she understood, and felt bad about it.

Archie still hadn't let go of my hand, but I didn't pull it back. His was trembling slightly, and I worried about what truths he was about to share.

"They drove me to the farmhouse, all of us in the Bentley. Olivia and I went in the back seat together, and every now and again she'd give me a hawkish look. That whole night plays in my head on a loop, and whenever a Gravesdown looks at me, I'm prey. I have nightmares where I'm a fox or a mouse or a pheasant. Something to be hunted, but toyed with first.

"'Now, Alfie, is it?' Olivia said as we pulled into the drive of the farmhouse. The lights were on inside, and I knew my father was away. It could only be Eric, or Eric and one of his friends.

"'Archie,' I corrected her. It was instinctive, to give her my proper name, and I wish I hadn't done that. It would have made the whole thing feel more amusing to her, that she threatened me and got my name wrong.

"'Of course,' she cooed. She reached out and ran a hand through my hair, and it felt like nails running down a blackboard. Her husband had switched off the engine, and he and his father were having a conversation in the front seat, low and urgent. 'Now, your brother, Eric, has been extremely naughty,' she said. I felt myself recoil when she said 'naughty.' She pouted when she talked, and it made my stomach churn. I felt for her son, Saxon. 'We've given Eric everything, my husband and I—and he's repaid us by going behind our backs with someone who works for the police. But you're a good boy, aren't you?' She cupped my cheek with her hand, and I swear I was considering biting one of her fingers off. Then she suddenly sprang into action, opening the car door and grabbing me by the arm to pull me out behind her. 'Eric!' she yelled. 'We know you're in there. Come out and see this adorable little lamb I've found!'

"Her husband and father-in-law didn't get out of the car, and when they turned to look at us, they both seemed almost bored. Edmund turned to her slowly as he lit a cigarette. Then he exhaled smoke in an annoyed way and made a gesture like he was shooing us away.

"'Round the back of the house,' he barked. 'We'll watch the drive. If Eric doesn't give us what we want, it'll be a tragic drowning accident for this one.'

"I thought of pulling the knife out then, but there were three of them. I knew that around the other side of our farmhouse, Eric and I could deal with Olivia and then escape into the woods."

"Something tells me that's not what happened," I said. I didn't know how to feel, because even as Archie told his story, sitting there holding my hand, I was afraid for him. These events were years past, and still my mind felt tricked into worrying for his sixteen-year-old self.

"It's not what happened," Archie confirmed. "Because Eric wasn't in the farmhouse; she was." He nodded across from us. "And you ran out of the back door of the farmhouse when you heard Olivia shouting for Eric. When Olivia saw that we weren't alone, it was like her anger doubled. It would be inaccurate to say that Olivia supported her husband's crimes—it was more that she felt that powerful people had the right to do whatever they

244

wanted. She didn't like the weak or the disadvantaged having the upper hand in any way.

"I think that was the moment when she decided to kill me," Archie added.

I inhaled sharply and felt his hand squeeze mine in a quick pulse of reassurance. It both worked and didn't. It told me that this story was one of kill or be killed, and I was glad Archie hadn't been killed, but I knew who had. The conflict of knowing she was a terrible person was at war with my sense of justice, but then— what was justice? What was fair, if Samantha was being threatened and paid to destroy evidence, and the police were happy to look the other way?

"Olivia pushed me toward the canal that wraps around the farmhouse. The bank back there is less pristine than around the front of the house—there are rocks littering one side of it and I used those rocks to my advantage, skittering among them and pretending to lose my footing. I grabbed the knife from my waistband while I was doubled over, but Olivia pushed me hard from behind, sending me sprawling over the rocks and to the edge of the water. I felt her hand around my neck, and she pressed my face into the water while I struggled to keep hold of the knife.

"I wasn't the burliest sixteen-year-old, but when I felt someone take the knife from my hand, panic made me able to throw Olivia off my back so that I could come up for air. But I only managed to gulp half a breath before that knife blade was at my throat. Olivia was wild, hissing in my ear—'You need to have a nice, neat drowning, so be a good boy. But don't think I can't make your body disappear if I have to cut your throat. Maybe I'll make big brother do it, hmm?'

"And that was when I grabbed the rock from under my knees, thinking that if she was going to cut my throat, she'd at least get a rock in the face for her trouble. It happened almost instantly—

I whirled around and smashed the rock into her forehead. She collapsed onto the canal bank, the blood on her face looking black in the moonlight.

"'You had better pray you haven't killed her,' Edmund Gravesdown said to me a in a low, menacing voice. He was looming over us, but his face was stern rather than furious. He still had a cigarette burning in one hand, and he took a long drag of it while staring at Olivia with calculating eyes. 'The bodies of two reckless teenagers can be explained away, but the death of my wife cannot.' He reached down and felt for the pulse at her neck but gave no indication as to whether he felt it or not. 'I would be hard-pressed to find another wife as loyal as Olivia,' he said, and he spoke about her more like she was an employee than someone he loved. It was clear from watching Edmund stalk around his wife's limp form that he was someone who saw people as things— women especially. Olivia just happened to be a thing that was very useful to him.

"'I'm afraid you'll have to come for a drive now,' he said. 'You'—he pointed to me—'help me get her into the boot. And you'—he pointed again—'get in the back seat.' He threw his cigarette into the river and grabbed Olivia's legs. Terrified, I grabbed her arms, and we struggled to carry the weight of her toward the Bentley.

"'What the devil . . . ?' Harry Gravesdown—Lord Gravesdown—was still in the passenger seat of the car, and he turned to see Edmund and me carrying Olivia like she was a heavy sack of grain. Edmund put down her legs and I let go of her arms, while he ran to get the keys to open the boot. I should have noticed her ring then, but I was too dazed by what we'd done, too worried about the consequences, to take in any details properly."

Archie looked up blearily, focusing on a spot on the wall above everyone's heads. "It was then that you told me to run. I didn't *want to leave you, but I knew I was the faster runner and I could get help. I hated the fact that I ran," Archie said. "I look back and wonder how things would have been different if I'd stayed. But I ran—and after that, it all becomes your story."*

We both look expectantly at the person across from us.

"The first thing I want to tell you," she says, "which I've never told anyone else before, is that although Archie and I thought we'd killed Olivia, I soon learned that she was still alive. Only a minute into the drive, we heard her screaming and pounding to get out. And her husband just kept on driving."

CHAPTER
35

JENNY RETREATS TO HER BEDROOM TO ANSWER SOME urgent work emails, so I'm left to face the piles of papers and my own frustration. But then I think of the dagger—how the last time I was staring at a dead end, Jenny and I focused on loose ends that we might have already had information for.

I open my phone, and my thumb pauses over the security camera app. I've looked at the footage from the morning Peony Lane died countless times, but maybe I need to focus less on who was coming and going, and more on the details that might tell a story I've overlooked. I scroll through to find the file the police isolated—the small span of seconds where Beth comes to the door, opens it, delivers the deli basket, and secretly lets someone else in through the double door.

It was wet that morning, so Beth was in her tan mac, but she had her umbrella open as well. It actually obscured her face, and had it not been for the familiar deli basket and the general shape of her, I'd have thought it could be anyone.

My heart hammers as the full realization of this hits me. *It could be anyone.*

I rewind the footage and watch it over and over again, looking closely at every detail. I zoom in on the person's hand, and it's the keys I recognize first, followed by the paint under her fingernails.

It's Mum.

Those are her keys, the ones I gave her when she last came to stay—I recognize her key ring from the Barbican dangling down.

"The ceramic cat," I whisper. "No one else would have known where to look for the file keys. Damn it, Mum!" I smack my palm down on the nearest bookshelf, hard enough that it stings, rattling several of the ornaments sitting there.

After that, the events come tumbling into my mind like dead leaves shaken from a tree. Birdy and Mum have become closer lately, with Mum suddenly deciding she was desperate for the file on Peony Lane. Mum posing as Beth would be easy—those tan macs are popular, and the deli sells those hampers prepacked. Beth's actual delivery probably didn't get made because the house was cordoned off by police just after lunch. I'd told Beth never to worry about timing her deliveries consistently, just to fit me in whenever it was convenient to her day.

When I dial Mum's number, my hand is shaking. She doesn't pick up, so I call again, and again. I fire off several text messages, call one more time, and get sent straight to voicemail.

I'm heading out to look into something, I text Jenny. *Don't worry, will call Crane for backup. Stay here xx*

I peel out of the gravel drive in the black BMW, seething with worry and anger at what Mum could now be mixed up in. Sparrows may not migrate, but this bird seemed to be returning to my orbit again and again.

———

I TAKE THE twisting backroads toward Castle Knoll at a speed that's far less gentle than my usual meander, but I slow down slightly when I recognize the bend in the road where the Gravesdown crash occurred. The road is empty, save for me, so I pull the car over onto the verge and turn the engine off.

I approach the fateful tree cautiously, but when I reach it there's nothing but a wide expanse of moss-covered trunk. Its branches reach out over the road, and they look almost cheerful with their changing leaves still clinging to them. Evening is closing in, and there's a golden haze hanging over the field just beyond the tree. I don't know what I expected. Some kind of scar where the car hit, maybe? Or perhaps I just wanted to stand in this spot—the place where everything changed for the Gravesdowns forever.

As I turn and walk back to my car, I look over the open field behind the tree and something strikes me. The village is really close to this spot. I can see the church spire above the tree line on the other side of the field, and even the backs of a few garden fences. It would take me all of two minutes to run from where I stand, through the field, and end up on the high street.

Someone could have easily gotten to the crash site from the village and returned again before being seen.

I have the yellow diary on the passenger seat beside me, and before I start driving again, I phone Crane. He picks up on the second ring, and I can't help but smile at the idea that he'd see my call flash up and rush to answer it.

"Annie, are you okay?" Crane sounds a little breathy, like he's walking somewhere.

"Yeah, I'm fine, but thanks for asking," I reply, my voice

betraying a little of the warmth I was feeling a second ago. "I just wanted to ask about Saxon and Elva—can you tell me if their alibis check out?"

Crane pauses. "I mean, technically that would be giving you a bit too much information into the investigation . . ."

I sigh. "It's more because I want to visit Saxon on a personal matter. I've got some of Aunt Frances's diary entries about things she learned about his mother, Olivia, and the rest of his family. These are things that I think would help bring him closure but that he might not like hearing. I'm just doing my due diligence when it comes to my safety—if Saxon is still a possibility for having killed Peony Lane, I'd like to know." What I don't say is that I'm hoping my candor in bringing him the diary might make it easier to get him to tell me anything he might remember about the night his parents died, or anything significant that happened after. Specifically, I'd like to know if he ever crossed paths with Birdy Sparrow.

I hear the shuffle of feet on gravel—he's thinking. "Okay," Crane says finally. "Yes, his alibi checks out, as does Elva's. Saxon was staying at the Castle House Hotel because he and Elva are having marital problems, apparently. He was seen by several staff members throughout the morning; he never left the restaurant and he read a whole book, cover to cover, to pass the time. Elva's gardener is her alibi—at the time of the murder she was shouting at him for planting the wrong color hydrangeas. He has no reason to cover for her, because she fired him later that afternoon—so he's not lying to try to keep his job."

"Thank you," I say.

"I'd still advise caution where Saxon is concerned," Crane says.

"Don't worry, I know that better than anyone," I answer, and hang up.

The drive to Saxon's house only takes another ten minutes, and he answers the door as if he's been waiting and I'm late.

When he sees the yellow diary in my hand, his brow creases, and he ushers me inside wordlessly. When we're settled in the pristine living room again, I try to choose my words carefully.

"Have you seen this diary before?" I ask.

Saxon gives me a long look, like he's considering how much truth to tell.

"Look, I know we aren't close," I continue. "And I'm not trying to change that, but I had a revelation today—I don't know my dad; he ran out on my mum while she was pregnant with me. But I have a file on him. If I wanted to learn about him, even if that means learning about his crimes or his secrets, I have that choice. If I wanted to dive deeper, I could."

"I've never seen that diary," Saxon replies. His voice is soft, and the lines in his face deepen. Saxon has always looked good for his age—I think he's somewhere in his sixties, but he could easily pass for fifties—but in letting his guard down, it's like I can see the years creeping over him.

I hold it out to him. "There are things about your parents and grandfather in here that, if they're true, will be hard to learn. But I just thought—I mean, if it were me, I'd at least want the choice of finding out. I know you've been looking into that crash, and I think there are answers in this diary. I think the death of Peony Lane holds clues too. I just need a little more time to make sense of them. But I wanted to offer you the chance to know what's in here, if you wanted it."

Saxon doesn't take his eyes off the diary, and it's a long time before he speaks again. "I'm betting the things in there you're referring to have been whispered around town for years. Some of it has reached my ears and I'm under no illusions that my parents were completely upstanding people."

"Has that affected your need to look into the crash?" I ask. "Because you said you've been trying to solve this puzzle for years."

"I have, and I don't think it's a coincidence that when I finally get closer—finding a key piece of evidence—someone dies."

"What do you mean?" I sit up a bit straighter. "What piece of evidence?"

"Why don't I make us a drink," he says, "and I'll tell you what I know."

CHAPTER

36

KNOWING THAT ARCHIE DIDN'T KILL ANYONE SETTLED *my nerves a little. I looked away from him and across the room again, at the two women sitting on the sofa. "How did you survive the car crash? And how did Olivia's body get in the road?"*

"These are all things I want to know too," Archie said. "Eric never gave me a straight answer—it was like you all closed ranks, leaving me out."

"Because we didn't want you any more involved in this than you had to be. The truth is, I was knocked unconscious when the car hit the tree. When I came to, the boot was open, Olivia was dead in the road, and her wedding ring was missing. What I do know is that whoever came on the scene while I was unconscious not only released Olivia from the boot and killed her, but also left me for dead—or left me to take the fall if it was discovered that Olivia had actually been murdered. So I ran. And I never found out who came along while I was unconscious."

"Do you know how the car ended up hitting the tree?" I asked.

"That's the easy part. I reached from the back seat over Edmund's shoulder and jerked the wheel, causing the car to spin out *of control. I only meant to get the car into a ditch or something, so that I could get away. I didn't count on how fast Edmund was driving, and I only realized later how close I came to being killed myself. The last thing I remember hearing, as my vision blurred and I smelled burned rubber and petrol, was a woman screaming."*

"As in, screaming from inside the boot? Or screaming out in the open air?" I asked.

"It's hard to be sure, but it sounded clear to me. Not muffled," she said.

"And you don't remember anything else?" Archie asked, and his expression was strange—his eyes were tight with some emotion; worry, maybe, or perhaps anticipation. It was like there was an answer he was looking for, but either she couldn't remember what it was or she wanted to keep it to herself. The latter didn't make any sense, if whoever had left her behind was willing to let her bleed there unconscious, without any help.

But some knowledge passed between them then, and instinctively I knew something wasn't right.

CHAPTER

37

I DECLINE THE WHISKY SAXON OFFERS ME, SO HE JUST shrugs and tops his own up another inch. He's wheeled an antique wooden bar cart next to him, and I swear I saw a photo of that exact piece of furniture in the Gravesdown insurance inventory files, but I don't mention it.

We settle into chairs in his all-white sitting room as the last of the sun sinks behind the hills beyond his huge windows. He pushes a button, and a gas fireplace contained behind smoky glass springs to life instantly.

"What do you remember about that night?" I ask gently. "You were what, seven years old? Eight?"

Saxon nods. "I know my childhood memories probably can't be wholly trusted, so take them with a pinch of salt. Most of the things I remember about that night are the nonsense things that children find important, rather than the facts you'll want. I remember things like Peony Lane giving me boiled sweets and teaching me how to shuffle a deck of cards. It took all evening, but she was patient with me, and I got it eventually. I even remember the cards—they had American flags on the back; it was a souvenir deck my father had given me, from his recent business trip to New York."

"Wait—that's interesting, Saxon, can you go back a bit? Start with Peony Lane. Do you mean you saw her when she came to bring Ford the evidence file against your father?" I ask.

Saxon nods. "All I remember is the adults arguing, honestly. One minute Peony Lane was there talking to my uncle, the next she was ushering me into the kitchen because my father came in and started shouting. I can't be sure, but looking back on it all now, I think Uncle Ford got irrefutable evidence against my father and confronted him right away." Saxon leans over toward the bar cart and opens one of its wooden doors. He pulls out a silver flask, but it's encased in an evidence bag—it's even sealed and dated.

"I thought I saw something that night," he continues, "but I could never be sure, until I found this hidden in the house years after the crash."

"Frances wrote about Ford drinking from a flask like that," I say, and Saxon hands it to me. "Why is this in a police evidence bag?"

"That isn't Ford's flask; it's my father's."

I turn it over in my palm and notice the inscription— *Edmund James Gravesdown, Fraternitas omnia vincit.* "Brotherhood conquers all," I whisper.

Saxon nods again. "It's in the evidence bag because I paid to have it analyzed a few years ago. I didn't even remember what I saw that night until I found the flask in a hidden drawer in my uncle's desk. But once I saw it, it came back to me. My father raging around the library, his flask open and abandoned on the end table. And my uncle holding that file, with a plastic bag from inside it, containing several white pills. When my father's back was turned, Ford slipped those pills into the flask. The recent forensic tests done on the flask confirm this—there were still traces there."

"I . . . Oh my God," I say. "Does this mean Ford caused that crash? That Edmund hit the tree because he lost consciousness, being dosed by the same drugs he'd given his victims?"

"I don't think my uncle intended that; I think he was actually trying to incapacitate my father so that he didn't hurt himself or anyone else and the police could be called. When he found out that my father had taken the flask with him and got behind the wheel of his car, Uncle Ford ran to his own car to follow. I think he was trying to stop him; I honestly think he didn't want anyone hurt."

"Frances's diary obscures all of this," I say. And I realize those passages she wrote about the night of the crash are strange. Something about them is off; they don't read like her normal keen-eyed observations and theorizing. Her addendum at the start of the entry at Peony Lane's house even admits as much: *It is I who hold the pen, and the shadow in this story was never mine to begin with.*"

"Well, she would have obscured the details, wouldn't she? She was protecting the man she loved," Saxon says.

"I suppose," I say slowly. "I just . . . don't see why she had to. Hiding the flask would've been all she needed to do to conceal Ford's involvement."

I sit there for a moment, lost in thought. When I don't say anything more, Saxon stands.

"You keep that," he says, gesturing to the diary. "When I decide I'm ready for it, I'll find you."

I reverse out of Saxon's drive and take the road back to Gravesdown Hall, going at least ten miles over the speed limit, not bothering to slow down even when I pass that fateful tree.

CHAPTER

38

MY PHONE RINGS AS I ARRIVE BACK AT GRAVESDOWN Hall, and I answer as I'm rushing through the hallway toward the library. "Detective Crane," I say, and I'm a little breathless. "Perfect timing—I'm onto something, can you—"

He cuts me off, and the seriousness of his tone sends my stomach to the floor. "This is a courtesy call, Annie, just so you're not shocked when a group of officers arrive to bring you to the station for questioning."

"I— What? Why?" I try to think through the fake phone call evidence of me "calling" to complain about Peony Lane coming to my house, and the appearance of the dagger in Peony Lane's back. How could that possibly matter *right now* of all times? If they were going to take me in for questioning, or arrest me on suspicion of Peony Lane's murder, why didn't they do it days ago?

"We found some evidence that links you to Samantha's death," he says gravely.

"You can't seriously think that I—"

"I'm not saying I do," he says.

I feel relieved—partly because it means I still have an ally, and also because I hate the idea that Crane might think I was capable of killing someone. "But we just got the results back on Samantha. She was killed by ingesting a large amount of lead that was mixed with water, and not by something planted in her pillbox, as we initially suspected. So we tested the water bottle at her desk, and it came back positive for those amounts of lead. Annie, you're on the police security footage handing her the exact water bottle, and standing there watching her drink it."

"It was on her desk—I was only being helpful! I didn't bring it to the police station with me, that must be clear from the footage. You can't seriously arrest me over this, it's absurd!" I start to feel my shoulders loosen because the police have no leg to stand on, if this is what they're building a case on.

"There's more," he says darkly. "Hair and fibers from Samantha's body were found in the boot of the car you've been driving. The BMW. It looks very likely that Samantha's body was transported to Foyle Farms in your car."

"That's not my car! And when did you manage a forensic examination of it without my knowledge? And her body couldn't have been in there; she came to Foyle Farms on her own, she—" I stop talking, wondering how many steps ahead of me Samantha's killer is. "Wait, don't you need a warrant to search my car?" I splutter.

"Yes, and we got one, and issued it to Archie Foyle, the owner of that car. The search was executed while the car was parked in front of Gravesdown Hall yesterday." Yesterday, when I'd spent hours in the library with Jenny, not bothering to so much as look out the window. What Crane says about the warrant makes sense—I don't own that car, so how could I have given permission for it to be searched? The betrayal of not being told is what stings more than anything. I want to believe it was Marks calling the shots, but Crane's hands can't be clean in this.

"That's rubbish!" I shout. "Why didn't you warn me?"

"Legally we didn't have to, but, Annie, I promise if I'd known I'd have talked to you about it. I was left out of the loop, presumably because it's known that we're . . . friends." He hesitates on that last word, and I feel the hurt and anger mixing together in my chest.

"Someone planted that evidence! Why not arrest Archie? It's *his* car! He was even here late last night—he said Samantha collapsed at his farm and he put her body in the boot of the Bentley to conceal it."

"Annie, the only facts the police are interested in right now are that you've been the only one seen driving the BMW in the past few days, and that multiple witnesses saw you driving it to Foyle Farms, where you were then seen poking around the wreck of the old Bentley."

"Let me guess, the police's key witnesses in this case are Beth and Eric Foyle, am I right? And maybe Archie himself? Come on, Crane, you know this is a complete setup."

Jenny rushes in and looks at me frantically. "Annie," she says. "Sirens, coming up the long drive."

"Shit," I say. I steel myself and shoot Jenny a determined look. "Okay, I'll handle this," I tell Jenny, and I hang up the phone before Crane can say anything more. "I think I need to run," I say, not quite believing my own choices. "Chief Inspector Marks doesn't like me *or* Crane, and I don't think he's going to play fair at all. I just need a little more time to put the rest of the pieces together to clear my name—but I'm close, Jenny."

The sun has gone down, and the full dark that's descended makes the flash of the police lights even more prominent.

Several loud booms come from someone pounding a fist against the front door, and I hear someone call my name in a rough growl.

"Come on, I'll go with you," Jenny says, and she grabs my arm. "Nothing like a quick exit through the solarium, right?" The irony of how circular this all is isn't lost on me.

That line from Archie's fortune slithers through my mind: *One death with three to blame, or three deaths with one to blame— the circle must complete.*

I don't have time to think about what completing the circle means, but the worry about the inevitability of all this plants a seed in my mind. What if I have my own fateful part to play?

I pocket my phone, and we both run for the solarium. "Wait, the file! And the diary!" I turn to sprint back to the library, but I hear the creak of the front door opening.

"No time! And how the hell did they get in so easily?" Jenny hisses.

"I was distracted; I didn't make sure the door was closed properly behind me," I say, cursing myself. Aunt Frances wouldn't have made a mistake like that; she valued her safety above everything. We both reach the edge of the kitchen, and I hear voices echo from the hallway.

"Wonderful, Annie," Jenny says, pulling me by the arm. "If the door is technically open, the police can legally just come right in. It's like an invitation."

"Annie Adams!" a male voice I don't recognize calls out. "You need to come with us and answer some questions. Running will only make you look guilty—please consider that!" The voice sounds reasonable, like he's trying to be authoritative but nonthreatening. I don't believe it for a second.

Jenny reaches up and deftly slides across the bolt that keeps the back door to the solarium locked. She shoves the door hard with her shoulder and lifts it at the same time as she turns the handle, and it swings open. We race out into the cold, our breath coming out in clouds as we head straight for the edge of the woods. It's a clear night and the moon is nearly full. It glares down at us from above the newly pruned rosebushes, and the garden feels like it's hiding weapons of its own.

I nearly stop short when I see a figure at the tree line, practically glowing against the dark branches behind her. She's like a ghost, and for a minute I think it's Peony Lane. But as we get closer, I recognize the neat overcoat and long white hair of Birdy Sparrow.

"Hurry now," she says. "I've got a car parked off the side of the main road. Let's get lost in the woods first, though, shall we? These woods keep all kinds of secrets, and they'll cover our tracks nicely."

CHAPTER
39

WE HURRY THROUGH THE WOODS, STOPPING EVERY few minutes to help Birdy around some brambles or over slick stones. She isn't the fastest, but she's got sturdy winter boots on, and a torch to pick out the path to the road.

"There," she says, pointing toward the thinning trees up ahead. "Let's get in my car."

Adrenaline is still coursing through me, but I feel my instincts pulse out a new warning. There are details in the back of my mind, something I'm missing about all this that I'm struggling to see clearly.

"Birdy, I know it was you who Mum let into Gravesdown Hall on the day Peony Lane was killed," I say, approaching the car cautiously.

Birdy turns and looks at me in the moonlight. Her eyes are clear, and she reaches toward my face gently, in a grandmotherly gesture like she wants to pat my cheek but thinks better of it. It feels like a deliberate reminder that we're actually family—she's technically my great aunt.

"I only ever try to do what's right," she says quietly. "Laura genuinely developed a fascination with Peony Lane, and she really does want to work Peony into her newest paintings. I saw a way to get the old file out of the house and away from prying eyes, so I encouraged her. *That* was the right thing to do, and when you didn't want to help, she and I took matters into our own hands. Laura said you'd understand eventually. But I couldn't have fresh eyes on that file coming to the wrong conclusions. It's a shame I didn't manage to get to the file in time. Frances's filing system was a mess; I ran out of there empty-handed."

It's not an admission either way, but I find myself temporarily relieved at the idea that Mum was just looking for inspiration and Birdy took advantage of her access to the house. Though it's not quite enough to exonerate her.

"That must be why Mum called a second time," I say. "Because you were unsuccessful the first time."

We hear voices in the woods, and the beams of torches start bouncing through the trees behind us. The police are getting closer. I could turn around and tell them that something's off with this old woman, that she's keeping secrets, and we all just need to talk and the truth will come out. But then I remember something Saxon said, and the cloak Frances tried to throw over some of her diary entries finally makes sense.

"It was you," I say. "The fourth passenger in the car, the person who was with Archie at the farmhouse when Olivia tried to kill him—I thought it was Peony Lane, but Frances's diary entries are careful not to mention which one of you was speaking. And earlier tonight, Saxon told me that Peony Lane was with him at Gravesdown Hall on the night of the crash. I didn't focus on the detail at the time, but he mentioned cards—he said Peony taught him to shuffle a deck of cards, and it took all evening. Peony didn't leave Gravesdown

Hall that night, because she was looking after Saxon once Ford sped off after his brother."

Birdy looks at me for a moment, then nods curtly. "We need to go," she says, and her voice is thick, like she's on the verge of tears.

"Annie," Jenny hisses, and grabs my elbow. "Is this smart? Do you think she killed Peony Lane? Remember last summer—let's not get into cars with murderers."

I'd laugh if I wasn't so focused on the torch beams becoming ever brighter through the trees. "I don't think she killed Peony. I think someone killed Peony to protect Birdy," I say.

"Oh my God, because Birdy killed the Gravesdowns," Jenny whispers.

Now Birdy is in the driver's seat, starting the engine, and she looks tiny behind the wheel. I still don't trust her completely, but we get in the car. It's a nice new SUV, and she immediately turns on the heated seats. I'm in the front seat, and Jenny is in the back, and I feel a little silly to be suspicious of a seventy-seven-year-old lady and her sensible car. We aren't the Gravesdowns, speeding off in a Bentley with a body in the boot.

"Birdy, this isn't a good road to drive this fast on," Jenny says. Her voice is weak and I look back and try to give her a reassuring glance.

Moonlight floods the car for a moment as we pass a gap in the trees, and my eyes catch on her keys sitting limply in one of the cupholders. The car is so new it starts with a button push, but Birdy's got them by the steering wheel out of habit, or to keep track of them. They're just ordinary keys, but that's the final piece I've been missing.

"Whoever had the keys to the boot killed them all," I

murmur. "You didn't actually kill any of them, did you?" I say to Birdy, louder this time.

"They deserved what they got," she says through gritted teeth.

"Those keys, with the eagle key ring, the Stars and Stripes. Those were *Edmund Gravesdown's* keys. Saxon's playing cards with the American flag on them—Edmund brought them back from a recent trip to New York. I never asked Archie how he opened the boot to get Samantha's body in there, but those keys fell out of her bag. Archie recognized them from all those years ago, but he didn't realize who'd had them last—he thought Samantha must have got them at the police station somehow, perhaps from an evidence file relating to the wreck."

"We were vigilantes, you know?" Birdy says, her knuckles white on the steering wheel. "Taking down the rich and powerful, doing whatever it took to make things right with the world."

"You *did* jerk the wheel, trying to cause as much damage to Edmund in the driver's seat as you could. But *everyone survived that crash.* Didn't they? Olivia was in the boot, pounding to get out, and Edmund and Harry were bruised but alive. *One death with three to blame, or three deaths with one to blame . . ."*

"How did you know?" Birdy takes her foot off the accelerator for a second, and the car loses a small amount of speed. My knuckles are white from gripping the door handle, and I feel my fingers start to flex and unclench.

"You took the knife from where Olivia dropped it, after her altercation with Archie at the farmhouse. You wanted a weapon with you if you were forced into that car. The ruby found in the road from that dagger was what made me realize that whoever had the knife last was the person who had been in the car. But you and Peony lived together back then—when did she find that knife among your things?"

"She didn't find it; I gave it to her. She asked me about it just after the crash, because she knew I'd been forced into that car. When the paper reported the ruby found in the road, she asked to see the dagger. We argued over it, and in the end I told her to just take it, give it back to the Graves-downs for all I cared. She took it, but she kept it secret. Until you found it."

"*It begins with a secret revealed,*" Jenny adds from the back seat.

"Exactly," I say. "Something made that fortune start to come alive in her mind again. . . . She realized it was hers all along. She was the bringer of death after all; she just realized too late that the death she'd bring was her own.

"When Archie ran from the farmhouse to get help on that fateful night, the first place he'd go to was the village. And the only person he could trust was Eric. Earlier tonight I stood at the site of the crash and saw that the high street is only minutes away on foot. It's a shortcut everyone takes if you're walking from the village to the Gravesdown estate—Eric would have cut through that field and stumbled on the wreck."

"Eric was the best of us; he always has been," Birdy said. "He saved me, you know that? In so many ways. Edmund never would have stopped coming for me. If Edmund wanted something—and he saw women as things—he got it. And that had to stop." Her voice got thick with emotion as she said, "I've never stopped thinking about how no one was there for Emily. All those years of wondering where she was, and knowing that the Edmunds of the world were lurking around every corner. I wished for years that maybe Emily had an Eric of her own, to make sure good people always won." Her foot is heavy on the accelerator now, and when she takes the next curve, I feel my weight shift into the window with the force of it.

"Birdy?" My voice cracks as panic squeezes it. "Birdy, listen to me, you've got to slow down!" I raise my voice until I'm shouting, hoping it will get through to her.

"Annie!" Jenny shouts from the back seat. "There's someone in the road!"

I notice with horror that she's right. I take it all in, in a fraction of a second—looming through the mist that hangs above the road is the familiar form of Archie, clutching his flat cap in his hands, shoulders hunched as he walks. He must have cut through the field from town, possibly hurrying up to the Gravesdown estate. He's crossing the road, on his way to join the footpath as it continues on the other side. Half a breath and he turns, blinded by the full beams of Birdy's headlights, and he stumbles.

"I love Eric," Birdy whispers. "He's the only real hero in this town, and everyone overlooks him." She isn't going to stop—either she doesn't see Archie or she doesn't care.

I have seconds to decide what to do—I check that all of us have seat belts on, and I release my grip on the door handle. In one swift motion, I reach over and pull the wheel from her grasp. The car spins off the road, and I lose all sense of which way is forward and which way is back. In my disorientation, the figure of the man hitting the car only registers after it happens, after we feel the impact against the hood.

The rush of the night air fills the car, and I look at the spiderwebbed glass in front of me, wondering if I imagined it. But Archie's there, shaking me alert—my head hit the airbag when it deployed, leaving me dazed but not concussed. Jenny moans from the back seat, but Birdy is motionless in the driver's seat, her eyes closed.

I reach over and check that Birdy's still breathing, which she is. Thankfully, we're all free of any visible injuries, but I'm concerned Birdy might have suffered something internal from the force of the airbag. Archie's talking to me—no, shouting. I shudder and my head clears further.

"Ambulance! Annie, are you listening? I need your phone! She hit him, I can't believe she hit him. Please, call an ambulance!"

Jenny's voice floats disembodied from the back seat. "I already am, okay? Just . . . who? Who did she hit?"

"Eric," Archie says, and his face contorts. "Eric was running across the field after me—he was shouting something. There's no way Birdy would have seen him."

I wobble out of the car and come around to see. My teeth are chattering, and I feel nothing but cold and terrified. I find in that moment that I don't care if the police come and I get arrested. I think the people of Castle Knoll are right—Gravesdown money has always been cursed.

And killing Peony Lane didn't stop her fortunes from coming true. The bird did return, but it was me who completed the circle.

CHAPTER

40

I'VE KILLED HIM, OH MY GOD," I CAN'T STOP BABBLING while the paramedics swarm around Eric Foyle, torches shining, shouting instructions. "Or we've killed him? Birdy was driving; I grabbed the wheel. I grabbed it in the same way she did, all those years ago, speeding toward the same tree. What does that mean?"

Jenny catches my arm, looking pale. "No fortunes right now, Annie," she says. We watch as Birdy is checked over by someone—she's conscious but disoriented. She answers questions about what day it is and lets them shine a light in her eyes, making sure she's not concussed.

I'm so worried that I've inadvertently caused Eric's death that I don't hear the additional car arrive. Crane gets out and talks in low voices with the paramedics. I worry I'm about to be arrested again—but this time for something I actually did. Vehicular manslaughter, that's a thing, right?

"He just came out of the dark, I swear." The words rush out of me when Crane comes within earshot.

He shocks me by pulling me into a tight hug. I didn't

realize how much I needed it, and tears prick my eyes as I breathe deeply into the softness of his shirt. He's warm and he holds on to me until I stop shaking. When he releases me, his professional posture immediately returns, and it somehow makes me feel colder than I was before.

"You're not going to be arrested," he says. "But why did you run?"

"Marks," I say, scanning the figures in the dark. "I didn't want to end up in a situation where the cards were unfairly stacked against me. I just wanted to buy more time."

Crane nods solemnly. "You've been under a lot of strain, Annie, and I think you made an impulsive decision to run based on something that wasn't really a threat. Not everyone is out to get you."

I clench my jaw to hold back my reply, because he's not wrong. And more than that, his explanation of my actions sounds unnervingly like something Aunt Frances would do, in the same circumstances. "I thought you didn't get along with Marks," I say. "He's been picking at you, the whole power struggle thing."

"We've had some interesting conversations in the last day or so," Crane says, not looking at me. "He's been a dick, and he admitted it, but I can understand why now. It was his way of trying to push me to be better. I'm not saying I agree with his approach; it's a bit old-school. Just that I get it."

I don't know what to say, so I remain silent.

"Just . . . I wish you'd trust that I've got your back," he says, and the look he gives me is so steady I feel like he can see through me.

"Hey," Jenny says, coming up to stand next to me. "I just have to ask . . . if it was Eric who killed Peony Lane, it was because she knew he killed the Gravesdowns, right? But she only discovered this because of that wrecked car?"

"Wait," Crane says, turning to Jenny. "Eric killed Peony Lane?"

"Yeah," I say. "I'll fill you in on all the details in a bit. But that car is what started the whole thing. When that pub collapsed, and the wreck was inside, Eric was out with his tow truck picking up a different car for Archie—that old petrol station constantly has old cars being dropped or dumped there. I think it's a common place for Archie to arrange to pick up the cars he buys. Peony Lane was walking into town—you told me she was seen by drivers passing that morning."

"Wait, so the old pub collapses, exposing the wreck, which was presumably hidden by Ford to sweep his family's secrets under the rug," Jenny says. "And Peony passes by and is shocked to see it, after all these years. But what about the wreck made her think of Eric?"

"Eric was at the petrol station picking up the other car, and he saw Peony Lane going off the path to check out the pub wreckage. He already had the tow truck, and when he saw that wreck, he knew he needed to get it out of the way fast. His secrets had been safe for so many years—Birdy would never have betrayed him, but he didn't know what Frances might have on file that I could dig up to expose him," I say. "And Peony Lane must have seen that he had the keys to that Bentley. And she realized that the person who let Olivia out of the boot was the person who killed all the Gravesdowns."

"Why carry the keys all those years, though?" Crane asks. He's watching the two of us in the still-flashing police lights, looking impressed but cautiously so.

"It's something we'll have to ask him, if he pulls through," I say.

My phone buzzes in my pocket, tearing my thoughts

away. It's Mum, and I grind my teeth when I remember she conspired with Birdy to sneak into Gravesdown Hall to try to take Peony Lane's file out from under my nose.

"Mum," I say, walking a few steps away from Crane to answer the call. "It's not the best time to have this conversation, but I recently discovered that you broke into *my house* and secretly let in one *Birdy Sparrow.* Care to comment on that?"

I hear her breathe down the phone, her typical frustrated blast of air when she's trying to come up with a retort and she's absolutely convinced she's in the right. "Look, Birdy was very persuasive, and I *did* try to ask you about that file. I knew you'd just be overprotective about it and—"

"Overprotective? Mum, how on earth can you just take *everyone* at their word? Birdy wanted that file because she was the sole witness to three murders in 1961, and she wanted to know how much Frances knew, in case I'd read it and was going to come and investigate her!" I'm shouting, but the darkness and din of police voices seem to muffle everything.

"I don't know anything about murders, Annie—Birdy and I only ever talked about my art, and how interesting Peony Lane is as a focus for some new paintings. I promise, if she'd ever said anything about people being killed, I would have told you."

As she's talking, I can hear a low voice in the background. "Mum?" I say. "Who's there with you?"

"Oh, just Reggie Crane again—he popped by for tea," she says tightly.

"I saw Reggie Crane earlier today; I passed his taxi on the road. He's not anywhere near London. Can you just be open with me, for once?" I'm not shouting now, but my voice wobbles a bit.

There's a long pause. "I've been seeing someone. He's—

It's someone from years ago." She huffs, like I'm dragging the information out of her, when I haven't even spoken. "I might as well tell you—lord knows you'll be interrogating Reggie for the information and he'll crack in seconds." I roll my eyes but don't say anything. "It's your dad. It's Sam. He recently came back into my life, and a lot of things I thought about him turned out not to be true. I'm really happy, Annie. He's making up for lost time, and then some."

Several beats pass. Then more. I'm quiet for so long that Mum starts repeating my name, thinking the call has dropped.

"I'm here," I say, feeling a bit like I'm at the bottom of the sea. My eyes dart to Crane, and I feel slightly self-conscious.

"I wanted to bring this up gently," she says. "So we could talk through what he's like now. How he's changed."

"But, Mum, *everything* you've told me about Sam Arlington is terrible. I can't just believe you're happy and he's treating you wonderfully . . . especially when you've suddenly got lots more money at your disposal. You *know* his reappearance isn't a coincidence."

"Annie, let's not discuss this right now. Just give everything some time to sink in, and then maybe, when you're ready, you can come up to London and meet him. I'm sure you're just a little curious, right?"

"Actually, no. I don't care what he does for a living, I don't care what he looks like, or how charming he probably still is—because if he's wormed his way back into your life after twenty-six years of you hating his guts, that's some dangerous charm. Mum, I just care that you're safe and not making bad choices."

"Hey," she says, her voice heating up. "I'm the parent here."

"Not really," I huff. "We're both adults. And it looks like I'm the only adult who doesn't just believe anything anyone ever tells them, so I think I'll be opening a few files of my own. And changing my locks," I snap. And I hang up. Which is childish of me, especially considering I've just been telling my mother how much of an adult I am.

But suddenly I don't care if I'm following in Aunt Frances's footsteps. I'm coming round to her way of doing things. I want to know the truth. Even if it means uncovering unpleasant secrets. Even if those secrets are dangerous.

CHAPTER

41

March 20, 1967

I'VE LEARNED SOMETHING ABOUT UNANSWERED QUES-
tions, and secrets, and mysteries. Some mysteries are concrete—
an act of murder or theft or fraud. You can trace evidence, gather
your theories, and find the one answer to who, and why.

But some mysteries are emotional. And rooting out their so-
lutions isn't a question of following a trail of physical bread-
crumbs. The sharp mind won't inevitably find answers when the
problems presented are questions of the heart. The best you can
do with those mysteries is watch people with your own heart
turned inside out—feel your way through the interpretation of
someone's long looks, or held breaths, or stuttered lies.

And the conclusions you draw will never be answers. Those
don't exist when your mystery is emotional. Realizing this has
been something of a release for me of late, where my concrete
mysteries got tangled with my emotional ones, and everything
has been crashing together while still pulling me apart.

Archie Foyle will always be my unsolved emotional mystery. I
think he knows this, and it's why he took the marriage certificate

out of my handbag. I don't know what he's done with it; perhaps it never left Peony Lane's house. Perhaps he's hidden it for safe-keeping. But I admit I forgot that it existed shortly after we signed it. It's only a piece of paper, I suppose.

But as Archie and I drove back to Castle Knoll, the familiar landscapes of my life started appearing through the window. The landmarks were just as drab as they'd always been, drenched in rain. Archie didn't want a life in London, and even though he'd entertained the idea of Southampton, I knew he didn't really want that either. He wanted his farm back. I knew he and Eric weren't speaking, but deep down I think Archie wanted to ensure that neither of them had to rent rooms at the Dead Witch ever again.

Ford might have been understanding about me ending things with him, but he'd never give Archie his farm if I was Mrs. Foyle. I winced as one of the wipers squeaked across the windscreen. Mrs. Foyle—only days ago, that name had felt like a new beginning. Peony Lane hadn't predicted the murder of Frances Foyle; she was another me, someone who didn't believe in fortunes, who was going to start a new life doing . . . what exactly?

I watched Archie driving, and I knew, deep down, that all he wanted in the world was for us to live in that farmhouse, have babies, and run my family's bakery. Tears started to prick at my eyes, but I swallowed them down. I'd done so much crying already, when I found out how much he'd been keeping from me. It was a blow to the foundation of my feelings for him—knowing that he could be so simple but so secretive at the same time.

"I know what you're thinking," Archie said.

"Do you?" I had the ruby ring clutched in one fist, unsure what to do with it. I was horrified by its presence, and my own superstition started to flood my mind again. Archie had married me, and he'd given me a murdered woman's ring. It felt like a bad *beginning. But more than that, I was staring at a future with Archie that I didn't know if I wanted.*

"I was thinking that I'd like to see your fortune," I said. "The one Peony Lane just gave you."

Archie shook his head, keeping his eyes on the road. "I meant to get my lighter out and burn that," he said. "It doesn't matter, whatever it says."

"What if it matters to me?"

"It shouldn't," he said plainly. He took the turn onto the high street and parked the car in front of the Dead Witch.

"Why shouldn't it?" I asked. "Archie, you've always been one of the few people who never made me feel like my belief in the fortunes Peony Lane tells is silly. You never made me feel small about it. You made me feel like my worries about my future were understandable. Relatable, even."

Archie sighed. "I never said I related, Frances. You assumed I did because I didn't say any different. But just because I never argued with you over your belief doesn't mean I agree with you."

I blinked at him, feeling my features shift with confusion. "You helped me find Peony Lane. You actively encouraged me in my quest to find out more about her and the fortunes she tells. Are you telling me you were just humoring me?" My voice was rising, and heat crept up my neck. Suddenly I felt so stupid, and with that feeling came a rush of hurt. "So were my beliefs just a joke to you too?"

Archie gave me a look that was horribly condescending. "We all have our phases, Frances, and I never thought you were a joke. I knew if I was patient with you, this fortune phase would pass."

I opened my mouth to reply, but I felt constricted with tears and outrage, so I shut it again without speaking.

"Let's smarten up before we see your parents," he said. "They might not be the happiest with me, but I want to make a good

impression." He reached over and tugged my earlobe again, but this time it was definitely patronizing. I must have looked worried, because he said, "I'll do right by you, Frances, you'll see."

Maybe I shouldn't have pushed him—maybe I should have just gone up to his little rented room above the pub. That's what a woman in love would have done: basked in the glow of her new relationship, the small pub accommodation just one part of a longer adventure.

"What if I really wanted to go to university?" I asked.

"With what money? We have to be realistic, Frances. Things like that are expensive. We can have a good life, but university is a frivolous use of money. It's for people who aren't us, love."

Love. There it was again, something that could be affectionate but actually felt patronizing. I rallied, letting him know who he married. I wasn't going to walk away from him unless I'd explored every compromise, every avenue. Would he be willing to do the same? Even meet me halfway and spend a few years taking in the larger world?

"Education doesn't have to be formal, I suppose," I offered. "There's a huge world out there, and I think we can learn amazing things in unconventional ways. Let's buy a van and drive it to Greece. We can learn new languages and cook different foods, and take in history and art just by wandering through the right ruins."

"Greece?" He laughed. "I love your imagination, Frances." He leaned over and kissed my cheek. I knew what he was going to say after that, even before he said it. "I've taken you to interesting places—"

"You took me to Southampton."

"But there was so much to do there! I think people who have to travel far to be entertained are just trying to outrun themselves. You don't need to do that, now that you've got me."

"It's not about being entertained. And . . ." I felt hot tears spill *down my cheeks as I fought not to admit the worst part of it, what I was quickly coming to realize. But it had to come out eventually. With every passing second, it was becoming more true. "I think I have been outrunning myself, Archie, but I did it by hiding behind you."*

Archie's face fell, and my heart broke. But in the creases of his forehead and the way he dragged his hand through his hair, I could tell he could see it too. He was disappointed but not surprised.

"What are we going to do?" he asked, and his lost expression made him look like a little boy. I wanted to take all those words back and reexperience all the feelings I'd had when I'd been swept away by him. But every emotional hit I'd taken had knocked an old me out of the way, and someone new had grown in the cavern left behind. Someone who filled the same shape as who she'd been before, and heard the echoes of old feelings like important sounds to be treasured and remembered, but never felt in the same way again.

My lips trembled as I reached for him, and I kissed him fiercely. He could sense it was good-bye, and he grabbed my face with both hands, diving into the kiss like he wanted to memorize the sensation of it forever. It was fuel for both our memories, and knowing that made it hurt all the more.

CHAPTER

42

IT'S LATE, BUT THEY'RE ALLOWING US TO VISIT ERIC because this is police business. Although I'm technically not police, Eric is requesting me, and the hospital staff seem okay with it.

Jenny is waiting in the hallway as we approach Eric's room, and I'm surprised to see her holding Birdy's hand. Beth is on the other side of her, her expression grim. I pause and bend down in front of Birdy so I can see her face properly.

"Hi," I say quietly. "Birdy, I know you've been through a lot, but there's something I really wanted to know, if you don't mind?"

She looks at me, and her eyes are clear but sad. She nods.

"When Mum let you into the house to get the file, you were interrupted by the noise of Peony coming in through the solarium, followed by Eric. Did you see what happened?"

"No," she says, and she has to clear her throat a few times before the sound comes out.

"And you were still in the house when I arrived back from Archie's and came in with Jenny?" I ask.

She nods. "It was like time passed strangely," she says. "The shock if it all, I suppose. I was pacing for ages, panicking, wondering what to do. I've spent decades keeping Eric's secrets; he earned my loyalty when he saved me from Edmund all those years ago, and I'd never let him go down for the murders he committed in the past. I didn't want to suddenly stop protecting him."

"So when you heard Jenny and me come in, you tried to go out through the solarium but passed the kitchen first and saw that knife—a knife Eric has never had any connection to," I say.

She brings a hand to her mouth, fingers trembling. "When I heard you in the hallway, I ran into the solarium to try to exit that way, but that's when I saw Peony's body—there's a pathway near the windows that's hidden by dense planting, and I went that way to try to remain unseen. But I panicked when I saw Peony through the ferns, and doubled back into the kitchen. I hid in the pantry until you and Jenny had settled at the table, and I watched you through a small crack in the pantry door. It was then that my mind put together everything that had happened, what Eric had done to Peony."

She pauses for a moment, drawing in a shaky breath. "I know putting the knife in her back was a horrible thing to do, but Peony was already gone. I was able to do it while staying hidden because I went back around that side path in the solarium—it's completely screened by plants from where you and Jenny were sitting. I thought if I put that knife in Peony's back, it might obscure any evidence that was left by Eric. I don't know much about crime scenes or forensics, but I covered my hand with my blouse and closed my eyes and put it in her back. I told myself I was doing it for Eric and that she was only a body now. And then I crept out the back when you were looking down the hill at the approaching police cars—I remembered there's a door off the boot room that's rarely used."

Crane is hovering by the door to Eric's hospital room, and he gives me a nod. "Thank you, Birdy," I say solemnly. It seems like the wrong sort of reply for the circumstances, but I don't know what else to say.

When we enter the hospital room, the first thing I notice is that a dark bruise is already forming across one of Eric's cheeks. But his eyes are clear and alert, and full of something like conviction.

Archie is sitting in a chair on the opposite side of the room, looking lost. I wonder how much Eric has told him, or how much Archie has guessed.

"Annie, Detective," Eric says. "Please." He gestures toward a pair of extra chairs that seem to have been dragged into the room in anticipation of our visit. You'd think we were in his sitting room, visiting for tea and cake. The arm he gestured with is hooked up to an IV, and it shakes a little as he lays it back down on the bed next to him. "Birdy told me what happened in the car," he said. "I'd followed Archie, you see. I needed to keep an eye on him."

Archie doesn't reply, but the anguish on his face is plain.

"Archie, why were you in the road?" I ask.

He sighs. "I felt guilty about not telling you about that warrant to search the BMW I'd lent you. I tried to call you, but you weren't picking up, so I just headed off on foot. I'm sorry, Annie, about . . . so much." He puts his head in his hands, and I can see just how much these circumstances are hurting him.

"It's okay, Archie," I say gently. "I'm just after the truth here. I want to ask Eric about the murders, and if this is too hard for you to hear, I understand if you want to go and sit with Birdy and Jenny outside."

He takes a long breath in, and his eyes dart to Eric for a fraction of a second, then back to me. "I'll stay," he says.

"Okay," I say. "Then let's go back further, to the calls logged by Samantha, the lie that I was calling the station over and over again claiming Peony Lane was harassing me."

Eric's eyes are sharp, and his mouth twitches upward slightly. It's an almost satisfied look, and it's unsettling. "Samantha didn't log those calls," Eric says, and he coughs. "I did. I dropped her off at work every morning, and I often came to pick her up if she didn't get a lift home from someone else at the station. She never logged out of her computer, and it wasn't hard for me to open her call spreadsheet and log a bunch of harassment calls and backdate them. PC Asha Singh never followed up—she was an easy one to put in the spreadsheet, because I knew she'd just moved to another station."

"Why make it look like she was harassing me?" I ask.

"I wanted the focus on you," he says, and he gives me a look that could almost pass as a glare, if he didn't seem so tired.

"So you wanted to make me seem paranoid? Or possibly guilty?" I ask. "Why me, Eric? If it was just about the files, you would have gone after Frances much sooner."

"It was Peony who set it off." He pauses to drink some water from a feeble paper cup on the hospital tray next to him.

When he's settled again, he continues. "Peony and I crossed paths when the pub collapsed, and I wouldn't have brought those keys out of my pocket if I'd known she'd recognize them."

"Why did you still have those keys?" I ask.

Eric pauses and picks at the hospital blanket he's under. "Well, I suppose there's no use for secrets anymore."

"Can we go back a bit, please?" Crane says. "I want to know how Peony Lane ended up in that solarium, and how this relates to Olivia Gravesdown."

We all wait to see what Eric will say, but his expression is blank. When he does speak, his voice is cold again. "It started with Archie, when he came for help. The night of the crash, when Birdy told him to run, he ran all the way to the Dead Witch to find me."

Archie's fingers clench around the plastic arms of his hospital chair. "I ran to tell you they had Birdy in their car. I told you Olivia tried to kill me."

"Exactly," Eric says. "And I knew what I had to do. I ran through the field, but when I got to the place where the road intersects it, the car had already crashed."

"Birdy said she pulled the wheel and that she was responsible for the crash," Crane says.

"She did pull that wheel. When I got there, she was going in and out of consciousness. When she woke up properly, the Gravesdowns were all dead. I didn't realize she'd witnessed what I did, but I'm not surprised she protected me. I made it look like the Gravesdowns all died on impact. But really, they died after I hit them. They were injured already, so it didn't take much. Just a few blows from a heavy branch that had fallen. But I had to stop them. I had to stop them from hurting my family, from hurting Birdy, and I had to stop them from ever hurting anyone else in this village again."

"And you took those keys, after you let Olivia out of the boot and killed her too. You still haven't said why. Why not just leave them?" I ask.

"Ford had raced after his brother, and he turned up just as I was still holding that bloody branch. It was clear what I'd done. But his reaction was strange; he seemed secretive himself, almost like he was party to it all. He hadn't done anything, but when he came across that scene, he seemed guilty," Eric says.

I think of Ford putting those pills in his brother's flask, then chasing after him when he got behind the wheel of the Bentley. Ford probably did feel guilty, like he'd had some part to play in their deaths. I think of that line again, *One death with three to blame, or three deaths with one to blame* . . .

Ford had drugged his brother, likely making it easier for Birdy to jerk the wheel out of his grasp toward the tree, and then Eric finished them off. We'd been thinking it was Olivia who was the only murder victim, in which case the three of them could have been to blame for that one death. But it was all three of them who survived, despite the actions of Ford and Birdy, so it all came down to Eric.

"So Ford covered for you," I say slowly. "All those years, he's covered for you. In Frances's diary, she mentioned him pulling you out of a police car. She thought you were an informant, but you weren't, were you? The young policeman was trying to get some answers about that crash, and he wanted to question you, but Ford used his status to protect you. Why?"

"He found out that night just how insidious Edmund, Harry, and Olivia were. They were his blood, but not his family. I heard him say that once, and I know he believed it. But Ford was a careful planner. He didn't just let it go; he saw an opportunity in me. He told me he'd keep my secret, but he said that I needed to keep those keys as a reminder that if I stepped out of line, I always carried evidence that could put me away. 'I want to see those keys, whenever I ask you,' he said. 'Just so you always remember your choices tonight, but you know that I can always take you down.' After years of carrying them, I started to add my normal keys to the ring, and out of habit I never took them off."

"When Frances and Archie started investigating that crash, they came to you in the Dead Witch and asked about that night. Why did you give them any information about it at all?" I ask.

"Archie already knew I had some knowledge of that night, though I told him that when I went to help Birdy, the car had already crashed and Birdy had run off. He never knew more than that. But he already knew how horrible the Gravesdowns were—they'd threatened him that night, after all, and Olivia even tried to kill him. I couldn't think why he wanted Frances to hear it all from me, but I gathered he was trying to play it off to her like he was never there. In any case, I gave Frances only the details I suspected Archie already knew, plus some small things to focus on to throw them off the scent. Details that might distract Archie, keep him from circling too close."

"And after Archie and Frances had their falling-out, it all went quiet," I say. "Until that day I met Peony Lane in the woods." I pause, thinking. "How did that dagger end up in the waterwheel?"

"After she saw me, Peony walked straight to the farmhouse and stuck that dagger right in the front door. I don't want to believe she could see the future, but all I can think is that she put that knife in her bag that morning in one of her uncanny impulses, feeling it would reveal its importance at the right moment. She probably put the knife in the door to show me not only that she knew the truth after all these years, but that she wasn't afraid of me. I found it before anyone else noticed it, and I pulled it out and threw it in the river right in front of the house. I was hasty; I should have realized that chucking it away right by the front door was a bad choice. It was a nasty twist of fate that the waterwheel caught it, bringing it right back to you."

HOW TO SEAL YOUR OWN FATE

The word *fate* echoes around my head like a bad song.

I think back to when we found Samantha's body, to how upset Eric seemed. "When we found Samantha," I say slowly, "you said, 'Oh, Sammy, what did you do?' I thought you were wondering what she did to get herself killed. But because you were the one who switched her water bottle, you weren't thinking about that. You were thinking about what she'd done *before* the lead took effect. She had the file. She got it from evidence in the police station, after Marks took it when he came to investigate the murder of Peony Lane. You meant who had she talked to, who had she told about the things she'd uncovered in that file, after all those years?"

"I'd taken Edmund's key ring off my normal keys after that meeting with Peony Lane, and hidden them in the glove compartment of my car. That was how I found out Samantha was onto me—when I dropped her off at home the evening before she died, I realized Edmund's keys were gone. She'd looked in the glove compartment for something and found the Bentley keys. She was always nosing around. I should have hidden them better. And, same as Peony, she worked it out quickly. And with all the police files and detectives at her fingertips, Samantha was a real threat to my secrets."

"Why frame me, though?" I ask. "I had no reason to want Samantha dead, or Peony Lane for that matter."

"When you and the detective opened that boot, I knew right away that Samantha had died on the farm, and that Archie had found her, panicked, and put her body in there. She would have walked up to the farm from the police station. More of his fingerprints at the scene of the crime, more of Archie not thinking about how this was going to look for him."

"So you quickly went to your car, the one you drove

289

Samantha around in constantly," I said. "Her cardigan was still there, and you placed it in the boot of the BMW I'd been driving, shaking the hair and fibers out in the process. You thought that even though it was Archie's car, it was obvious who'd been using it exclusively recently."

"What really convinced me that you needed putting in your place"—he sits up straighter in his hospital bed and leans toward me—"what told me you were just like them, was when you started putting all that money into Archie's car restoration business."

I'm completely taken aback; of all the reasons for Eric to dislike me, this was not on my bingo card. "I'm sorry, what?"

"You heard me," he says, settling back against his pillows. "Gravesdown money getting its claws into the Foyles, just like always. We've been free of the Gravesdowns for decades, and then you had to try to get a piece of us again. This is why I've always fought against people like you—you think you can just buy whoever you want." His voice rises as he speaks, and color flushes his cheeks.

"Why on earth would I want to do that? I like Archie! I want to help! And you think you're fighting something by trying to make me look guilty, when you went and worked for Archie too? If you hated the idea of his business being funded by me, why go anywhere near it?" I say, leaning forward in my own challenge.

"Someone with the right morals needed to be in the thick of it, keeping an eye on things," he says plainly.

"Morals," I say sharply, ready to give Eric a speech about his own selective morality, but Crane interrupts me.

"How did you and Peony get in the house?" he asks quietly.

"Mum let Birdy inside," I say.

Archie finally speaks. "I don't know the rest, but when I

found out Peony Lane had been killed, I thought it had to have been Birdy who'd done it. I couldn't think why she'd kill Peony all of a sudden, but I knew Birdy had been the passenger in the car all those years ago, and I suspected she was the one who'd killed Olivia Gravesdown. I think Frances thought so too, but she always worried Ford might have known something about it and kept it quiet, so she stopped digging. So then on the day Samantha died, when she approached me on the farm with the file—which she'd taken from Marks's desk—and she suddenly collapsed, I knew she'd been poisoned. I panicked because I thought I was next, or Eric was. I thought Birdy was going through the whole group from the night of the crash, picking us off one by one. The only thing I couldn't understand was why she'd start with Peony Lane, one of her oldest and closest friends. Or what on earth Peony Lane was doing inside Gravesdown Hall in the first place."

"That brings us to the mechanics of the whole thing," I say. "On the day of Peony Lane's murder, Eric was driving Samantha to the police station for her morning shift, and I was there with the ruby knife, saying it came from Archie and telling Crane that Peony Lane was talking about the Gravesdown crash. Eric decided he had to act fast. He knew the house was empty, because I was at the police station. But he also knew, from what I'd said, that Peony Lane was somewhere in the woods near Gravesdown Hall. So he followed the path he knew she'd take and approached the house from the back."

Crane coughs lightly, as if to remind me he's still there. "But how did they get inside? I assume Birdy was still in the house—did she let them in?"

I wince. "This is where my repeated examinations of the solarium doors, and how bent out of shape they are, helped me realize a huge mistake I made. That and my failure to

291

close the front door behind me properly when the police were on their way to question me. *I* was the one who didn't close the solarium door properly. I wasn't thinking clearly that morning; I'd never left through the solarium before, but if I'd been paying attention, I'd have realized that the door didn't lock from the outside."

"I wasn't counting on it being unlocked, but when I saw it was slightly ajar, it felt like fate," Eric says. "I had my gardening knife in my pocket, and I was going to kill her somewhere on the property so that it looked connected to you." He gives me a look that's so cold it makes me want to shuffle my chair back a few inches. I resist the urge. "Inside your house was even more perfect. I didn't see or hear anyone else in there, but Peony was facing away from me in the solarium when I went inside, and I stabbed her in the back. She screamed and fell into the plants and stayed face down there. I talked to her gently for a moment and told her it'd be over soon. I'm not a monster, you know." I give him a look that says I strongly disagree. "She and I were close for years," he counters. "I wish it hadn't had to end that way, but I made sure it was quick. When I could tell she was dead, I slipped out of the back door again, carefully shutting it behind me."

"Your compassion astounds me," I say, my voice monotone and harsh. "But Birdy was a few rooms away," I add, trying to keep on track and not let my emotions take over. "She must have gone to see what happened, found Peony's body, but panicked when she heard Jenny and me come through the door moments later. So she hid, watching us, wondering what to do."

"What I don't understand is why Birdy didn't just come and tell you what had happened," Crane says.

"And look guilty herself?" I raise an eyebrow at Crane. "But more importantly, Birdy was eternally loyal to Eric. She was the sole witness to his crimes all those years ago, and she'd spent decades keeping his secrets. That kind of loyalty becomes an identity; it crystallizes and makes it possible for a person to even go so far as to deface the body of one of their closest friends, just to obscure evidence. Birdy did what she thought would help keep suspicion away from Eric—she took the knife out of the sink while Jenny and I were still having lunch and put it in Peony's body. Eric tried to frame me out of malice toward the Gravesdown money and what he thought was me trying to control his family's assets, but Birdy just saw an opportunity to shift the blame."

We're talking about Eric as if he's not in the room with us, but when I look at him, his features are stony, and I doubt he's planning to say any more. It's like he's finished his story and is resigned to his fate now. Which is appropriate, considering that's what he's brought on himself.

CHAPTER
43

June 1, 1967

*I DIDN'T SEE FORD FOR SEVERAL WEEKS AFTER ARCHIE
and I signed our secret divorce papers. I tried to give the ring back
to Archie, saying that if it really did belong to the Foyles in the
first place, he should keep it. He looked at me sadly and said it
was better off with me. I didn't know what else to do with it, so I
squirreled it away in a plastic bag, among my notes and pieces of
evidence from the time Archie and I spent investigating the crash
together. Maybe one day I'll make a proper file, inspired by that
evidence file Samantha and Peony Lane put together against Edmund Gravesdown.*

*Archie and Eric remained in the rooms above the Dead Witch,
Eric pulling pints and Archie coming and going from odd jobs
and gardening in the village, or working on neighboring farms.
After a few awkward run-ins in Castle Knoll Library, things
started to smooth out between us. It was a relief when I could
bump into Archie and finally not feel the squeeze of heartbreak.
The more distance I got from those frantic days in March, the
more clearly I could see that he and I weren't a good match.*

Ford wasn't on my mind much, if I'm honest. I spent my days working at the bakery while hardly paying attention to anything but my own thoughts. If I went to university, what would I study? Were there scholarships? My marks in school and sixth form had been excellent; I'd just never considered going further. It just wasn't something that people in my family did.

But I sent away for some brochures anyway, and spent my evenings in my room looking through lists of courses, thinking about London. On a whim, I applied to read psychology at University College London, which included a scholarship for women from rural areas. I wondered if Castle Knoll counted as rural—we did have a post office, after all—but I thought I'd try my luck anyway. To people in London, Castle Knoll probably felt like the moon.

It was on one of those sunny days in May when it feels like spring is practically waving at you through the window that Ford stepped in through the bakery door.

"Can I help you?" I asked, and for once I simply felt friendly around him. Not guarded or suspicious, or wondering what he was doing there. Having an application to university pending made my days at the bakery feel far less onerous, and Castle Knoll less stifling. It was a potential new way to have a future of my own making.

Ford gave me a warm smile and looked around the empty bakery. It was midafternoon on a Thursday, and I was on my own in the quiet, basking in the warm light from the big front windows.

"I do need some bread," he said, and he looked almost shy. "And I also just wanted to say hello. I considered ordering a delivery so that I might see you up at the house, but you've taught me to be better than that. I know you don't like feeling summoned."

I laughed. "Good, I'm glad you've learned. And it's nice to see you. How have you been?"

"Honestly?" His eyebrows lifted and his expression was surprisingly unguarded. "I've been rather in need of my sharp-minded friend who doesn't let me get away with anything. I mean, if you're okay with us being friends again?" He asked the question timidly, like there had been some falling-out, or he was worried I wanted nothing to do with him ever again.

I gave him a reassuring look. "I'd like to be friends," I said. "But surely you have a lot of people in your acquaintance who have sharper minds than I do."

"No." Ford leaned on the glass case between us, the one that holds all the iced buns and scones and things. His look was slightly humorous and conspiratorial. He may have asked to be friends, but the air between us would never feel that way. And I smiled at him in return, because I found that this didn't bother me. Some people just have a spark between them that never fades. "There's no one in my acquaintance quite like you."

He took a step back as someone came into the bakery, and I helped with some loaves of bread while trying not to let my eyes keep darting to where Ford was standing, his hands confidently in his pockets but his expression soft. The woman buying the bread kept looking from me to Ford and back again, and rushed back out as soon as her purchase was completed, probably keen to fuel village gossip about us once more.

"Tell me, Frances," Ford said, once we were alone again. "In your recent investigations, did you find out much about the mythical character that is Peony Lane?"

"I . . . No, actually. She's been the one person I've still not managed to track down, or learn much about at all," I said. It was a lie that tasted a little stale in my mouth, but from the night Archie and I had gone to Peony Lane's house, I decided I wasn't going to pursue any more truths about that crash. Bad people died, and fates were balanced out. Knowing that was enough.

"I'm not surprised," Ford replied. "I've tried to find her again too, and I haven't been successful."

"You?" I said. I felt surprise shift my features, and I regarded him carefully to make sure he wasn't trying to make fun. I didn't think he would, but after things had gone so badly with Archie, and Archie's outright dismissal of my belief in Peony's fortunes, I was wary of not being taken seriously.

He smiled, and it was gentle. "You know me, Frances. I'm curious and I like to philosophize about the world. Humans have been interested in fortune-telling throughout history, and I find that the concept is growing on me. It's fascinating."

"I agree," I said slowly, "not just with fortunes being fascinating, but with wanting to know about things. Lately whenever I find out about something dangerous and unsolved, I seem to have to uncover everything I can about it. There's something about the search for truth that is extremely compelling to me."

Ford smiled broadly. "Then we'll have to get you some more notebooks," he said. "When do you finish work? I'd like to take you for a walk this evening."

"I'd like that," I said. "I finish in an hour."

CHAPTER
44

I SPEND THE REST OF THE AUTUMN LETTING THE events of those fateful few days breathe a bit. I have a restoration company come and refurbish the solarium, including replacing the back doors. It takes a month, since the whole structure is historical, and they have to replace everything in a way that is "in keeping with the original time period." But I had to do something to change it or I'd only ever think of Peony Lane, lying there among the plants. I'm debating giving the library the same treatment, since that's where Aunt Frances died, but it seems like the beating heart of the house in a way. One thing is clear about Gravesdown Hall, though— it's well past time that I put my stamp on it, even if it's a gradual process.

Jenny returned to London shortly after Eric was arrested for the murders of the three Gravesdowns, Peony Lane, and Samantha. Archie and Beth visit him whenever they can, but it will be hard to shake the sadness of Eric's warped understanding of his own Robin Hood persona. In a strange way, Eric was the "foil" mentioned in the fortune. But he wasn't

Archie's foil; he was Aunt Frances's—they both obsessed over justice and exposing criminals, but they let those ideas rule their lives in different ways.

Eric got control over the injustices he saw through violence, and Frances got control over hers through information. And I can't stop thinking about how the Frances in her diaries is such a clever, independent, and logical person—what must she have seen to convince her the world was truly a frightening place, and that the comfort of Castle Knoll was a false one? The yellow diary feels like one step farther down the path of her turning into the paranoid recluse she became, but it's hard to reconcile that, after reading about what a deeply feeling and vibrant youth she had.

As I ponder the new solarium designs Jenny sent me throughout November (each one beautiful but demonstrating her complete inability to understand the needs of plants), I keep coming back to what Crane said about Aunt Frances: *She was a collector of secrets, not a solver of crimes.*

And soon, that fact becomes embedded in my thoughts. As I walk through each room of her house, thinking about how I might make space for myself here among a lifetime of artifacts she left behind, I realize there is room for us both. We are a strange sort of team. She was indeed a collector of secrets, and I've proven yet again that if I work hard at it, I can be a solver of crimes.

HAVING A PARTY in a space where someone was previously murdered is a strange sort of way to usher in Christmas, but when the solarium is finished, I have a Christmas cocktail party in there. I'm committed to the mentality that creating new memories in a room where bad things happened might rescue its soul a bit.

The solarium is still packed with tropical plants, some old, some new—orchids have become a new fascination for me, along with bananas, tree ferns, hibiscus, and ginger. Aunt Frances's cacao tree has been given pride of place along one side of the glass room, near the vanilla pods and ginger. The gardening team I hired found several rare and interesting species that have been properly revived and placed in better positions so that they can thrive.

The whole space retains some of the old Victorian feel— the tiles have been scrubbed up and repaired, and the intricate venting system has been replumbed and works properly so that the space has a tropical humidity about it. But it's also more of an arty, plant-filled space now—a deep twisting archway of porous wood snakes its way from one end of the space to the other, with Spanish moss dangling among a myriad of aerial plants. In the dark wintry evenings, lights come on at the base of the taller palms near the back of the solarium (the previous dodgy wiring has been replaced), which are where the table used to be. They cast amazing shadows while illuminating the vibrant greens of the fronds.

The old pond has become a rectangular reflecting pool, and tonight I've floated votive candles in it, in a sea of fresh cranberries. The red seems to glow with the little flames dancing in it, and even Jenny is impressed with my decorating skills. In the center of the room, under the large glass dome, there's a table that seats twelve, decorated with every mismatched candlestick and cocktail glass I could find.

Jenny has come up for the weekend, and she's brought one of her brothers with her—Wes, who is an architect and lives in Winchester. I'd be suspicious that she was trying to play matchmaker, but lately I've learned that I enjoy hosting here, and introducing new people to the weird and wonderful land of Gravesdown Hall is a rare pleasure.

Beth has been here cooking since this morning, even though I told her this was just going to be cocktails and some hors d'oeuvres. But I think she needed to reintroduce herself to a Gravesdown Hall without Frances, and it's just taken a few months for her to be ready. The spread she lays out could rival the work of the most trendy London chefs, and I take that as a sign that the reintroductions are going well.

In an effort to make peace between Crane and Chief Inspector Marks, I've invited them both. And then I overcompensated by inviting a few too many other people I haven't seen in a while either. Around one side of the table sit Dr. Owusu, the village GP; John, who is technically my grandfather on my mum's side; Walt Gordon, Aunt Frances's former lawyer and close friend; and Mum.

Mum and I have made an uneasy peace, and though I still refuse to go and meet my dad, she's agreed to be a bit more cautious in what she shares with him. Even though Chief Marks is a bit of a dick, he's better than everything I've ever heard about my dad, so part of me is actually hoping that sitting them next to each other creates some kind of spark. Across from them are Jenny, Wes, Detective Crane, me, Archie, Beth, and Miyuki, who has recently returned from Japan. Saxon and Elva declined my invitation, to my relief.

Birdy Sparrow said she wasn't feeling well, and Mum has promised to visit her after dinner with some leftovers. I think for Birdy, there's been a lot of loss and strange events in a small span of time, and it's taken quite a lot of the fight out of her. She's been cleared of any involvement in or knowledge of the murders—both past and present—as Eric has vehemently denied she ever witnessed any of his actions. Birdy herself refuses to talk about it, but I get the impression he's still protecting her, after all these years.

For the most part, we eat and drink and converse in a

happy but rather subdued way. It's not the easiest, getting together and trying not to think about the people who aren't there, and all the complicated reasons for that. With Archie next to me and Crane on my other side (and two glasses of champagne loosening my tongue), I decide not to tiptoe around the conversation so completely.

"Archie," I say slowly. "Can I ask you something?"

Archie nods and finishes chewing one of Beth's vol-au-vents. "The Gravesdown car is gone now, if that's what you're wondering. It's finally been destroyed—crushed at the scrapyard."

"That's good to know, but what I really wondered was . . . did you ever know? About that crash, about what really happened?"

"No, not truly. I mean, I had my suspicions, but I always thought it was Birdy who'd killed Olivia. When I found the ruby ring in a box of old jewelry Eric had salvaged from the farmhouse, I just assumed Birdy had given it to Eric, knowing it truly was a Foyle heirloom. But looking back, I should have questioned everything when Birdy was shocked to see the ring on Frances's finger, that night we went to Peony Lane's. That ring was like a bad penny, always turning up, changing luck for the worse."

"So you believe in luck, but not fate?" I ask.

Archie grins. "'Course," he says simply. "Luck is a nice explanation for how life isn't fair but sometimes has good things in it. Fate—now, that's just an excuse to give up control and let some invisible force drive things. And I could never do that."

I laugh lightly. "No, I can't see you doing that at all." I pause, sipping my drink. "Archie, I know that there are three more diaries on your shelves." I narrow my eyes at him, but in a way that has the edge of a joke to it. Yes, those diaries mean a lot to me, but I now know that they mean a lot to him too.

Archie shifts in his chair. "I suppose you're due your turn with those," he says. "And there's more about Peony Lane in those too—Frances and Peony had a long, rather interesting history. I swiped four of the diaries back in October, when I was still coming and going from the house, because I just didn't know what she'd written about me and her . . . about that winter we went to Southampton." His face falls, and I instinctively put my hand over his, where it rests on the table. He reaches over with his other hand and covers mine briefly, a silent acknowledgment of all the feelings contained in that little yellow book. "I'll get the others to you soon," he says.

"Thanks."

Archie twists the stem of the wineglass in front of him, which has been full all evening, never refilled. "Annie," he says eventually. "Why did you never ask yourself—or the Foyle family—why we weren't included in that fight over the inheritance last summer?"

"I . . . I made an assumption, about your relationship with Aunt Frances. It was a snap judgment on my part, but when I first came to Castle Knoll, I just saw you as her gardener, and Beth as her cook. And the farm being on Gravesdown land just sort of made you all her long-standing tenants. I know now, obviously, that there was so much more to it. But if you don't mind telling me, why *weren't* you part of the inheritance setup she so carefully planned?"

"Because years ago, we asked her never to include us," he says, his voice tinged with a solemn edge. "I've always felt that Gravesdown money is cursed, and I didn't care if I lost the farm again. Sure, at the time, Beth and I were worried things might not go our way. But we both decided the risk was worth it, to be kept out of all that scheming."

"But," I start, trying to reconcile the Archie in Frances's diary entries with the Archie sitting here now, "your farm, that's always been the most important thing to you, hasn't it?"

"I've always wanted a *family*. And I got one—I've got Beth and Miyuki, and . . . Eric." His face falls as he says Eric's name, and his eyes dart to his plate. "The farm was a special place for me, sure. But it's as haunted as it is joyful. If we lost it, we'd be all right, somewhere new."

I look at Archie, and I want to hug him—this man who has just bounced back from so many ups and downs in life, and held the people he cares for close. I think of him carefully tending to Frances's plants, bringing her fresh flowers from the garden every morning. Did they ever reconcile? And why didn't he tell anyone about his past with Frances? He must have been going through a horrible private grief when she died, but he kept it all locked tight behind his quick smiles and his cheesy sense of humor.

At the end of the evening, I walk out to the front with the people who aren't staying—Jenny and Wes each have a room upstairs, though Mum has opted to go back to London. I look for my winter coat, because a thick frost is already forming on the lawns and across the gravel, but I can't seem to find it so I opt for the raincoat I haven't worn since the weather turned properly cold. I wave to everyone as they head down the long gravel drive, now lit with elegant white Christmas lights that spiral up the rows of manicured cypresses, and realize the lonely restlessness I felt back in the autumn has been gone for weeks now. Having a massive estate has its perks, when you have friends you like spending time with.

As the last car leaves the gate, I put my hand in my pocket, and my fingers catch the stack of envelopes still in there from when Crane and I went to Peony Lane's house a few weeks ago. I'd honestly forgotten about them, in the flurry of the fallout from Eric's arrest, dealing with my own feelings on settling properly into my new Gravesdown life, and tackling my first house renovation project on top of that.

I swallow hard and decide that I'm up for another challenge. I'm going to choose one at random, open it, and look into all the possible things that fortune could contain—past and present.

My fingers shake slightly as I flip through the fortunes in my pocket, feeling for a likely candidate. Finally, I take a deep breath and pull one out.

And it is—predictably—my own.

ACKNOWLEDGMENTS

Second books are notoriously tricky animals, and this one grew claws and fought me from start to finish. But throughout that battle, the voices of encouragement, feedback, and confidence for me and my work not only made the battle worth fighting but led me to emerge victorious.

My fantastic team of agents at the Bent Agency—Zoë Plant, Jenny Bent, and Martha Perotto-Wills—the three of you always make me feel in such safe hands, and I could not have asked for better champions of my work. I've had fantastic support from so many other members of the TBA team—a special thanks to Aminah Amjad, Victoria Cappello, and Emma Lagarde. Additional thanks to Emily Hayward-Whitlock at the Artists Partnership for championing *How to Solve Your Own Murder* in the wider world of film and television.

My editorial dream team, Florence Hare at Quercus and Cassidy Sachs at Dutton—I'm still pinching myself to have landed with such a perfect pair. When the three of us get together and chat all things Annie and Frances, it's like lights clicking on in dark hallways, ideas floating out of forgotten spaces, and feeling pushed to be better but supported all the way at the same time. Thank you both for your unceasing enthusiasm for my stories and my characters.

A huge thank-you to the UK team at Quercus—Stefanie Bierwerth, Katy Blott, Charlotte Gill, Ayo Okojie, Ella Patel, Emily Patience—for their hard work promoting my book from all directions. And a thank-you also to the UK copyeditors, cover designers, and people designing the amazing materials to promote my books; you're all amazingly talented and I appreciate you.

The to the US team at Dutton—Emily Canders, Isabel DaSilva, John Parsley, LeeAnn Pemberton, Dora Mak, Shannon Plunkett, Hannah Poole, Erika Semprun, Clare Shearer, Melissa Solis, and Amanda Walker. Also to the US cover designers, copyeditors, and team members working beautifully to shout about my books from the rooftops: a heartfelt thank-you.

To all the brilliant translators and foreign publishers, marketing, publicity, artists, and designers—thank you so much for all the work you do. Every time I see a new translation of my work, my heart swells, and I still can't believe I have the exceptional privilege of having my work in so many countries.

Writing is a lonely business, and I am forever grateful for the writers I've connected with who have offered friendship and support, joy and commiserations, with all our ups and downs. My lovely Harrogate group (you know who you are, you rock stars) and my fellow writers who have been there to give publishing insights and advice in an industry that can be so confusing to navigate alone—Faridah Àbíké-Íyímídé, Hannah Brennan, Jessica Bull, Samuel Burr, Rose Diell, Amy Dillmann, Henry Fry, Jennie Godfrey, Alex Hay, Fiona McPhillips, Cara Miller, Orlando Murrin, Tania Tay, and Teri Terry.

To my wonderful network of critique partners who patiently read early material for *How to Seal Your Own Fate* and offered their invaluable feedback or listened to my wild ideas during brainstorming calls—Ashley Chalmers, Mary Osteen, Kate Poels, Tyffany Neiheiser, and Hannah Roberts—I couldn't have done this without you all.

Family and friends on both sides of the Atlantic who have read and shouted about my books, thank you so much. I love your pictures snapped in bookshops, reports back from book clubs, and general excitement so very much. My husband, Tom—I don't need to tell you all the ways you are fantastic because I tell you all the time, but for the nosy people who wonder who the most essential part of my support network is, it is undoubtedly you. And my gorgeous kids, Eloise and Quentin, who are reaching those wonderful ages where they love to tell everyone about my books even though they aren't allowed to read them yet, you make all my days brighter.

And finally, to the booksellers and readers who have been above and beyond in showing their enthusiasm for my book and this series—thank you for your love of these characters and Castle Knoll, and for trusting me to steer you through a mystery and back out again a second time. I have so much gratitude for you for sticking with me, and I hope we have many more adventures together.

ABOUT THE AUTHOR

Kristen Perrin is originally from Seattle, Washington, where she spent several years working as a bookseller before moving to the UK to do a master's and PhD. She lives with her family in Surrey, where she can be found poking around vintage bookstores, stomping in the mud with her two kids, and collecting too many plants.